The AFRICAN SORCERESS Series

Book 2

War on the Sahel

By

M.E. Skeel

Revised 2nd Edition

2023

To order additional copy of this book, contact:
2708 Armidale Road Blaxland's Creek
New South Wales 2460 Australia
info@bilbybooks.com

Fate whispered to the Warrior,
'The storm is coming.'
The Warrior answered,
'I am the storm'.

Contents

Dedication

To all who lost their lives and freedom in the holocaust of the Atlantic Slave Trade, called the Ma'afa in Africa.

To my friend Kwame Dabbisah, who first told me the story of the sorceress who saved her people from slavery. To Malcolm Boyd, the pied piper of Uralla – Somunye, my brother. And to dear Ugochi. We miss you, my sister.

'Songs we would never hear! Histories we would never know! Art we would never see! Because the European had the capacity to destroy and didn't have the moral restraint not to.'

Maulana Karenga

'The word Ma'afa is derived from a Kiswahili word meaning disaster, terrible occurrence or a great tragedy. The term today collectively refers to the Pan-African study of the 500 years of suffering of people of African heritage, through slavery, imperialism, colonialism, apartheid, oppression, invasions and exploitation. The African Holocaust or Ma'afa, is a crime against humanity and is recognized as such by the United Nations, scholars, and historians who have documented the primary and overwhelming culpability of European nations for enslavement in Europe, in the Americas and elsewhere. However, this history would be incomplete and unbalanced without also reflecting on the rape, genocide, slavery, and warfare that Africans have also engaged in against other Africans.'

Synopsis

Book 1   A Warrior is Forged

In the early 1600s, a young African girl, Kisa, grew up protected in a small village hidden from the outside world by a cleverly constructed maze in the forest until it was discovered by an Arab-Swahili slave trader, Mbwana Sefu. In one raid, Kisa's beloved father was taken away and she vowed to kill the slavers.

Her mentor, the village sorceress called Grandmother, taught her all she knew. But she could see that Kisa had to become a warrior as well as a sorceress. In dream-travels, Grandmother found Yasuki, the Black Samurai and convinced him to come back to Africa from Japan to teach Kisa to fight. He also taught her twin brother and sister, Kwame and Shani, and other members of the tribe, including a young orphan, Kojo, who fell in love with Kisa.

When the slavers returned, Kisa and the villagers were ready. The slavers were defeated and Kisa killed their leader, Mbwana Sefu, but three slavers escaped. Sefu's half-brother Badru captured Kojo's sister, Afia, and fled with Sefu's lieutenants. Kisa and Kojo vowed to rescue her.

The war against the slave masters had begun.

Prologue

Father never let the story be told without the proper rituals. After the evening meal, he made an offering of palm wine on the sacred stone at the head of the fire pit and built a large fire. At last, our Obeah woman walked out and took her seat near the Stone. We sat around her in the fire's warmth while she told the story of our ancestor, the great Prophetess who fought to save our tribe from the slave masters.

She always began with prayers, to Nyame the Creator and to the Goddess, Asase Ya, embodied in our Mother Africa. 'Mother, sing me a song. A song that will ease our pain, mend broken bones, bring wholeness again. A song that will catch our babies when they are born, sing our death songs, teach us how to mourn. Mother, heal our hearts that we may serve you, for you are the tree of life for us.'

Then in soft words she told us the story of the mother of our tribe, Kisa, the greatest sorceress who ever lived, and how she saved our tribe three hundred years ago.

'Many tribes disappeared in the terrible time of the slave forts,' she began. 'The people did not fight back and the price for slaves was so great that the slave masters took everyone. Only those that hid or became part of the Evil survived. We were among those who chose to hide and then, because of Kisa, to fight back.'

A hush fell over us as she continued.

'She grew up in our secret village in the forest. It was surrounded by a maze that protected us for many years, until the slave masters found us. Kisa vowed to fight them. She trained in the arts of magic and warfare and when the slavers returned, she defeated them.

Tonight, I will tell you how she fought the slave masters in a great war…'

Figure 2. Kojo's Map

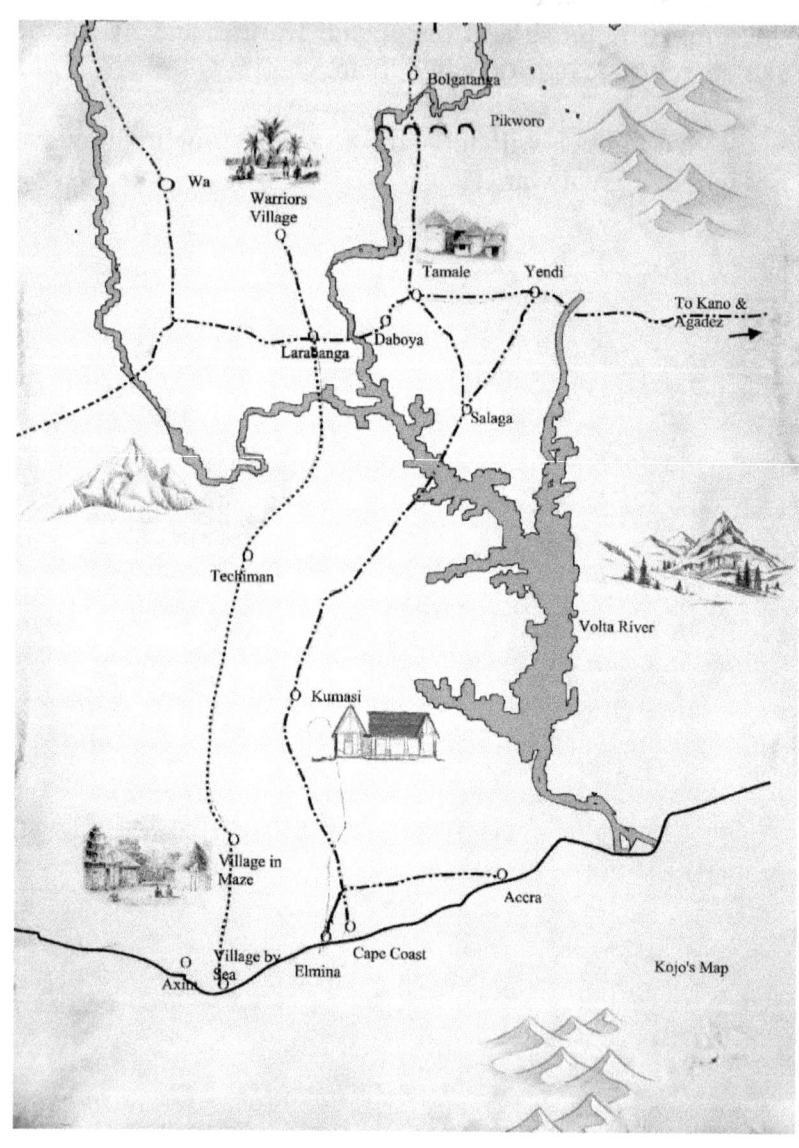

Figure 3. Map of West Africa

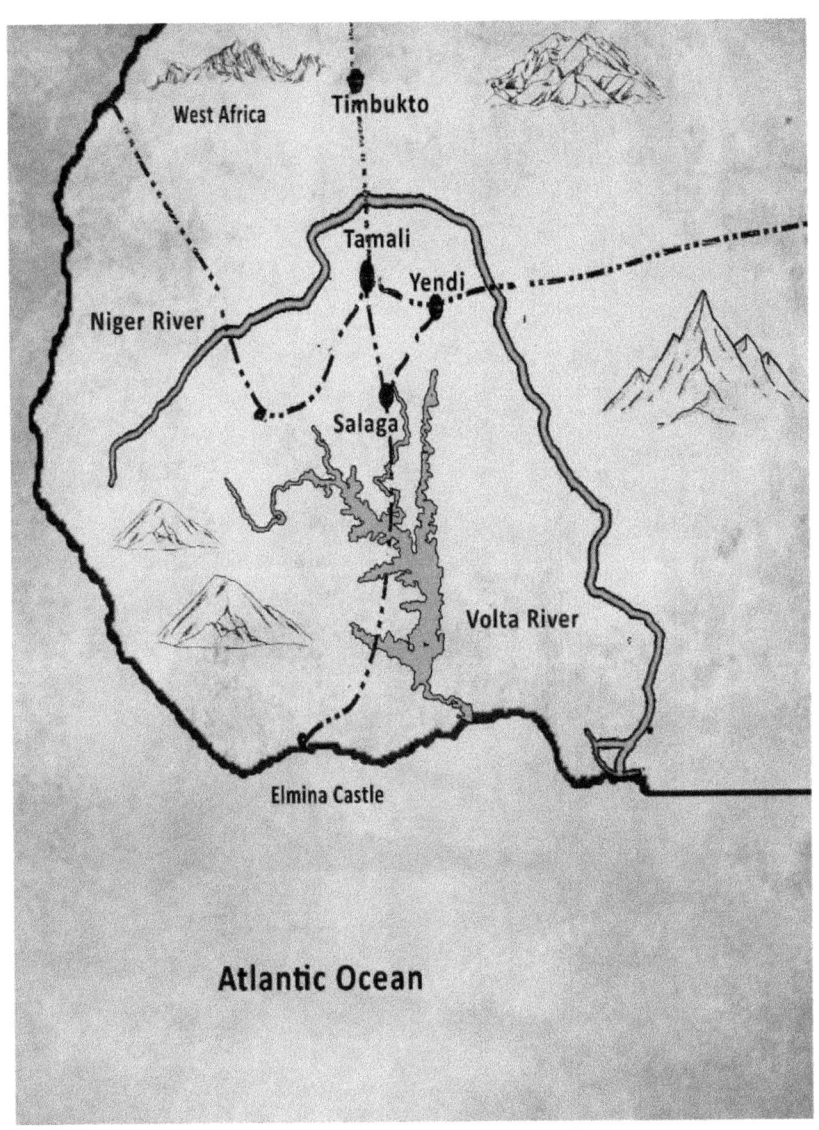

The

Vulture

Flies

Chapter 1
Battle's Aftermath

The one-eared man was riding fast, holding tight to the slim, young girl in his clutches.

High overhead a great vulture flew, screaming.

Afia had been thrown over the pommel of the saddle when she was captured. The stench of her captor filled her nostrils, her arms and legs hung uselessly, and her head banged against the leather saddle. A rough hand held her down. She shut her eyes against the horror. There was nothing she could do as the horse raced madly through the narrow forest path.

The one-eared man's companions were hot on his heels on their own tired mounts - racing away from the cursed village in the maze, that had turned from prey to predator with the coming of the sorceress.

Fear rose in their throats and they whipped their horses on.

The vulture followed them.

***

Kisa had led the battle against the Arab-Swahili slave masters to save the village in the maze. The survivors raised up Kisa as their Sorceress because she had brought them to victory with both sword and magic. In front of all, she killed the slave master Mbwana Sefu.

The villagers had also trained with her teacher, the mysterious black samurai, Yasuki, just as she had. They were filled with fear at the coming of the slave masters, but their young sorceress inspired them and gave them the courage to fight bravely. They killed most of the slavers and saved their children and their village.

The result was so unexpected that they had to rejoice and celebrate in their salvation. Raising the sorceress, as they called her respectfully now, was the first most important moment of the celebration by recognising that, without her, most would have been captured or killed.

It was clear from the size of the invading party that they intended to wipe out the village. In the end only one person was captured and only a few of the defenders died. It was seen as miraculous and the miracle worker was Kisa, the young apprentice to the old Obeah woman called Grandmother. But she was an apprentice no more. The battle had shown that to all.

The evening was spent in jubilant dancing and drinking, but Kisa and her lover and husband, Kojo, could not celebrate with the rest. Afia, Kojo's beloved sister, who had been taken. They retired early and spent the evening discussing the future with Yasuki and Grandmother. Somehow, they had to rescue Afia.

The next morning, Addie, the master drummer, summoned the villagers together. The Elders were calling a meeting so all could discuss what had happened in the battle. It was a day to be remembered forever in the tribe's verbal history. A sacred fire was lit, then all gathered around the great Sentinel tree, in the centre of the village.

First, Grandmother said prayers to thank the gods for the victory. Then a young man put on feathers and danced to frighten away the spirits of the evil dead, the spirits of Mbwana Sefu and the slave traders who had been killed in the battle.

Chief Abrafo and Grandmother spoke, and the people listened. They heard for the first time the story of the battle that they had lived through. It would be told over and over for all the generations to come, of that, they were sure. It sent chills through their bodies, and they muttered thankful prayers that they had survived.

The chief spoke the names of those who had died: Adwin, the carpet maker, Kofi the farmer, Kya, wife of Oko, who was killed protecting her babies. Grandmother made offerings and chanted prayers to the rhythm of the drums that eased the passing of the dead to the world of the ancestor spirits.

Then the Chief and Grandmother motioned Kisa and Kojo to come forward.

'Hail the sorceress!' The Chief cried out.

Grandmother and everyone else echoed this, including Kojo, who raised his fist. The others followed suit and then Kisa raised her sword high in the air with one hand and the symbol of her power with the other, the black spear carved out of the lightning-struck top of the Sentinel Tree – the tree that stood guard over the Village in the Maze.

'Somunye!' She cried out in her deep, loud voice. 'We are one!'

'Somunye!' The word was taken up as a chant by the whole village.

At last, Chief Abrafo called for silence and turned to Kojo to acknowledge his leadership in the battle as well. The Chief handed Kojo a ceremonial sign of office, a stick with feathers and small branches attached, to show that he was now a leader in the tribe.

After much clapping and cheering, the next part of the meeting began. Everybody in the village would be given the chance to speak about the events that had changed their lives forever.

Kisa could see that this was going to take hours. She chafed at having to leave Afia in the hands of the slavers and wanted to give chase, but Kojo whispered to her:

'The people need to release themselves and we must consult with them before we leave. It is the way.'

'I cannot protect Afia from here,' Kisa started to protest, but Kojo interrupted.

'Send Afia protection spells, my Love. I will see that decisions are made swiftly and no time is wasted. Have you looked through the vulture's eyes to find her?'

Kojo turned to the group and raised the ceremonial speaking stick for silence. Then one by one he allowed the villagers to speak their peace.

Kisa sat down and leaned against the Sentinel Tree, relieved to let Kojo take over the running of the meeting. She watched him talk, but her mind was already elsewhere. *Why didn't I think of that! Udele!*

As soon as the name crossed her mind, she felt herself lifted up and found herself looking out of Udele's eyes high above the village. As soon as Udele felt her presence, she turned and flew south down the path leading out of the village.

Grandmother saw what was happening and sat beside Kisa, staring fiercely at anyone who looked towards their new Sorceress. In the shade, Kisa's body rested against the trees, but her eyes were open and no one else noticed as her mind followed the slavers and Afia on the wings of the great she-vulture, Udele.

Meanwhile Kojo was addressing the villagers. 'We have won a great victory, but it is only the start of the war. It is important that all speak today but there are urgent matters for the Sorceress to attend to, so you must be quick. Chief Abrafo, what do you say?' Kojo asked as he handed over the speaking stick.

'I agree with all you say. We have won a battle, but it is only the first blow. If the sorceress does not strike again, our enemies will return. We are no longer hidden. And this goes far beyond our small village. All villages suffer as we have. This scourge must be met. These devils must be thrown into the sea! Let each now have his say, so that decisions can be made.'

Chief Abrafo handed the speaking stick back to Kojo who then oversaw the process in which every villager had his or her say. This covered everything from who had died or wounded to what to do about the capture of Afia, who was loved by the entire tribe.

Meanwhile, Kisa was flying with Udele's wings and using her sharp eyes to scan the partly obscured path through the jungle, searching for her prey. She found the horses, no longer running but still moving even after all the hours of the night. They were exhausted but the three slavers were so frightened by what had happened that they would not stop.

She saw the one-eared man on the lead horse, holding Afia down across his saddle. Udele screamed at the sight and, startled, he jerked on the reins, stopping his horse, and stared at the sky. His two companions pulled up beside him, glad for a brief rest.

One spoke. 'What do you see, Mbwana Badru?'

Badru! She had a name to put to the hated face.

'Badru! You will die by my sword!' She could not resist sending out the words to him through the vulture's voice. Her image rose briefly into each mind, enough to send chills of fear down their spines as they stared up at the circling vulture.

Badru nervously kicked his horse as he answered. 'It's only a vulture, Zuberi. Come, we must get to the fort! We cannot stop now!'

Kisa cursed her reaction. She should have remained calm. She rose high above them where she could see them, but they would have seen only a dot if they had looked up. However their eyes were fixed on the rough road to the great Dutch slave fort of Elmina.

I must slow them down, Kisa thought desperately. Then she remembered Kojo's words. 'Send Afia protection spells…'

But how? She remembered Grandmother's teachings on how to send thoughts to vulnerable minds, to influence them.

She began on Badru.

My captive is old. She is ugly. She has sores on her face. She smells bad...

A feeling of repugnance swept through Badru as he looked at the captive under his hand. Instead of seeing the young beauty he had captured, he thought he saw a sickly old crone. Badru swore and vowed to sell her quickly.

Other messages began flowing into the minds of all three slavers as Kisa saw Badru's reaction and gained confidence in her ability.

I'm tired. I must rest. I'm tired. I must rest.

Kisa was rewarded with the sight of her prey slowing down and bowing their heads, slumping wearily over their horses' necks. *They will stop soon. We will have a chance to catch them if I can get them to sleep.*

Back at the meeting, the names of the wounded were given with much praise for their bravery. Their care and chances of survival were discussed. Then people talked about what should happen next: burying their dead, burning the bodies of the slavers, repairing the trails and hiding the village. At last they came to the issue of Afia.

Kojo was running the meeting with brutal efficiency. The sooner he could leave to rescue his sister the better.

Kisa continued her assault on the minds of her enemies. Other messages were entering into Badru's head, unbidden and seemingly out of nowhere.

I can slow down now. Sleep, sleep. I want to sleep.

They won't follow me – they are cowards hiding in their stinking village.

Slow down.... Sleep, sleep....

And he did, nearly falling off his horse.

'Kondro!' Zuberi called out. 'Stop! Mbwana Badru must rest.'

Kisa heard the third name and was pleased. *I shall kill all three of you*, she thought.

Udele wheeled at her command and flew back towards the village. Kisa let go and returned to her body, satisfied that she could continue her mental assault on her prey and their journey would take considerably longer than they had planned.

Kojo was just informing the villagers that he and Kisa intended to follow the slave masters and rescue Afia when Kisa suddenly stepped forward and raised the symbol of her power, the black spear from the Sentinel Tree.

'Kojo and I will rescue Afia. We will take the war to the white devils and the slave masters. They have unleashed a storm by coming here!'

Silence fell. Some wanted to disagree, to ask their new leaders to stay to protect them, but no one argued with her.

Kojo filled the gap. 'Then it is decided. Chief Abrafo and Grandmother will guide and protect you while we are gone. We will return with Afia and an army at our back!'

Afia's fiancé, Adwin, raised a cheer. He was not brave enough to confront the slave masters, but his love for Afia was strong. He knew her only hope lay with Kisa and Kojo. The other villagers took up the cheering and the matter was decided.

Several of the young warriors begged to come with them but Yasuki, the black samurai who had come to teach Kisa and the others to fight, intervened.

'This is a job that the sorceress and Kojo must do. And they will raise an army as they do it. You must stay here to protect your village and continue your training with me. When the real war begins, you must be ready to join her army. Your sorceress will need you to be strong, because the enemy will fight back!'

Everyone stood up as Kojo and their sorceress prepared to leave.

Kojo spoke first. 'I go to save my sister. Protect the village while we are away.' He turned and gave a short bow to Abrafo and also to Yasuki.

Kisa stood on a stump and spoke.

'I will free Afia and start a war! It will not end for me till the slavers are defeated – no matter how long that takes!'

Kisa leapt down and strode towards the trail out of the forest. With a wave of his hand, Kojo set out with her. High overhead, a vulture cried.

Chapter 2

Following Afia

Kisa and Kojo ran smoothly, with long, loping strides, down the winding path of the maze that hid their village. The path was too narrow to run side by side and Kojo let Kisa lead the way. His fear for his sister Afia was matched only by the guilt he felt at her capture.

I should have protected her. She saved my life when I was a child and I failed her.

The thought spurred him on, and he overtook Kisa in a small clearing, but not for long. She matched his speed and passed him again, determined to lead.

That brought a smile to Kojo's face and then faded as another thought came to him. *I once believed that she would be the mother of my children. When did I realise the truth of the matter?*

Memories flooded back. After the first time that the slave master Mbwana Sefu discovered the village in the maze, Kisa, still a mere child, had told Kojo angrily that she was going to kill the slavers. He told her to stick to women's business and her anger had turned on him for that. He went to Grandmother for support, but she sat him down and told him how it would be.

'She will be a great sorceress and a great warrior. She will never be a mother.'

Grandmother had not softened the blow.

'But you must be there for her anyway. You must become a great warrior. You must protect her, while letting her lead. Some lesser men will look down on you for this, but you will rise above their jeers and the gods will reward you. There will be no hearth or hut for you, Kojo, filled with the laughter of children. There will only be a life of hardship and battle - if you truly love her.'

'I do,' he had answered without hesitation. *And I still do,* he thought now as he ran after her.

Kisa's mind was not in the past. All her efforts, physical and mental, were focussed on rescuing Afia and killing her enemies. Kisa had no doubts, no guilt, no hesitation. She had trained for this for years, yearned for this day to come, and now it was here.

Her mind turned to her spirit animals: leopard and vulture. She remembered the great she-leopard who stood eye to eye with her when she was hardly more than a toddler. She felt the strength of the leopard in her heart – always with her.

Then she remembered the night that Grandmother gave her the drink and she was led to her second spirit animal, Udele the vulture, matriarch of her clan. Out in the open, she could be her eyes and, on her wings, she could always find the slave masters. But not here in the jungle. She would have to find the one-eared man herself, especially if he reached that castle. No vulture or leopard could attack him there!

She quickened the pace again, eager to reach her enemies. She gripped the spear and thought of the great tree that had nurtured her in her childhood, allowing her to see beyond the narrow confines of the village.

Her other hand grasped the hilt of her sword, the sword she had received after her years of training, from her teacher, the Black Samurai, Yasuki. She felt a different kind of power flow through the sword, steeling her for battle.

Her hand left the sword and touched the amulet hanging from her throat. A different power flowed from it to her, the power of the earth and the mother goddess, Asase Ya. She felt strength pour into her and her legs stretched out, longer and faster. She felt as if she could run forever.

***

It was still early when Badru stopped at a stream in the forest and declared it time to rest. His companions, Kondro and Zuberi, were surprised. Their former leader, Sefu, would never have stopped till he reached the castle.

Zuberi tried to argue with him. 'We should try to get to the main road south. We could get there this afternoon if we keep going now…'

'Silence!' Badru barked back. 'I am the leader here! I too am the son of Mbwana Abbas! You are working for me now. I am the slave master of this band and I say we camp here!'

Zuberi swallowed his words. He knew Badru was wrong and hated him for it. The band was now only three men! Memories of the terrible raid gone wrong flooded his mind. The terrified villagers suddenly led by men with swords and in front of them, carrying a torch and a sword – a sorceress.

The fear Zuberi felt of that sorceress was intense. He knew she was tracking them. He had seen her in his dreams in the early hours of the morning when they stopped for the first time since fleeing the village that had fought back so unexpectedly.

'A damned sorceress!' Zuberi muttered as he unsaddled his horse. He couldn't stop thinking about the battle that had gone so wrong. He remembered the big black man with the strange robes and stranger swords. *Who was he?*

The villagers that had been simple farmers with only forks and hoes as weapons on the first two raids. Now they were armed with spears, knives, and the knowledge to use them. *How did that happen?*

Sefu and the rest of the raiders had been killed. There had been close to fifty in the raiding party and all they faced was a woman and two men with swords. The rest were just villagers. Who were the swordsmen and what connection did they have with that sorceress?

She struck first with her fire and her sword and two raiders fell. The swordsmen were right beside her, cutting and slashing with their bright steel and more raiders fell. Behind them came the villagers, many armed with only hoes and rakes, but using those farm tools like weapons! More raiders fell and Zuberi had moved closer to his leader, Sefu, but the sorceress was closing in on Sefu as well.

Zuberi saw Badru race for the village huts, just as the sorceress reached Sefu. Zuberi turned back to see his leader losing his horse, going to his knees, and dying on her sword at her feet. It was over in minutes. She stood over his body with a great black spear raised above her: the image burned in Zuberi's mind. A great fear rose in him at the sight of her and suddenly all Zuberi wanted was to get away from her as fast as he could.

He had turned his horse and signalled to Kondro, another mounted raider, to follow him. As they raced away, Badru galloped up with a captive over his saddle.

Now only he, Badru and Kondro were left alive, and yet Badru thought they would not send out a party of warriors to get their own back! Zuberi found himself longing for Sefu to ride up and take over again. He would have known what to do.

Zuberi looked over at their captive. He too saw an old crone, but he had a thought. *Maybe she is a respected elder. Perhaps if we can get to the Castle, we can bargain her back for a much better price than the white men will pay. And then we can get home.*

Then a soothing voice on the breeze said:

It's hot

Rest...

Drink from the stream.

You are far enough ahead.

Rest...

Zuberi looked around. Kondro was tying up his horse. Badru was washing, trying to get the blood of battle off his skin and clothes. The prisoner was bound and slumped on the ground between them, her eyes shut. Zuberi

15

sighed and gave up, with Kisa whispering in his ear *sleep*. Soon they were all asleep in the warm sunshine.

Far behind, Kisa and Kojo were running as fast as they could after them, but for all Kisa and Kojo's speed they could not catch up. The horses gave the slavers the advantage. Even with her mental commands to slow them down, it was not possible to catch Badru and his companions before they reached the safety of Elmina.

Hours later, the raiders woke suddenly and even Badru realised they had slept too long. Grabbing their captive, they remounted and raced off, a renewed fear of the sorceress driving them on. Far behind, Kisa felt their fear and knew that nothing would slow them now. She gritted her teeth and forged ahead.

Just before sunset of the next evening, the three raiders reached the castle. Badru left Zuberi and Kondro with the horses and dragged Afia inside. The men guarding the inner sanctum looked with disgust at the disfigured man and a captive who looked old and worthless.

Badru had never been inside before. Sefu always carried out the job of selling captives. Hesitantly he approached his first white man, a clerk of the Dutch West India Company, sitting officiously at a desk. The man had red hair as well as his pale pimply skin. He looked sick to Badru, but he had an air of authority much like Badru's feared father, the slave master, Mbwana Abbas.

After ignoring Badru for long minutes, the man raised his head from his paperwork and said, 'The slave masters are busy. You will have to wait. The palaver room will be open for business in two days.'

'What is the palaver room? Can you not buy this slave now?' Badru was anxious to do his business and leave.

'All business is conducted there!' The clerk was clearly annoyed as he shuffled his papers and Badru knew he was being dismissed.

Badru's nerves were raw and his fear of the sorceress was growing again. But he needed the money, so he had to wait. He jerked Afia to her feet and went back to the outer courtyard. He found Zuberi and Kondro drinking palm wine, in a vain attempt to forget what had happened in the hidden village. They offered Badru a drink. He handed Afia's chain to Zuberi and took the flask. He too had a nightmare to forget.

***

Kisa and Kojo continued to follow their prey, running day and night, with only brief rests and to drink at streams that crossed the path.

At the first stop, Kojo saw something strange: three ravens landed in the tree above where Kisa was drinking. They were staring at her from a tree that seemed to be bowing its branches towards her. Kojo froze, watching the ravens, sensing something was about to happen.

Kisa rose and looked up. Kojo could see that she had known they were there all along. She saluted them with an upraised fist and to Kojo's astonishment, all three bowed to her - wings outstretched, heads lowered, great yellow eyes meeting hers. Suddenly they flew up in a tight spiral above Kisa's head. Their cries were in unison and Kojo heard two words... *sorceress... somunye...* echoing in their cries.

They turned and flew in the direction of the castle. Without waiting for Kojo to finish drinking, Kisa took off after them. Kojo swallowed a mouthful and sprinted after her.

Night came and they kept running.

Kisa finally stopped at another stream crossing and Kojo leaped forward to drink and wash. When he looked up, Kisa was motionless before a tree that was also bowing before her.

Kojo looked up into its branches to see a huge owl staring with great yellow eyes at Kisa. Kojo froze. Kisa and the owl stared as if they were communicating to each other. Kojo waited, his muscles tightening in the cool night air.

A second owl flew in. It was much smaller, a different species that Kojo was familiar with – a little fishing owl. It sat on a branch between the great owl and Kisa and Kojo saw it bow to them both. Then the little owl ruffled its feathers and stared hard at Kisa.

Kojo waited for a long time, while Kisa communed silently with the owls. Then Kisa turned and started running again. The small owl flew after her, while the great owl sat and watched them go. Kojo stumbled through the water and took off after Kisa again. High overhead, the vulture called.

Long after midnight, Kisa stumbled. Kojo caught her arm just as she got up and tried to start running again.

'We have to rest my love,' he began. Kisa tried to pull away as she shook her head but above her the small owl hooted.

'He agrees,' Kojo said. 'It's time to rest.'

Kisa sighed and gave in. Kojo pulled her to the ground beneath the tree where the owl sat. They laid aside their weapons and he gathered her into his arms. She put her head against his shoulder, closed her eyes, and slept.

And dreamed...

She was alone. All around her were grey clouds and no earth and yet she could walk. All weapons and leather protection were gone. She was clad only in a thin brown cloth shift. The air felt colder than any she had ever felt before in her short life. Frozen it felt.

Sefu was riding towards her on a great black horse with fiery red eyes. Kisa was barefoot and bare handed. She looked around. There was nothing. No Kojo. No Yasuki. And no weapons.

The horse charged, Sefu screamed and swung his sword. Kisa leaped to one side, turned, and watched as Sefu yanked his horse around to charge again. Kisa knew in her heart that he had come back from hell itself to kill her.

He charged and charged again and each time she danced out of his way with the skills her teacher, the Black Samurai, had given her. But that was all she could do. She did not know how to kill him, mounted as he was on the horse of the dead. She feinted and dodged, wondering how long her strength would last – and what then?

Kisa heard Kojo calling her and Sefu disappeared. She opened her eyes, felt Kojo's arms around her, holding her, heard him saying: 'Wake up, it's a dream.'

She looked into his eyes, now fully aware of what had happened.

'Yes. I had a dream. I was fighting Sefu. I had no weapons, nothing, he was on a horse from the world of the dead. I did not know what to do – no sword, no spear, nothing.'

'It was a lesson, I think. You must be prepared to fight without weapons,' Kojo mused as he pondered her dream. 'Next time you will find a way to send him back to the land of the dead. Sleep now. I am here to protect you.'

Kisa sank back into his arms and rested for a while, but as soon as the sky lightened, she was on her feet and on her way again. Another day and half a night of running, then a rest in the darkest hours. In the early morning, Kisa and Kojo came over a low hill and saw the castle by the ocean, its white-washed walls gleaming in the first rays of sun.

The sight was entrancing and the smell of the salt air refreshing. Palm trees swayed in the morning breeze. In the distance they heard the sounds of village life, children crying, mothers singing, fishermen preparing to launch their canoes. And over it all hung the beautiful but brooding presence of the castle. Everything else faded into insignificance.

Kisa stopped and reached out for Kojo's hand. He looked into her eyes and saw the young girl he had always loved looking back at him. He smiled and squeezed her hand in silent acknowledgement that he was there for her, that they could do this together.

She sighed and looked at the formidable power of her enemies. The walls were high and thick and looked impenetrable. The gate, built of wooden beams crossed with metal braces, was firmly shut. A strange flag flew high above the gate, waving in the sea wind. It was coloured red, white and blue in horizontal stripes and in the centre, there were strange symbols. Kisa saw a lion and a bird.

'My leopard and Udele are stronger' she said quietly.

Kojo squeezed her hand and stepped forward.

'Yes… and smarter,' he said as he walked toward the white fort of their enemies.

Overhead the vulture called. Kisa held her spear hand up to Udele in answer and then followed Kojo.

Chapter 3

Inside Elmina

The closer they came, the bigger the fort looked. The massive white walls soon towered high above them. They watched as a group of ragged prisoners were marched through the great wooden gates, which shut with a boom behind them.

A thought unbidden swept through Kojo's mind: *I will never see Afia again!*

'No! We will rescue her! I don't know how yet, but we will do it, Kojo. And I will kill that man! These walls will not protect him.'

Kojo jumped. He had said nothing out loud. Kisa touched his arm, and he looked in her eyes. He saw her strength and it poured into him, giving him hope.

He drew himself up tall. 'Yes. I know we can do this! It is what we have trained for all these years... but...' His eyes slid back to the formidable castle walls.

'I don't know how yet either, Kojo, but you know that these devils will not win. I have disguised Afia in their minds – they think she is an old woman; they will not touch her body. She is safe for now.'

Kojo let out his breath in a sigh as Kisa continued.

'Somehow, we will get her back. There must be other ways in and back out again. For now, let's explore the town and learn what we can. What will be her fate? How long will she be in there and how will they take her out to send her across the sea? That is when our chance will come. For now, we must find a safe place to camp and then we must find out more about this place. My birds will help us.'

It was the first time Kisa had talked about the birds. As she spoke, the three ravens called out from above him. He looked up to see them circling overhead. He wanted to join them – to see what it all looked like from above.

'Perhaps they will let us do that.' Once again Kisa heard his unspoken thoughts. 'Tomorrow.'

She turned and strode back into the forest, looking for a secluded spot, hidden from the paths used by the villagers. The paths had been there for hundreds of years before the white men arrived and the villagers, creatures of habit and superstition, never wandered off them.

The fishing owl flew silently in front of them, leading them until he stopped in a glade with a small opening in the forest next to a creek. Kisa dropped onto the mossy ground and Kojo saw her utter exhaustion.

He sat beside her and gathered her into his arms. She collapsed into his chest, breathing deeply. Despite the dire situation, Kojo felt himself arousing to the touch of the woman who was his wife. He gathered her in close, wanting her with all his body and soul, yet constrained by Grandmother's orders.

Kisa felt his rising manhood and to her surprise, even after the days of running, felt herself aroused by his presence and his musky, sweaty man-smell. They were young and their bodies were coursing with hormones. They sank into each other's arms, touching each other and feeling the electricity. They grappled in what was almost a mock fight as they strained to not give in to their passion.

Then Kisa whispered into his ear. 'I have herbs… Grandmother gave them to me…'

Kojo stopped, stunned at the implications of those words. Kisa giggled and snuggled in close.

'But first my love, I need sleep,' and she was gone.

He held her softly for hours, protecting her. Overhead the little owl watched them. Far above the trees, he saw Udele circling. Kojo knew that if anyone approached, the birds would alert him. He too could sleep. He found himself whispering to the owl.

'Akwaaba – welcome, little friend.' He touched his chest with his free hand, 'Kojo.'

To his surprise, the little owl made a soft brief two note noise in response 'Koo – book!'

'Koo-book,' Kojo repeated.

'I follow her too, Koo-book. For you she is the sorceress. But for me, she is my wife, and I will give my life to her and for her – always.' He fell asleep with her gathered in his arms.

Kisa slept soundly , but Kojo woke at the slightest noise, thoughts crowding his tired brain. Memories of Afia rescuing him came to him in his dreams.

They were memories he had thought forgotten, but there they were – the burnt remains of the village, the dead grandmothers and babies, picking up his drum, Afia leading him by the hand into the forest. Walking, walking, walking… killing a baby monkey and eating it after days of nothing but grass and water. And then at last, walking into the sunshine and seeing Kisa for the first time.

He woke, remembered, then slept and dreamt again.

This time he was older – Grandmother was shouting at him and Yasuki was kicking him. 'Don't touch her! Protect her but don't touch her!'

He woke in a sweat and drew her body closer to him. Not being allowed to take her was incredibly erotic now that he knew she had the herbs to prevent an unwanted pregnancy. But first, they had to rescue Afia. This time, Kojo drifted away into the most beautiful erotic dreams he had ever had.

Kisa slept the dreamless sleep of the exhausted and woke refreshed before dawn. As soon as she sat up, Kojo was on his feet and ready to face the day too.

They bathed and drank, then ate a quick breakfast from the food bag that the village women had prepared for them. There were dried foods in it, tasteless, but nutritious and sustaining.

Kisa looked up at the three ravens sitting patiently on a tree limb above them. She stared into the eyes of the largest, then spoke: 'She is the mother. Her children will let us ride in their bodies, look out of their eyes. I have the herbs for that also.'

Kojo knew what she meant. Grandmother had used herbs to help Kisa and Kojo discover their spirit animals. Kisa found the birds of prey, had flown with Eagle Owl, the great Tawny Eagle and the White-headed Vulture, Udele, who circled lazily above them even now.

Kojo's experience was different. He became one with his drum and the trees that night instead – hearing them tell him that they could speak to him through his drum.

He had not flown before. The thought that he too could fly, roused him almost as much as holding Kisa the night before.

Kisa was busy getting ready. She took some herbs from her bag and began to prepare the tea.

'If we are both gone, who will guard our bodies?' Kojo asked.

'The little owl. If anyone comes, he will call. Udele and mother raven will hear and bring us back.'

Kojo looked up. Udele was circling them.

Kisa handed him the cup and he drank. He sat down in the shade and leaned against the tree. He drew his sword and laid it beside him. Kisa drank her tea and joined him.

'Put your head on my lap, my love,' Kojo motioned her down. 'Be comfortable and I will be ready.'

The three ravens sat on the limb of a nearby tree, waiting. Overhead Udele cried once.

Kisa lay down as he bid, closed her eyes and within moments she was looking out of the eyes of the mother raven's daughter. Mother raven looked back, aware of the profound change. Daughter raven gave her mind up to the sorceress as a horse gives control to his master.

Kisa shook her wing feathers and then looked to mother raven's son.

Kojo looked back at her in amazement and excitement. He shook his wings in answer and let out a low aaaah.

Kisa turned back to mother raven.

'Show us!' She cried it out in the language of the ravens. With an answering 'aaaaah', the mother raven took to the skies, and her children followed.

They flew swiftly to the town and over the great white castle, where they circled, cawing on the wind. Kisa and Kojo looked silently below through keen eyes, soaking up as much detail as they could. Overhead Udele circled, watching.

The ravens flew to the rocks and the sea behind the castle. They flew up and down the beaches where the fishing boats rested and over the village that surrounded the great white walls.

Suddenly the mother raven cried out and headed out to sea. In the distance, Kisa could see a great black ship, much bigger than any canoe she had ever seen. It had three huge posts on it that held cloth sails, also much bigger than she had seen on the canoes of the villagers.

The sails filled with the brisk sea wind, driving the ship towards the castle. A terrible smell penetrated her raven nostrils as she flew above the ship. All three ravens circled the ship once and then with loud cries that caused the startled sailors to look up from their duties, headed back to land.

The sailors saw the ravens. And far above them, they saw the vulture. They looked quickly away, returning to their chores on mast and deck, but shivering in superstitious fear.

Mother raven led them back to the wood where their human bodies waited. The raven's children landed back in the tree. Nestling down, they closed their eyes.

Kisa's and Kojo's eyes opened. They were in their own bodies, back as suddenly as they had left.

Kisa sat up. 'That black ship! It must be used to take the captives across the sea. It is waiting there to take Afia and the others away. What the runner told us when he came to the Village last year. He said the white men in the slave castle send the captives across the sea to grow crops for their masters. That ship must take them there, to that new land.'

'It stank of worse than a toilet pit in the heat' Kojo shuddered.

'What must it smell like when it is full of captives?' Kisa added.

'The fort is full of soldiers,' Kojo continued. 'But did you see how the outer courtyard had tents and townspeople selling their wares? I wonder where they keep the prisoners. I could not see enough.'

'It was good to get that view. It will help us find our way around.' Kisa was reaching into the food bag as she said this. The journey had given her a fierce hunger, as if she had run for miles.

'It would be even better if we had something to remember what we saw.' Kojo was hungry too, but he picked up a stick instead as he smoothed the dirt in front of him. He put a stone down to represent the castle and then drew some lines for the roads and paths, to, from and inside the town he had seen from the air.

'Before we can get into that fort, we must get to know the town. We will need clothes and food. We can steal what we need but we must know our way around.'

'I like that, Kojo. Put in the market,' she said as she handed him some pebbles.

Together they ate and discussed the details of the map that Kojo was drawing, while making plans for getting into the fort.

When they finished, Kisa sat back and took a drink of water from her skin waterbag. 'That was a great help. I feel like we know the town well enough to find our way around and do what we must do. It's time to explore the town, meet the people and decide what our next steps will be.'

The bustling town that had once been a poor fishing village was profiting from trade with the white men. They passed merchants and hawkers, eager to display the goods now available for all who could pay: bars of copper and iron, brightly coloured cloth, finely made ceramics, salt and spices.

Kisa and Kojo put some of their skills to work, picking pockets and then spending the money on clothing that they could use for disguises. Round and round they went, winding through the paths, learning their way around, but always with their eyes on the white castle. They had to get inside. But how? A plan slowly formed in Kisa's mind.

'Kojo, you must disguise yourself as a slave trader who is looking for work. Get into the fort, find out what happens there and where the captives are kept. Learn as much as you can, and I will do the same out here. If I dress as an old woman, I can ask questions without raising suspicions.'

They made their way back to their camp. It took the rest of the day to get their disguises made, faces painted, and strategies planned. Kisa took off her bracelets and dressed in rags. She used charcoal to create wrinkles in her face and painted a nasty unhealed wound on Kojo's face. If he passed the raiders of their village, they would not look close enough to recognise him.

At last, Kojo stood up, looking the part of a wounded soldier of fortune, willing to sell himself to a raiding party. He saluted Kisa, who was dressed in rags with her face painted in black grooves to make herself look like a wizened old woman. Then he turned and strode away.

'Return to me, my love,' she whispered to his back.

Kisa walked back to the village. She hobbled through the narrow lanes between the mudbrick huts, observing the activities of the locals. Learning nothing useful, she headed down to the beach, where the fishing canoes were tied up.

Offshore she saw the great black ship, sitting silently, all the sails gone. It was much larger than a dozen canoes laid end to end. She disliked it now as much as she had when she flew over it. It was black and ugly, and it stank of evil, even from this distance.

She saw a fisherman mending nets next to his canoe, overturned and steaming dry in the hot sun.

'What is that?' she asked him as she pointed to the black ship.

'Slave ship,' he answered, without looking up.

'Where does it take them?'

'I don't know. Far across the sea. Long way away... what do you care, old woman?' He looked at her suspiciously. Most locals knew little about the slave ships and didn't want to know more.

'Why? Why do they take them across the sea?' Kisa whined insistently.

'They worth big money. They work in sugar cane fields for white masters. That all I know.' The fisherman was getting irritable, so Kisa walked away.

She hung around the shore, trying not to attract any attention from villagers or soldiers alike. She spoke to one of the villagers, who had a cloth stall in the marketplace.

'I am from a village far away. What is that place?' she said as she pointed to the castle.

'It is called Elmina, which is a white man's word for a mine. In it the white men from the north live in the style of their people. They come to buy gold and wood and slaves. They bring many goods such as this fine cloth from their country,' he said and held up a brightly coloured bolt of cloth. 'You should buy some, mother, and have a new dress made.'

'No thank you. Not now. But why do they call it a mine? It is not a hole in the ground.'

'I don't know,' the merchant said and turned away. If there was no money to be had, he could see no reason to talk to this poor old woman.

Kisa turned her attention to the Dutch soldiers who were wandering about aimlessly in their spare time. They were forbidden by their officers to spend time in the village, but they did anyway. They liked whoring and drinking as much as soldiers anywhere, rules were made to be broken and discipline in this hot, distant outpost was slack.

Kisa watched them swagger around the village. They were dressed in blue jackets and white pants with metal-buckled leather shoes. They all wore broad hats to protect their pimply faces, already bright red from the tropical sun. Most had ugly facial hair and all of them stunk in their sweaty, unwashed clothes.

Their smell didn't seem to put off the local whores. They clung to the soldiers, dragging them into huts to satisfy their animal needs and then relieving them of their coins. The soldiers ignored Kisa as they would any old African woman, not worthy of their attention. She felt invisible to them and that suited her. She could watch and learn as much as she wanted.

But it was the fort and the ship, not the soldiers, that held the key to Afia's future. Kisa's eyes turned to them often, as she wandered around the village, wishing she could magically see inside them.

She went back to the shore to have another look. She saw a boat leave the large black ship and watched as it was rowed ashore. There was a big gate at the back of the castle. She expected it to open but instead she saw men in chains emerging from a tunnel below the castle that ended at the rocky beach.

The men were guarded by several black soldiers, overseen by a red-faced Dutch soldier, who loaded the captives on to the boat. Suddenly the gate opened, and a few wailing women were led down to the boat too. Then the sailors, both black and pale-skinned, rowed back out to the black ship.

When the captives were loaded, the black ship raised its sails and headed south, but just off the horizon, Kisa could see another black ship coming to take its place. Watching them, Kisa began to see way to rescue Afia.

***

Two days later, she saw Kojo emerging through the castle gates and breathed a sigh of relief. She had feared for his safety in that terrible place. By separate routes, they went back to their camp to plan their next move.

Kojo spoke first. 'It was easy to get in. I walked up to the gates and a guard asked me what I wanted. I sent the suggestion to his mind to believe whatever this handsome, but wounded, young man had to say.' He grinned. 'I may not be as good at that as you, but it was enough. I told him I wanted a job with a raiding party, and he let me in.'

'I found my way to the big courtyard we could see from the air. All around the edge against the great wall are mud brick rooms for the soldiers and slavers to use. Between these, tents are set up with food and other goods for sale. Whores were wandering around and slipping away with men into the rooms. It was a very busy place, like a little village.

'I spoke with several soldiers and guards - the black ones of course. There were a few white soldiers around, but their rooms are in past another set of gates. They do not talk to the black soldiers, except to give orders. They ignore the rest of us.

'I was told I could sleep in one of the huts and that the next day I could go up to the palaver room to talk to the traders. I was told I could find myself a job, or if I wanted, sell myself to the white devils. The soldiers said I could get a very good price for myself even with my wounded face. They were laughing, but I think it was a threat. I could tell I needed to learn as much as I could and get out fast, or one of them was likely to chain me in my sleep and sell me. I did not sleep much that night!'

'The next day I went to the palaver room where they sell the captives and I saw the white devils themselves. Not the soldiers, but their masters. They dress in strange clothes. They wear heavy coats in bright colours. They had white stockings on their legs and leather shoes with bright metal buckles. They were sweating like donkeys in the heat. They had slaves to wave great feathered fans over them, but it did little good.

'Then the captives were brought in. The slavers bargained with the devils. Men fetched a few hundred seashells, women more, but none of them brought as much as a good cow.' Kojo shook his head.

'I saw the one-eared man who took Afia - Badru. He brought Afia up while I was there and sold her. I wanted to kill him right then, but it would have cost me my life. They made me leave my weapons at the door, so I could not save Afia that way.' Kojo sighed at the thought.

'She did not recognise me. She never looked at me. She was in a trance, not seeing anything that was happening to her. Your suggestions worked. Badru thought he was selling an old woman and took quite a low price for her, but I fear that the guards will not see her that way.

'After she was sold, she was taken through the door into the inner castle. I was told the white men live there in fine splendour while their prisoners rot in filthy dungeons below them.' Kojo spat these words out in disgust.

'I did not get to see the dungeons myself, but I talked to one of the guards in return for a drink of palm wine. There is one prison for the women and one for the men. He said the men are taken through a tunnel to the sea where they are put on boats. The women go out through a big wooden door instead. I fear for Afia. She will be at the mercy of the white soldiers in there and they are known to carry many foul diseases.'

'Then I must go into the castle to protect her.' Kisa spoke in the tone she used when there would be no discussion.

Kojo protested anyway. 'It will be easy to get you in, but how will you get out again with Afia?'

'I have seen the other gate. It is around the back of the fort. I will show it to you and the slave ship too. It sits in the harbour waiting even now – a black ship like the ravens showed us. That is where Afia and I will be taken. You must keep watch until they bring us out to take us to that ship. Then you must kill one of the sailors and get on that ship with us!'

'Then what?' Kojo said in surprise.

'You cannot free us by yourself on the land. There are too many guards. But on the ship it will be different. There will be strong men in the hold, men crying out for freedom. We can lead a revolt, Kojo. We will take that ship and free everyone, not just Afia!'

Kojo stared at her in awe. It was such a brave, unexpected idea.

'But we could take nothing with us... no weapons... my drum...' he said at last.

'We can fight without weapons. That is what Yasuki taught us. But your drum...' she paused, knowing how important it was to him. It was all he had left of the village of his birth, the little Kidi drum he had picked up from the smoking remains of his life when his sister Afia saved him from the slavers - the drum he had carried ever since and was as much a part of him as the amulets that Grandmother had given her were to Kisa.

'I can wrap it and bury it. The gods will keep it safe. When we have rescued Afia, we will come back for it.'

Kisa looked deep into his eyes and took him in her arms. 'I love you,' she whispered.

'This idea of yours, it could work,' he finally agreed.

'It is the only way, Kojo. We will make it work.' *But first,* she thought, *I will find this Badru and kill him!*

Kojo swallowed his fears for Kisa. She was right. It was their only chance to save Afia.

Chapter 4

Imprisoned

Kisa changed out of her old woman's disguise. 'What shall I wear to the castle? How shall I appear to the devils?' Kisa spread her arms and looked down at her slim form.

'Do not tempt them too much with your beauty,' Kojo smiled. 'Or you will be fighting them off at every corner.'

'I wish I could show them my teeth,' she hissed back, not amused. 'But I want to fetch a good price for you to spend on our first gun!'

'Yes, you need not dress as old or sick… but not as a warrior or a whore either.' Kojo stood with his hands on his hips, staring at his beautiful young wife and wanting her to stay safe, but seeing also the sorceress he must follow.

'I will cover myself in the fashion of the women of the Prophet,' Kisa mused, remembering what she had seen on their northern journey before the battle.

'Fake shyness, my love,' Kojo grinned a gain. 'That should test your powers of deception.'

Kisa grinned and turned to search through the pile of clothes they had obtained from the village. She chose a dark brown dress suitable for an older married woman and wrapped scarves around her head and face.

Kojo brought more scarves. 'Put them inside your dress above your belt to hide your slimness. Let them see a fatter woman than you are. And put touches of grey in your hair.'

Kisa put the finishing touches on her costume and stood back for Kojo to see. 'It suits,' he agreed, swallowing his fears for her again. He could hear Grandmother's voice in his head. *She will walk into the lion's den many times... this is only the first.*

Kojo tied her hands and led her to the castle gate. The guard let them in and Kojo took her up to the palaver room, set with tables where the slave masters sat. The walls were white, the floor polished and there were large windows to let in the light.

Kisa took it all in as she was led up to a freckly-faced white man with bright red hair who eyed her with a disgustingly sexual look. She stared hard back, and he turned his eyes away. She longed to send him a message of his own death, but she didn't want to affect the price Kojo got for her.

Kojo and the man haggled for several moments while Kisa sent him the message that she was worth a good price. Kojo was offered a thousand cowrie shells, more than usual. His stomach in knots, he watched as they took Kisa away. He collected his shells and went down to the outer courtyard, where he traded the shells for a pistol, powder, and balls. He bought a soldier a drink of palm wine in return for showing him how to use it.

***

A black guard took hold of her chains and lead Kisa through a high-ceilinged hallway. They descended the stairs to the inner courtyard. The smell of the dungeons assaulted Kisa's nose. She was led to a wooden door with another guard in front, who laughed when he saw her.

'More meat for the...' he started to sneer till her eyes met his and he caught a glimpse of the leopard. He lowered his eyes and hastily opened the door. Overhead three ravens circled, crying loudly, as Kisa disappeared from sight.

Kisa's eyes took a moment to see in the darkness. Then she saw rough stone walls and a group of women huddled together on a bare stone floor. Beside them were two buckets, full and stinking with their wastes.

'Kisa!' Afia's eyes had adjusted to the gloom and when she saw the sorceress, she stopped crying and stood up. The guard removed Kisa's chains and swiftly left the room, an unreasoning fear overwhelming him, despite his contempt for the women.

Afia sobbed and clung to Kisa, thinking that she had been captured as well.

'No! I am here to protect you. Kojo and I have a plan. We will free you and these other women too.' Kisa looked around at the other women.

'How can you do that? An army could not take this place,' Afia protested.

'They will be taking us to a ship. On the ship we will fight. Have faith,' was all Kisa would say.

***

That night a soldier came in to choose a woman for the fort commander. Kisa sauntered up to him and gave him the suggestion to take her. He led her up the stairs to the governor's private quarters, a beautiful room with large windows, polished floors and a large bed in the middle.

The governor was sitting in a chair being fanned by two slaves. He was naked except for his white breeches and, to Kisa's eyes, was repulsive to look at. His long greasy hair was a strange reddish colour, his skin pale like the belly of dead fish. It was pockmarked and flushed, not just with the heat but with a look of sickness about him. He had a large stomach hanging out over his pants and there were long, ugly hairs sprouting from his flabby chest and arms.

He stood up, waving his slaves and the guards away. He started suddenly at the cry far above him of an unknown bird. *An eagle perhaps,* he mistakenly thought.

He walked up to Kisa, took her by the arm and led her to the bed. She kept her eyes down, allowing him to lead her that far. Then she looked up into his red, watering eyes.

He didn't have time to be startled by this. Soothing thoughts flowed into his mind, and he found himself becoming very sleepy. He sank down on the bed.

Kisa marvelled how easily the man was hypnotised. She gave him thoughts of a satisfying night with a pretty woman. Then she slipped herbs into his wine that made him too sick to want another woman for many days. She waited for a while so the guards would not be suspicious, then slipped back out. Unsuspecting, they led her back to her cell. Overhead Udele called again.

41

With the governor under control, Kisa decided to go hunting for Badru the following night. She was sure he was in the outer area of the Castle, where the traders and soldiers camped. Now was the time to find and kill him.

'I am going out tonight,' she whispered to Afia. 'I am going to kill the man who captured you.' She got up and moved towards the guard. He followed her into the passageway, hoping to taste the merchandise. He got the suggestion of a great sexual experience as she knocked him out with one slicing hand to his neck.

She slipped into the darkness and moved silently to the inner gate which separated the Dutch masters from their underlings. Only one guard manned the gate, and he was facing outward and distracted by the unaccustomed sound of a vulture crying above him.

Kisa used a hand chop to bring him down and then left a suggestion in his mind that he had fallen asleep on duty. She slipped past him into the outer courtyard. A few minutes later the guard awoke with a headache and a guilty feeling. He quickly straightened up and resumed his duties, while hoping that no one had noticed him sleeping.

Kisa walked around the courtyard that she had seen through the raven's eyes. She stole a whore's scarf, so she fit in as she searched for Badru. He was nowhere to be found. Finally, she offered various traders a good time if they could give her information as to the whereabouts of the slave trader with the missing ear. One man told her that he thought the man had left the castle, but that one of his companions could be found with the prostitutes.

Kondro was with an older woman who was all he could afford, but he thought his luck had changed when a much younger and far more beautiful woman beckoned to him to follow her. She looked vaguely familiar, but Kisa sent him a powerful suggestion that he did not know her.

She took his hand and led him into an unoccupied tent. He reached for her but suddenly her hand was around his throat and his own knife slipped up through his ribs and into his heart. Kondro, blood bubbling out of his throat, sank to his knees and died silently at Kisa's feet.

'For Afia!' she said quietly, wiped the blood from her knife on his robe and left him without another thought.

She slipped out past his companions and said, 'he will be out soon!'

Then she made her way back to the inner courtyard. No one was expected to want to break in, so it was much easier to convince the new guard to let her through. When they found Kondro's body, they would search among the whores, not the women's dungeon.

***

A few days later, soldiers came and took the women to the inner courtyard to be stripped, baptized, and branded. The baptism was nothing more than a bored priest sprinkling water on them and declaring them to be Christian.

The branding of their buyer's mark on their shoulders was painful but Kisa glared at the man with the hot iron and uttered no cry. His hand slipped at her stare and left only a lightning-shaped mark instead of the intended letters.

When he was finished, the women were led through the gate of no return and down to the shore, to be taken by longboat to the ship. Overhead, the three ravens and Udele circled and cried out in distress.

***

By that time, Badru had returned, discovered Kondro's body and left again in a panic. He was sure the sorceress had a hand in Kondro's death and so he rode hard, heading home to safety. Zuberi was his only companion.

He had two reasons to go back home to the slaving capital of Agadez. The first was to escape the sorceress but the second was to get a new raiding party. His father, the slave master Mbwana Abbas, would surely see his worth now.

My raiders, Badru thought with satisfaction. Sefu, his half-brother and tormenter, was dead and the sorceress was far behind him. *Good riddance to them both!*

Chapter 5

Goede Fortuin

Outside the castle, Kojo wandered the foreshores, blending in with the townspeople and minding his own business, but always watchful.

At last, he saw longboats launched from the black ship and rowed to shore. He watched as the captive women were led through the heavy back door of the castle and down to the waiting boats. Kisa and Afia were among them.

Kojo moved behind a black sailor standing furthest from the boat. A hand over the mouth, a knife drawn across the throat and the man sank down silently behind the rocks. Kojo stepped over him and took his place.

The attention of the other sailors and the guards was focussed on the women. This was due more to Kisa than any determination on their part to do a good job. She was looking directly into the eyes of each guard and sailor, influencing them to think only about her and the other women.

This was the first time she had used hypnosis in such a life-or-death situation, but it was easy. These were simple men. They never noticed when Kojo slipped on to the boat instead of their dead colleague.

When the women were loaded two of the castle guards pushed the boat off the rocks and the sailors began rowing. The women wailed louder as they left the shore and headed across the choppy water to the black ship.

Kisa and Afia held hands and Kisa chanted a calming prayer to the women. 'Mother, protect us. Mother, gather us into your arms. Mother, do not abandon your children.'

One woman was on the verge of jumping into the water, but the prayer settled her. All the women heard a gentle whisper on the wind.

'Wait, wait, help will come… wait, wait…'

As the boat approached the black ship, the women gasped at its size. Giant letters that they could not read spelled out its ironic name: Goede Fortuin – Dutch for good luck.

Then the smell hit them. It was so disgusting that several women vomited. Kisa closed her nostrils, put her tongue on the roof of her mouth and breathed through her clenched teeth. The smell still permeated her pores.

It was worse than any latrine she had ever used, worse than the smell of death. Instead, it was a horrific combination of the two: human faeces mixed with the bodies that had been allowed to half rot before being dropped in the sea. No matter how the crew cleaned it between voyages, a slave ship never lost the stench of its cargo.

The sailors stopped rowing and the man in the bow caught the rope ladder that the crew lowered. They made the women climb it into the waiting arms of the sailors on deck.

One by one they were shoved across the deck and down into the forward hold, away from the male prisoners. The sailors laughed and manhandled the women, squeezing their breasts and feeling between their thighs while telling them in the coarsest language what would happen to them later that night.

That was until Kisa stepped on to the deck. As she scaled the ladder, she willed the hands away from her and not a man touched her, though all eyes were on her. Suddenly three ravens flew from out of nowhere, circling above the ship, screaming insults. They landed on the topmost mast and fell silent. Kisa looked up and all eyes followed hers. But the eyes of the ravens were fixed only on Kisa. Then she looked at the sailors.

A wave of fear went through each man's mind at the eyes now staring at him. Even the white captain at the helm felt it. Afia came on board behind her, and the two women walked proudly untouched to the hold. When they were out of sight, the ravens screamed a warning to the terrified sailors. It seemed a warning to the superstitious crew and they hesitated, but the captain and first mate angrily ordered them back to their tasks.

The rest of the prisoners were brought on board. Kojo was the last to climb the rope ladder. While all eyes were on Kisa, he moved quickly into the shadows so that none of the sailors could see that he was unknown to them. After the longboat left, he stationed himself as the women's guard. Kisa sent mental suggestions to the crew that he belonged there.

The captain and sailors were eager to leave this place. The mainsails were hoisted, along with the special black side sails that marked the ship as a slaver. These were spread on either side of the ship to drive air into the holds where the captives were held, though it was never enough. Overhead the three ravens circled and cried. The superstitious sailors cursed them as they went about their duties and felt some relief when the birds finally disappeared.

Kojo waited until they were underway and then managed a few minutes alone with Kisa.

'I found out where they are going. Not west across the sea yet, but south. Their holds are not full. They will visit other slave forts. They are going south to an island called Sao Tome.'

'Good. Then we won't have so far to sail to get back home.' Kisa grinned as Kojo melted into the darkness, only the gleam of his white teeth smiling at her visible in the cloudy gloom.

Because the women weren't chained, Kisa was able to explore the deck the first night out. She waited until Kojo was on duty and then slipped by him. Mental suggestions to the sailors kept them looking elsewhere as she got her bearings in this strange environment. She found the entrance to the deeper hold where the male captives were kept. She saw the ropes and the rigging and watched the sailors as they furled and unfurled the sails.

She watched the white man at the helm, turning the great wheel that controlled the ship and listened to his shouted commands to the sailors. She took great gulps of fresh air, so needed after the stench below decks and looked up at the stars. The sailors in the rigging reminded her of the cosmic trickster, Kwaku Ananse, and she said a quick prayer to him to help her in the trickery she needed to take this ship. Then she slipped back down to discuss her plans with Kojo.

'How many men are in the other hold?'

'Not many. Fewer than the sailors and they are chained, of course. But I have been talking to the sailors. They are going to buy more slaves at the next port, and they hope to get more men. I think we should wait till there are more strong men on the ship before we act. It will give me time to find out who has the keys to the chains and what weapons we can use.'

Kisa was impatient, but she saw the sense of what Kojo said.

'How far to this island, Sao Tome?'

'I am not sure. A few days at least.'

'I suppose I can put up with this stench for that long, if it means we have more men to fight with us. Do you think the black sailors would help us?'

Kojo snorted. 'No. They too make money from the sale of the slaves. And I have heard that the captain and his officers are harder on the sailors than the captives. Any sailor who disobeys orders is hung from those trees they call masts until he dies. The captives are worth money to the captain. The sailors are worth nothing.'

Kisa sighed and fell silent.

The journey took more than a few days, so they spent the time getting to know both captives and sailors. At night, Kisa surrounded the women with protection spells and left Kojo on guard to prevent the sailors from hurting them. Then she prowled the ship, looking for weapons. There were long spiked hooks that the sailors used to grab lines and short, fat belaying pins used to tie them in place, which looked useful.

They learned the ship's routines and Kojo learned the basics of sailing. He could see that just taking over the ship was not the only problem. They had to get it back to shore or they would all drown.

The sailors were mostly poor white men who were only interested in profits and surviving the voyage. A few were mulatto or black, but they too were seasoned sailors who had no problem with slavery for profit. The most important people on board were the captain and the surgeon, both Dutchmen. They were the lords of the ship, and everyone obeyed their orders without question.

Kojo also found time to explore the hold. He found bolts of brightly coloured cloth, kegs of alcohol and some strange, dried leaves with a pungent smell that the other sailors informed him was called tobacco. There were iron and copper bars, combs, mirrors, beads and bangles and he learned that they were all to be used to trade for slaves.

The only women on the ship were captives and the captain and his officers forbade the sailors to have sexual contact with them. The sailors were dirty, unhealthy, and likely to carry any number of infectious diseases. They brought down the value of these women when they arrived at the slave market of Mauritz in Brazil, so the officers were on the lookout for misbehaviour by the sailors.

A few days out, a sailor was caught trying to molest one of the women. He was taken on deck, whipped with the cat o' nine tails and tied to the mast for two days without water. When he begged for a drink, the other sailors laughed and poured salt water on his wounds instead or put vinegar in his mouth.

Kojo was watching. *They will leave him to die*, he thought, but, in the end, they needed him. Kojo saw the surgeon inspect the man and go to the captain. Words were spoken and the captain gave an order. Within minutes, a sailor cut him down and after a drink, the miscreant was ordered back into the rigging.

'They needed his labour,' Kojo explained what he learned to Kisa. 'The one with the white linen ruffles on his chest and sleeves and the blue uniform – he runs everything. They call him captain. His name is strange: Johann de Vries.

He struts like a rooster, above the others, with his broad hat and fancy jacket and gives all the orders. No one dares disobey him. His officers punish any disobedience worse for the sailors than the captives in the hold. There the men are chained, but the sailors are loose on the ship, and they have to be cowed into obedience. They are very poor in their country. Some were stolen and put on this ship. They are a sickly lot. It is best not to go where they sleep. The air is foul with their sickness.'

Indeed, two days out, one of the sailors died. His body, when discovered, was quickly wrapped in a sheet, weighted down, and sent to the sharks that always followed the slave ships. Kisa and Kojo watched the proceedings with interest. The ship's surgeon said prayers and read from a small book. The sailors took their caps off as the body slid into the sea. There was a moment of silence and then they returned to their duties. And the ship never faltered but continued to move south through the rising seas.

As the waves got bigger so did the discomfort of the prisoners. Kisa experienced sea sickness for the first time in her life and she did not like it. In the men's hold, it was much worse. Once the first man threw up, the smell was so bad that the rest quickly followed suit. There was nowhere for the vomit to go, and the smell became unbearable. The sailors avoided the hold, descending only to take food and water to the suffering men below.

Kojo saw an advantage in this and volunteered to take supplies down. No one argued with him. This gave him the chance to smuggle the first weapon to the captives. It would give them hope to see or hold a knife or a piece of wood and know that soon they could use it on their captors. It also could give them some faith in Kojo, who they were unsure of. He said he was on their side, but he was dressed as a sailor and the crew treated him as one of their own.

Kojo set about in earnest to befriend the men in the hold and earn their trust. He picked out a strong, young Ashanti warrior as the most likely leader in the group.

'My name is Kojo. I come from the forest lands to the west of Kumasi. I came on this ship with a great sorceress, who will lead a mutiny on this ship to free you.' As proof he handed the man a small knife.

'My name is Fela. I am Ashanti and come from a village to the east of Kumasi. I was taken defending my family.' Fela looked at the knife in his hand. 'I did not trust you before, but this knife shows me the truth of you. But who is this sorceress? How will she free us?'

'The women are not chained. The sailors think she is just another captive, but she haunts their dreams with fears of death, when they dare to sleep. She is weakening the crew of this devil-ship and she is sending strength to you. I will bring her here to meet you and the others. Then you will see for yourself.'

'When?'

'There is a storm in the distance. We are sailing toward it. The sailors have told me the seas will be rough. They will be too busy fighting to keep this ship from sinking to watch us ... and you down here will be much sicker than you already are. The smell will keep them away, but you must be ready – drink, but do not eat their slop. If your stomachs are already empty you will be able to fight instead. Expect us when things seem the worst!'

Kojo turned and left as suddenly as he had appeared. Fela palmed the weapon, taking strength from the feel of cool steel. He turned to the other captives, who had been together in the Elmina dungeon for a long time. In that nightmarish place, they forgot the petty differences and jealousies between their tribes, as they struggled to survive.

The weakest had died there. The strongest survived through cooperation as much as competition. They knew each other and had the potential to be forged into a fighting unit under a good leader. Kojo was determined to provide them with that.

Many had lost heart since being branded and loaded like cattle on this hellish vessel. They could not read its name on the prow as they were loaded but if they had, they would have understood the dreadful irony of a slave ship named the *Good Hope*. Leaving their homeland to the wails of the women in the other hold had sapped them of much of their will to resist.

Conditions in the hold were even worse than in the dungeon. One man was already on the verge of death and many others were sick. But Fela was young and strong. He wanted to live, and he wanted to be free. He moved to the healthiest men close to him, prepared to tell Kojo's story and convince them to pass the information on down the lines of the chains.

By that evening the whispers had carried the tale to all who were well enough to hear it. Most were sceptical and some were afraid that this was intended to be a betrayal, which would end in whippings and punishment.

'Why would they bother?' Fela argued with the closest naysayer. 'They want us strong and healthy, so they get good money for us. Not beaten and bloody! This weapon is the proof this Nzema man speaks truth.' Fela showed him the knife.

'But what about our chains?'

'He said there was a sorceress with him. He will bring her here. We will see what she can do about the chains. If we are freed of those, I will fight! If you do not fight too, you will be a fool and deserve to die in those chains.' Fela hissed back.

Then he sat back, cradling the small knife, and waited for the sorceress.

***

On the deck, Kisa and the women had cleaner air to breath but still they suffered as the ship pitched and rolled through the waves, which were getting noticeably larger. In the distance masses of black clouds loomed. The captain above them was watching them and muttering.

He cursed the weather but ordered the ship on. It didn't look that big. The seawater would wash the decks and the hold. The sooner they reached Sao Tome, the better.

Late that night the weather turned nasty, and rain pelted down. The waves were higher than the ship. The women were taken into the forward hold. Kojo brought them down, then slipped out again with Kisa.

In the dark they were barely visible, and the sailors, intent on keeping the ship on course, were too busy to notice as two shadows slipped from the forward hold towards the men's hold.

Kojo walked up to the sailor on guard and said, 'I have come to relieve you. You are needed on deck.' Both Kisa and Kojo's minds were sending suggestions of compliance to the man, who nodded, handed the whip he was holding to Kojo and headed up into the driving rain.

Kisa's nostrils were hit by the powerful stench of the vomit and wastes of the seasick men. She closed her nostrils and mind to it, forging forward, taking only the shallowest of breaths.

They stopped in front of Fela, who like the rest, was lying down. Side by side, they stood in front of the prisoners. They spread their legs and braced themselves against one another, but their knees bent with the waves – a trick they learned from watching the sailors, so they could stay upright.

Kojo spoke loudly enough for all to hear. 'Behold the sorceress!'

Kisa raised her free hand and a small blue light rose from her palm. Fela and the others hissed in awe, though it was only one of Grandmother's smallest tricks. Kisa had a small amount of the necessary substance concealed in her magic pouch for this occasion. A little magic light went a long way to convincing these men that she had the power to help them.

As the light went out, she spoke. 'I come to free those who do not wish to live in chains. I will strike hard and kill the crew. We will take this ship! Join me or die here. I do not care which. I will fight whether you do or not!'

She turned and strode out, leaving Kojo to map out the details.

'I know where the keys to chains are kept. It will happen after we take on more captives. The women will bring you pieces of steel and wood – the tools for sailing this ship will be our weapons. And even the chains that you wear. I will release you. They will arm you. The sorceress will lead you to freedom!'

Then he too left the foul hold for the rain-washed air above.

He found Kisa vomiting. He handed her a rag to wipe her mouth and kept watch, but the crew were still busy.

'If I had known how bad it was, I would have eaten nothing for the past days,' she muttered when she was finished.

'It's much worse than it was last time I went below. I should have warned you though.' Kojo put a cool hand on her face. She felt feverish.

'Are you all right?'

'Yes, yes,' she said impatiently as she pushed his hand away and headed back to the other women. 'But I think I will sit out the rest of this storm. Oh Mother! I hate this ship!'

Kojo wanted to join her but hurried instead back to his duty as the guard of the hold.

***

They ploughed through the storm for three gut-wrenching days but at last it subsided, and the sun came out.

The Captain had the women brought back on deck. They were allowed to wash in sea water and then told to sit in the sunshine and enjoy the fresh air by the man Kisa could see was the white man's witch doctor. Kojo had told her that the sailors called him the surgeon and were very respectful of him.

'He is the only one who can save them if they get sick. But his main duty is to keep the captives alive. Everyone who dies means less money to the masters.' Kojo spat in disgust.

Now the surgeon addressed the women through an interpreter. Kisa listened with interest.

'My name is Wilhelm Jansen. I am the ship's doctor. Your health is my concern.

'I know that you are frightened and confused. But we mean you no harm. We are taking you to a better life.'

Kisa stared at him in disbelief.

'You are Christians now. When you die, you are saved. Before you faced hell and damnation. We are your saviours. Do as we say and you will have a much better life than the one you had in the jungles. You are savages but you will be blessed with civilization.'

Kisa wanted to stab him in the heart right then and there, but she could see Kojo, on guard, willing her with his eyes to be silent. She took a deep breath as the surgeon finished and turned back to the captain.

After some discussion between them, the captain ordered the sailors to bring the captive men on deck, ten at a time. They were brought in their chains, to prevent any from attacking the sailors or jumping overboard.

When the first lot, including Fela, were assembled, they were doused with buckets of sea water to wash off the filth. Then they were ordered to dance.

'Dance, dance, dance!' the surgeon shouted while jerking his arms up and down.

'Show them!' he ordered the guards.

One sailor jumped up and down, waving his arms, while the other guards used whips to force the prisoners to do the same.

Kisa stood in plain view of the miserable captives as they danced. She seemed invisible to the sailors, but the prisoners could not keep their eyes off her. Fela was mesmerised. In that instant he fell in love with Kisa completely, totally and for life. Someday, perhaps, he would have a wife. But for the foreseeable future, he was a servant of the sorceress, bound to her by the chains of the heart.

Kisa saw it. She was only eighteen and still unused to her new effect on the men she would meet in this war. She stared back, glad that Kojo was at her side. She wanted men like Fela to follow her but not want her sexually. It was such a sword with two edges, one good, one quite scary. She had to be strong in herself.

Back at the wheel, the captain watched the forced dancing with approval. After some time, he ordered the dancing to cease. Then he stepped forward and explained through an interpreter that dancing and washing would occur regularly.

'My name is Johann de Vries. I am the captain of this ship. We are here to civilize you and save your souls. We want you to enjoy this journey. You are going to a much better life in the new world than the one you left behind. All that filth and disease.'

He snorted, unaware of the irony of the words on a ship wracked by the white man's own deadly diseases.

He stepped back and the surgeon took over. 'We want you to be healthy and happy. Washing and dancing are good for you. When you reach the end of this journey, you will see how much better your lives will be and thank us for bringing you there.'

The surgeon motioned to the guards to take them down below again and bring up the next lot for exercise and propaganda. Unfortunately for the surgeon and the crew, Fela and the other prisoners were so hypnotised by the presence of the sorceress, that they heard nothing of it.

After all the men were washed and exercised and safely back in their hold, Kisa managed a few words with Kojo.

'They think they are helping us to a better life?' Kisa was so angry that she was shaking and on the verge of tears.

But she won't cry, Kojo thought with pride. He had not seen her cry since her father was taken by the slave master Sefu years before. She never cried when hit or hurt in training and she would not cry now. Her anger always won out when her emotions battled within her.

Then she spoke. To his surprise, it was not about what the surgeon had said, but about Fela.

'Kojo, Fela is in love with me. He wants me. You must watch the men that are attracted to me. It worries me. I can fight the surgeon and his kind. But I need men like Fela to serve me - but that is not their first thought when I look into their eyes and will them to follow me. I see now why Grandmother insisted that we marry. You must protect me from the men who will serve me, Kojo. I see that now.'

Kojo was stunned. He saw before him his eighteen-year-old bride – who was still a virgin. He had been thinking of the dangers of the castle, the slave masters, the soldiers, and the guards, not the men in the hold. Now he realised that his duties as the protector of his young sorceress were far more difficult than he had imagined. There were far more dangers to face than just the obvious enemies.

Kisa sat down and put her head in her hands. Kojo ached to take her in his arms, but he could not. His disguise was being a sailor and her guard. All he could do was reassure her with words.

'I would give my life for you, my love,' he whispered while pretending to look the other way. 'I will see to Fela and the others. You will lead them. They will follow and that is all. I will kill them if they try to hurt you. When you sleep, I will guard you… always.'

For answer, Kisa smiled at him. It was enough.

***

After the storm, the winds were fresh and blew the ship swiftly to the south. A few days later, the lookout stationed high up the mast called out and pointed. All eyes turned to look. They saw a green mountain rising above the horizon and knew that the first part of their journey was over.

Chapter 6

The Fishermen of Sao Tome

A few days later, the slave ship approached the large, mountainous island of Sao Tome which lies in the Bight of Benin, about a hundred miles from the African coast. It was covered in green forests on steep mountainsides which rose above the small Portuguese settlement that was nestled in the only protected harbour. The narrow strip of flat land surrounding the small town had been cleared and planted with sugar cane, the first that Kisa and Kojo had seen.

The ship anchored in the harbour and the crew rested for the first time since the voyage began. The captain and the surgeon went ashore with some of the sailors. Kojo, by this time a trusted member of the crew, went with them. He came back breathless with excitement. As soon as he could, he spoke to Kisa about his first visit to a strange land.

'It is beautiful! So different from home. The town is filled with flowers and that huge mountain rises behind. It is a busy place with many white men and a big slave market. We spent most of our time there.

'The captain bought a lot of strong men who will be loaded soon. I think the captives mostly come from lands south of here. I learned that there are two great rivers that come into the sea close to this island. The chiefs of the people who live on those rivers capture enemy villagers and sell them to the Portuguese. Then they bring the slaves here to work on the farms we can see beyond the town.

'The captain has traded much of the goods in the holds for these slaves, but I heard him say that we will have to go to a place to the south for more. He was hoping to head across the ocean now but luckily for us, he needs more cargo. After we leave here – that will be the time to attack.'

Kojo was crouched near Kisa, who was sitting on the deck together with Afia and the other women. He was on guard and whispered cautiously to her while the other sailors were busy. Kisa pretended to be ignoring him but soaked up all he had to tell her of this foreign land that was so close but that she could not go to herself. She stared towards the inviting green forests on the great volcano at the centre of the island.

'What do they grow there that is so important?' Kisa asked, still not knowing enough about the Europeans to understand what was so valuable a crop to them. 'Not yams, surely.'

'Sugar – it's called sugar and they make it from that plant we can see growing in the fields. It's sweet like honey though not as nice. The Europeans want it. They put it in their foods. Remember the runner who came to the village to tell us about the Dutch? He said the slaves were to grow the sugar cane. Some were still convinced that the white people eat the captives, but the runner thought that was a ridiculous superstition. And here it is. Crops of sugar cane owned by the Portuguese and grown by the labour of black men.'

An officer walked by and Kojo coughed and stood up with a curse towards the women. When the man was gone, Kojo sat down again and continued.

'I learned something important. I talked to some of the local people, and they told me that there are many escaped slaves in those mountains. They are called maroons and they harass the white men and free people when they can!'

'Oh, I would like to meet them! I wish I could go ashore too.'

Kojo laughed. 'I cannot make that happen, but you will meet them. Some of the captives the captain bought were taken from the maroons. If they fought before, I am sure they will fight with us when the time comes!'

***

The next day, longboats rowed out to the ship with the newly purchased slaves. Some were from tribes that lived around the Niger River delta. Others were from the Kongo River basin. The men were brought on board with rough hands, chained, branded, and taken to the men's hold.

Then the sailors handed down the goods that had been exchanged for the prisoners. There was much shouting and arguing, but finally the occupants of the longboats were satisfied and rowed away with the profits.

Kisa waited impatiently while goods were loaded and unloaded. At last, two days later, the ship set sail for the mainland and more trading. A few more bodies in the hold and the ship would be ready to cross the sea to the New World.

***

As soon as he could, Kojo got down into the hold to talk to the new captives. They looked at this black sailor with suspicion.

'Who is your leader?' Kojo asked in Kiswahili, the common trading language across much of Africa.

'I am the leader of some here.' A big man with giant arms knotted with muscles, stood up. 'What do you want?'

'I am not what I seem, I am not a sailor but a warrior,' Kojo began. 'There will be a mutiny on this ship. When the time comes, join us.'

'You and who else?' The big man looked suspiciously at the young man. 'You won't be taking this ship on your own.'

'There is a sorceress on this ship. They think she is a prisoner with the other women, but she wields great magic. We will take this ship! '

The new prisoners felt Kojo's passion. All looked his way, but the big man still eyed him with suspicion.

Fela stood up and unexpectedly backed Kojo. 'We have met her. She has power. She says she is going to take this ship, with or without us. I, for one, intend to fight with her.'

He sat back down, and another man rose and spoke. 'I am Okocha of the Ibo people. I will fight with you too!' The other Nigerians looked surprised, but he ignored them.

Kojo continued. 'I must go now. I will bring her to you this night. You will see. Some of the other men in this hold already follow her, as you have seen. Talk to the

Ashanti man, Fela. We will get the keys to your chains. The women will bring us weapons. The sorceress will stun the guards. They will be fish in her net for us.'

Kojo turned and made his way back through the hold and climbed to the deck. As soon as he could, he squatted next to Kisa.

'I have met some of the new prisoners. Some are from the river country to the east, the Niger, which we know, and a river called the Kongo. One of them stood up and said he would fight with us as soon as I spoke.' Kojo looked around to make sure no one was watching him.

'The others are fishermen from the other side of this island. I met their leader, a man they called Amador. He is a big man and used to his freedom. He chafes at the chains, but he is no fool. He wants proof that we can do this thing. I told him about you - that you have magic and will lead us. He will have to meet you but if he is convinced, I believe they all will follow.'

***

That night, when all slept except the guards, Kojo took Kisa back to the men's dungeon below the deck. The guard was startled to see the young woman but as soon as she looked in his eyes, he froze and then slipped to the ground, hypnotised into sleep. Kisa slipped past him, leaving Kojo on guard.

A large, well-muscled man stood as the tall, proud woman approached him. She had no weapons or symbols of power, but her strength radiated out and he felt a strong suggestion of her abilities flowing from her dark eyes.

Kisa stared at him. *This is the man Kojo spoke of,* she thought. *I must convince him first, then the others will be easy.*

'I will free you if you follow me! I am trained in the arts of sorcery and fighting. I have defeated an army of slavers who threatened my village. I am on this ship to rescue one who was taken. Join me!'

'My name is Amador,' he answered her. 'I am the grandson of the king of escaped slaves who have waged war on the Portuguese for a hundred years. We nearly overran the island once and though we failed, we have continued the battle. If the Portuguese had known who I was when I was captured, I would have been tortured and hanged instead of sold. These are my companions.' He pointed to the other fishermen chained beside him.

'We have been living free all our lives on the wild side of our island, the descendants of a slave ship that crashed on the rocks in a wild sea a long time ago. We are fishermen now and when our canoes were blown into the path of the slavers, we were taken captive.

'They will follow me,' Amador concluded. 'Convince me that we can take this ship and we will fight with you, sorceress!'

For answer, Kisa raised her hand and a bright light blazed out from it, blinding all who were looking at her. When it died down, a stunned silence fell over the prisoners. All felt her power. All suddenly knew in their hearts that she could lead them to freedom.

Amador went down on one knee and lifted his chains up. 'Free us, sorceress and we will fight with you.'

'It is decided then,' she answered. 'Kojo will tell you when and how. Be ready!'

She turned and left.

Chapter 7
Mutiny!

'Tonight!' she whispered to Kojo when she and the other women were moved back out on deck, the day after they left Sao Tome. Kojo nodded and kept moving.

As soon as it was dark, Kisa slipped away from the other women, found the entrance to the men's hold and climbed down beside the sleeping guard. The captives were in chains. She went among them whispering words of encouragement. 'My companion and I will free you tonight. We have weapons and we will get the keys. Be ready!' She sent them a silent message of comfort and readiness to believe her words and then was gone.

She went back to the women and Kojo knelt beside her so they could talk. 'You must get the keys to the men's chains. There are spear-like weapons and short clubs holding ropes that we can give to each man as he comes on deck.'

'They are called belaying pins,' Kojo interrupted proudly with his new-found sailing knowledge.

'We will wait till it is dark and cold, after the moon has set. On my signal, kill the guards and free the men. I will have the women spread out and gather the weapons while I distract the sailors. We must move quickly to make this work!' Kojo nodded and moved away.

69

A little while later the guard with the keys died silently at Kojo's hands. Kojo signalled to Kisa and went down the ladder into the men's hold. Soon the second guard was dead too. Kojo worked swiftly to free the men from their shackles which then became weapons in their hands. Kojo led them silently up onto the deck.

Kisa had not been idle. She signalled to the women to be ready to gather weapons then she stood up and sauntered in front of the sailors. Their eyes turned to her as if hypnotised and she swayed in a sexually come-hither dance while entrancing them with eyes and swaying hands. They did not see the women handing belaying pins and spikes to the men coming up from the hold until it was too late.

Kisa grabbed a long pike and led the attack against the sailors. Amador and the Sao Tome fishermen raised a blood-curdling cry and raced up the deck to the ship's wheel, closely followed by Fela and Okocha. The first mate fell beneath the blows of the belaying pins and Amador took the wheel. He threw the ship into a sharp turn, which caused havoc on the decks as sailors raced to take in the sails while trying to fight off their suddenly lethal cargo.

The screams of the dying sailors brought the officers up from their quarters. The captain raced on deck in his nightshirt, frantically calling out orders. Fear cut off his voice as he saw a tall black woman striding towards him. Her eyes glowed yellow with anger and he had a sudden vision of a great she-leopard. He went weak at the knees and his bladder failed him as she approached him. *Who is she? Where did she come from?* He could not remember seeing her on his ship before this moment.

His thoughts were silenced as Kisa brought him down with savage blows to his head. All her pent-up anger spilled out on the captain, lying defenceless at her feet.

The other freed captives moved swiftly around the ship, killing most of the sailors outright or throwing them overboard. Kisa found the surgeon cowering in his quarters and was about to kill him, but Kojo came up behind and stopped her raised hand.

'He can be useful to us.'

'I want to kill him,' she hissed at Kojo but made no move to do so.

Kojo grabbed the sobbing man and tied his wrists together. 'You can always kill him later. There is no hurry, my love.'

Kisa spun round to the battle instead of answering. She watched as Amador took over sailing the ship. The first mate lay dead at his feet. The other freed captives were killing the white sailors, but three African sailors were on their knees, begging for mercy and offering to sail the ship to a safe haven in return for their lives. Kisa strode over to them.

'You deserve to die for serving the slave masters! But we wish to live so join us, swear allegiance to me, help us get to shore safely and perhaps I will let you live!'

The three sailors crawled to her feet, begging her to spare them. 'You are my queen,' one gasped and the others echoed.

Kisa motioned for the first to rise. 'What is your name and why do you serve the slave masters? Why should I spare you for that?'

'Please, my queen! My name is Sule. I was kidnapped as a child from my people, the Ewe. I was released from the hold of the slave ship during a great storm and forced to help with the sails. When I did not drown, they kept me as a sailor. But I was still a slave, my queen! And you have released me.' He sobbed and fell to her feet, touching them with his hands.

'Rise, Sule. You and your companions are free of the slave masters now, but you must serve me in my army. This will be a long war. It will not end here. This is only the beginning. Swear allegiance now!'

Kisa raised her hand and cried 'Somunye!'

All the freed captives echoed her. 'Somunye!'

Sule and his shipmates leaped to their feet, raised their fists, and cried out too. 'Somunye!'

Next, Kojo dragged the surgeon over and pushed him down in front of Kisa.

'Sule, do you speak Dutch? I have learned a little, but I want him to understand me.'

Sule nodded and walked up next to the surgeon, eager to help the sorceress in any way he could.

'Tell him that he is a fool to think his god will save us. We are saved by our own beliefs. We do not need to be the slaves of others to be saved.'

While Sule translated as best he could, Kisa turned to Kojo. 'Make him treat the wounded. I see several with blood on their bodies. Have Sule tell him that if they die, his body will join them in the sea.'

'Keep him alive while we decide what to do next,' Kojo ordered Fela, who was guarding the terrified Dutchman.

Amador, who was still at the wheel. steadied the ship as Kisa and Kojo approached him. Kisa stood proud and silent before him, and her eyes bored into Amador. He felt again her strength and power. Amador raised his arm in salute. 'Hail, sorceress! My men and I are in your debt for saving us. How can we repay you?'

'You are fishermen. Help us sail this ship to the land. Then join us in our fight against the slave masters.'

Amador looked at her and nodded. 'We can do that. My grandfather and my father fought against the Portuguese but were defeated. I and my people have continued the fight. We will fight with you, sorceress and may the gods reward us with victory!'

Amador raised his fist as he shouted the last word, 'Victory!' Fela, Okocha and the other freed captives raised up the call.

'Victory! We fight with the sorceress!'

'Somunye!' Kisa raised her own fist and answered them. 'Somunye! We are one against the enemy! Let this place become a graveyard for the white men! Somunye!'

The freed men and women took up the chant: 'Freedom! Somunye!' They danced around the ship as

Kojo drummed on a water barrel. Then Sule and the sailors joined in so that their captors could see their new loyalty.

Kisa turned back to Amador. 'We are not sailors, and my magic will not sail this ship. Get us to land! Beach the ship somewhere safe where we can decide our next step in this war.'

Amador nodded and with the help of his fellow fishermen and the three black sailors, who raced to the sails, turned the ship towards land as the sun rose in the east.

Afia approached Kisa and Kojo, touching each of them forehead to forehead. Then she turned to Kisa. 'You have saved me from a terrible fate. I thought I was doomed. I owe you everything.'

'No,' Kisa smiled. 'You gave me my husband Kojo by saving him when he was a child. I have only just repaid you for that great gift! I know that you are not a warrior. We will take you home now so that you can be married and have the life you deserve, Afia. We are sisters now and forever. Wherever our war takes us, you will always be in our hearts.'

***

The freed prisoners spent the first night of freedom celebrating and ransacking the ship for decent food and clothing. They found a hold packed with the most beautiful cloths they had ever seen. It was what the captain used to buy slaves – the finest 'India' cloth made in Manchester, England and bought by the 'Negrieres', the Dutch slave ship owners in Amsterdam to fill the holds of their slave ships to trade for what they called 'black ivory' - the sons and daughters of Mother Africa.

There was wine and tobacco for the captain and officers of the ship, this night consumed by their victims instead. There were copper bracelets that went on arms and feet, and fine China, which the freed slaves broke as the wine went to their heads.

Kojo kept drumming, beating out the rhythms he knew so well. Dressed in their new finery, the people danced while, with the help of the black sailors, Amador and his fishermen sailed the ship towards the African coast.

The next day, while the exhausted freedmen slept on the sun-warmed decks, Kojo made the surgeon treat the wounded captives. In the afternoon they took food and drink together and then Kisa stood up to address them.

'Because you took a chance and fought with me, you are free of the chains of these white devils. But you owe me a debt for that freedom. You must help me now to get us back to Africa... and then I will help you stay free... because it will not be as simple as going home to your families. Mother Africa is endless when you are on foot. You know this, and there will be many hostile tribes between you and where you came from.

'I called out Somunye when I raised you to fight. It means we are one, yet before this ship we were many, it was this ship that brought us together, but we must leave it behind for we are not sailors and where would we go?

'I want to wreck this ship as a warning to the slave masters. Then I am marching to war, not just running away like a hyena, but forward towards war against these devils and the traitors among us who support them. And I want you to fight with me… I propose that we become a new family, bound together by the fate that we so narrowly escaped.'

That night, when the freedmen and women laid down in their finery to sleep, they had much more than clothes on their minds.

***

It did not take long before the coast of Africa loomed before them. Lengthy discussions between the black sailors and Amador occurred as they made their way offshore, looking for a safe place to beach the ship.

Eventually they found a suitable deserted beach and ran the ship aground. Some of the black sailors ran off, just glad to be alive. The surgeon, who had treated the wounded in return for his life, was allowed to leave also. He slunk off into the jungle with little hope for survival. Kisa and Kojo watched him go.

'Do you think he will find the white men?' Kisa didn't sound as though she cared.

Kojo laughed. 'I think he will find the chiefs that sell men to the whites. Perhaps he will be lucky, and they will return him to his own kind. Or maybe they will eat him.'

Neither could find it in their heart to wish him well.

***

The freed captives gathered on the shore to decide what to do next. They set up a camp, gathered food and the stores of the ship. They made simple shelters and beds from the bolts of India cloth, then they waited for their rescuers to decide their next move.

Kisa and Kojo discussed this as the others were busy making camp.

'First, we have to find a common tongue that we all can speak.' Kojo was as practical as ever. 'The languages of the Niger and Kongo rivers sounded familiar to me but not enough that I can speak it. I have noticed too that many of the captives are having trouble speaking to each other.'

'Yes, we have many languages here,' Kisa mused. 'I noticed it first among the women and I learned that one group of them came from a place they call Old Calabar. A river called the Niger that runs far to the north of us comes all the way down and into the sea near here. Other people come from the South. They spoke of the rivers Kongo and Kwanza and told of their tribes who lived there.

'When we freed them did you notice that the women ran for men who spoke their languages? Some of them knew each other but others first met in the pens of Old Calabar and the city of Luanda to the south. They were captured from tribes of the two areas, sold to the same ship that then went north and bought us.'

'And then after Sao Tome, across the Middle Passage,' Kojo finished.

Kisa shuddered. Now that the battle was won, she could dare to think of what would have happened if they had not been successful. She shook her head. 'Let's concentrate on the future and how we get home again!'

'I think the language should be Kiswahili,' Kisa said, getting back to the need of a common tongue. 'I was able to use it with the women, and I have heard some of the men speak it too. Sule the sailor knows it. Everyone knows a word or two at least, so I think we can all practice it and use it.'

'If you can make them do it now that they are free. Somehow you must get their loyalty, Kisa, not for just one battle but many!' Kojo pointed out.

'I think,' Kisa began slowly, 'I must always be the sorceress to them. I cannot be me to anyone but you… and Afia, of course. To them, I must remain mysterious, powerful… do you know what I mean?'

'Yes, my love. Remember I am your husband. I don't want other men to look at you and want you for themselves. I want them to worship you from afar and do your bidding and always respect you, not as a young woman, but as what your heart is… sorceress.' Kojo stared earnestly at her.

'Is it shameful?' she said doubtfully. 'We were taught not to put ourselves above others. I can do it with the enemy, but with the people who fight with me. I want to be their friend, their sister, even their mother.'

'The mother leopard. It is powerful magic, Kisa. It is not you who is above them. It is the sorceress. Keep the two separate my love. Be my Kisa when we are alone – the sorceress and her general when we are not. It will expand our authority. These people are still lost. There is no way that they can find their way home alone, but we must make them soldiers.'

'Yes,' she agreed, 'if they slink off in all directions they will be caught and sold again. If we mould them into an army, however small, we have a much better chance of making it home. They need us and we need them as the core. The first of many, someday I will have an army Kojo, but right now it is these people I have in my hand, and I must keep them there!'

Kisa and Kojo called together the leaders of the various tribal groups who had been liberated in the mutiny: Amador the Sao Tome fisherman, Fela the Ashanti warrior and Okocha the Ibo man and his wife, Ugochi, who had been among the female captives.

Kisa spoke to them in Kiswahili. 'We must have a common language though we come from many tribes. This language is used by traders almost everywhere that we will travel. Let your followers learn it if they do not already know it and let it be the language that we use to communicate with each other.'

Sule the sailor agreed immediately. He understood more languages than any of the others, having spent several years crossing the Middle Passage on the slave ship. He translated for Kisa to those who did not know Kiswahili. They agreed to learn it from those who did, and the word was spread throughout the camp. Most already knew more than one language and were quick to pick up another. Soon all were making the effort to learn the language.

Then Kisa called a meeting of all the freed captives. When she stood up, she stood out from the others, Afia had helped her shape some of the cloth into the garb and headdress of a powerful Elder woman, a true sorceress. She lifted her hand and a small flame leaped upward as proof of her power.

'I have freed you from a terrible fate!' She began and all nodded in agreement. 'Without me, you would lie still in chains. You have a debt to pay for your freedom! We must all decide our future. You may wish to go home but it will be impossible for you to all go in different directions. If you want to survive, your only chance is to stay with me under the power of my protection. But I will not just take you to some lonely refuge. This is only the beginning of a war for me. I will fight the slave masters wherever I find them. Don't just hide! Join me! Fight with me and I will bring you glory!'

She stopped, stood strong, crossed her arms, and looked out to sea to give them time to discuss the matter among themselves. They broke into groups to decide what they wanted to do. Some of them did want to try to return to their homes. Others, whose villages had been destroyed or who had been betrayed by their own people, wanted to stay with Kisa. So did Amador and the fishermen of Sao Tome. There was some discussion back and forth, but Okocha the Ibo man pointed out the obvious.

'You may want to go home but how? You would have to walk alone through these jungles, cross rivers, and the lands of those who would recapture you and sell you again to the slave masters. How many of you would ever find your way home? None, I think. Let us join with this sorceress! Let us fight for her!'

'And I for one,' Amador said with burly arms crossed, 'owe her my life and my freedom. I will not leave her till that debt is paid. If you have honour, you too will acknowledge that debt and serve her.'

The two warriors, Fela of the Ashanti and Okocha of the Ibo agreed. 'We too will pay our debt to her. We will serve the sorceress.'

Their words swayed the rest. In the end, they all pledged their allegiance to the Sorceress. Then she told them her plans.

'We will go north, back to my village. Many of my people have trained for this war. We will gather others along the way, and we will form an army that will put the slave masters to flight and send the white devils back to their northern holes where they belong! Tomorrow we will go through all the food and supplies on this ship. Choose what we will take, form an order to our marching and we will also start training.'

Sule stopped translating and asked what this meant.

Kisa explained. 'We have a teacher who taught us how to fight, not just with spears or clubs as we used on this ship, but with our hands and feet. We are going to teach you how to defend yourselves. And then we will teach you new ways to fight the slave masters so that you will never ever have to serve them again.'

Kojo stepped forward. 'Let me show you. Who here will fight me? Without weapons.'

Fela the Ashanti warrior stood up.

'I will,' he said as he dropped the knife and the small wooden club he had taken as his weapons when he helped with the mutiny. He stepped forward and began dancing around Kojo. Kojo danced back and took out Fela's forward foot with a sweep of his own, then caught and twisted an arm behind his back as Fela fell forward.

Kojo stepped behind and pulled the arm up till it was close to breaking as he shot his other hand around like a knife blade on to Fela's throat.

He let go and stepped back so Fela could get to his feet. 'I could have broken your throat with that blow.'

Fela turned to Kisa, who stood impassively watching. 'I saw you do the same to sailors and the captain when you took the ship, I will gladly train with you and learn how to do these things.' The others muttered their assent.

'And after every evening meal, we will talk,' Kisa said unexpectedly. 'We must become friends, all of us. We must share our stories. Kojo and I will tell you of our gods, how our tribe came to be, our childhood stories of the trickster, Kwaku Ananse. and you will tell us your stories and we will become family too. We are family now because I have rescued you. I have been your mother. I came to you with the power of the she-leopard to save her cubs. Now I want you to honour that... become family... become united... it is called Somunye.... We are one. You knew it in your different tribes even if you didn't have a name for it, now you must know it here.'

Kojo looked at her in amazement. He had not thought much about how all these different people were going to be held together. He had concentrated on their rescue and left the rest up to fate but not Kisa. He could see how she was thinking to create this army out of such disparate peoples representing so many tribes.

'Now sleep,' she ended. 'Tomorrow, we take what is useful. Blankets, weapons, food... and we march. North.

Not as slaves escaping their masters but as an army marching to war!'

She ended with a blessing from the earth mother goddess for the safety of all of them and then she sat down with Kojo, and they wrapped themselves together and slept.

The next day, Kojo lined them up in marching order and gave them their first lessons. When they were finished, they gathered everything worth salvaging from the Goede Fortuin, wrapped it in India cloth, lined up and waited for Kisa to begin. She inspected them briefly, indicated her approval and moved to the head of the line. Kojo joined her and together they took the first steps back towards the village in the maze.

As they set out, a shadowy form left the forest and ran to the grounded ship. Wilhelm Jansen, former surgeon on the wrecked Goede Fortuin, was a canny man and had waited patiently in the forest for Kisa and her band to leave. He knew his chances in the endless African jungle were non-existent. His only hope was to stay with the ship. A few weeks later, the wreck was noticed by another passing slave ship. A longboat was sent to investigate. A thin and ragged Dutchman was found, the only known survivor of the mutiny on the Goede Fortuin. Wilhelm Jansen was taken to the next European fort and eventually made his way back to Holland.

When asked what happened, he told the story of a woman, who had been bought from Elmina, and had turned out to be a warrior and a sorceress. He had seen her lead the attack on the ship, killing the captain. Her fellow mutineer was a black man who had been a sailor on the ship. They freed the men and attacked under the cover of darkness. All were murdered by the slaves, except himself and three black sailors, who joined the mutineers. He was forced to treat their wounded but then was spared after they wrecked the ship.

The story spread far and wide and more guards were hired for the slave ships. The common opinion among the Dutch and other Europeans was that a woman was not capable of leading a mutiny. Village people who passed the story on were not so sure.

Chapter 8

Nights around the Campfire

At the end of their first day walking north, Kisa chose a campsite and told them to rest. After building a campfire, they ate dinner and drank tea. Kisa stood up and said, 'We have walked and we have eaten. Now before we sleep, we will tell stories so that we learn about each other. I will start.' She told them of her childhood, losing her father to the slave masters, training to be a sorceress, the coming of her teacher, the mysterious black samurai, fighting with him and the village to defeat the slave masters when they came and then chasing after Afia and rescuing her by starting the mutiny.

Then Kojo stood up and told his story of how the slave master Sefu came to his village and took or killed everyone. 'I was in the care of my big sister,' he said and pointed to Afia. 'She saved me. She hid us and after the slavers left, she took me into the village. I saw my grandmother ... dead... I saw my baby brother... dead... and all the rest were gone, our mother and other sisters, gone forever.'

Kisa was amazed. Kojo had never spoken before about his early life. She had only heard Afia tell this story. Kojo finished, 'She found the village, the village of the sorceress, the village in the maze.' And he named it for them for the first time, it would become legend one day... the village in the maze.

Silence fell. Afia stood up.

'It is my turn,' she said softly.

'When I was a girl, the slavers came, and I became my little brother's mother, just as my grandmother told me would happen. But now that I am a woman, my brother has become my father by saving me from those hyena men who captured me. That too was foretold by my grandmother, though I had no idea what it meant when I was a child. The little girl who led us into the village in the maze has grown into a powerful woman, an Obeah woman, ' and she pointed to Kisa.

The other women nodded and with their voices whispered their belief in what Afia was saying.

'Without her, my brother could not have saved me. Together, they have great power.' She walked up to Kisa and knelt before her, gracefully and with dignity. 'I owe you my life and my freedom. My brother who is my father has given you his allegiance. I give mine to you now too.'

Kisa, eyes shining, took Afia by her hands and gently lifted her up. 'Alone I am nothing, my sister. Somunye.' Then she turned to the others. 'Sleep now. Tonight, we have shown our hearts to you. Tomorrow it will be your turn.'

The next day came and went. They rose and exercised, ate and packed up for the day's march, skirting villages, fording rivers, scrambled through forests, and always moving north.

That night they stopped, exhausted, and unpacked blankets and food, while Kisa lit a fire with her magic. Dinner was eaten, water was heated for tea and washing. Then Kisa rose and opened the evening meeting.

'I am a warrior and a sorceress,' she began, 'but I cannot do everything alone. We must work together just as we would do if we came from one tribe. I have told you my story. Now I want to know yours. I want this to be a moving village. We will discuss our problems and come to solutions together. My word for this is Somunye – we are one.'

'Ubuntu!' A dark Nigerian warrior spoke up for the first time. He was a big, well-muscled man. 'Ubuntu is our word. It means 'I am because we are'.'

'Yes!' Kisa and Kojo both agreed at once. 'Übuntu,' they repeated. Others joined in, savouring the new word with their voices.

'My name is Nkrumah,' he said, folding his arms. 'I will follow you, sorceress, because I too owe you my freedom though you did not come to save me. I am grateful that the gods put me in your path. That is all I have to say for now. Let others speak too.'

Fela the Ashanti warrior stood and said, 'I come from a place close to this village in the maze, though I had never heard of it. My father was a revered goldsmith and I led a privileged life. We had slaves in my house, but I never expected to be one. My older brother became a goldsmith. I chose to learn to fight for my chiefs and my people. Mostly, before we warred with those who came from our gold, we had mines that are hidden from all outsiders. If they have nothing to trade for it, they try to steal it.

'And now they steal people too, to sell to the white devils. But I was not stolen, it was worse than that. My own uncle, my mother's older brother who should have been as a father to me, he sold me to pay his gambling debts; he likes the games of chance too much. He invited me to his house for a meal, fed me palm wine with something else in it. When I woke up, I was bound, gagged, and forced to walk through the night to the great white castle by the sea. I had never seen anything as beautiful before that was built by men, but then they took me inside and it turned out to be uglier anything I had ever seen before.'

Fela fell silent for a moment, remembering the hell of the castle and the horror of the slave ship. 'What do you believe in?' A Matamba man asked in the silence.

'Nyame is the creator god. Asase Ya the earth mother,' Fela answered.

'As we believe too,' Kojo spoke up.

'We call him Ochukwu,' Okocho of the Igbo people answered, 'but he is the same sky god.'

'In Dahomey, we call the creator Mawu-Lisa and that god is both male and female,' said a Fon woman.

Kisa held up her hand. 'They are all the same, I think, whatever you call them. We will continue to serve those gods, make offerings and prayers, together and ask them to help us. First to get home to my village, then wherever our journey takes us. Call to all the gods that our different tribes serve. If they help us, we will not be stopped!'

The discussion ended on that high note, and they rolled up in their blankets, eager for rest. Over the course of their weeks of travel, each night a different person spoke about their home, their people, their families, and their lives. Each day they warmed up with fighting techniques in the morning, followed by a long day's walk. They followed the coast, walking on sandy beaches lined with green forest, or skirted villages cut into the jungle. People saw them coming, but they looked to be a united force and not refugees, so they were given respect and allowed to pass.

Sometimes they stopped long enough to trade. With the help of Sule and the trading tongue of Kiswahili, they were able trade goods from the holds of the Goede Fortuin for food and other supplies.

Kisa and her band saw that there were other slave forts being built along the coast. She and Kojo talked to the people of the different tribes that they encountered. They found that along the coast there were many independent kingdom-states and that the different people were divided about the presence of the white men and their forts. They began to realize just how many people were profiting from the slave trade, not just the Europeans and the Arab-Swahili slave traders, but also members of many of these local tribes.

'I don't understand it, Kojo, ' she said one night as they rested by a campfire, eating the evening meal. 'How can they do this to their own people? Fela was sold by his own uncle!'

'Greed.' Kojo spat out the word.

'You know what that means? It will be hard to raise an army if they only want to make money.' Kisa sighed and poked the fire with a stick.

'Perhaps,' Kojo countered. 'I heard today of one tribe in the Eguafo kingdom who are fighting against the

Portuguese. I was told that they have plans to attack a fort on their land and that their village is not far from here. Perhaps we could join them. If one fort falls, then other fighters may be willing to join us.'

Kisa liked the idea and explained the plan to the others. The next day they headed towards the Ga tribe that wanted to be rid of the European fort being built in their midst.

Chapter 9

Storming the Fort

Kisa walked proudly at the head of her band. Amador was on one side and Kojo on the other. Behind Amador were Sule and the sailors as well as the other Sao Tome fishermen, all capable of handling a knife or the short-curved blade favoured by the tribes of this region. Behind Kojo were Afia and the other women and men who had been freed from the Goede Fortuin. There were almost fifty in all. Some of them were not yet fighters, but all were willing to learn, after the horrors of the slave ship.

I have an army! It is small but it has begun!

Another day's walk took them to the outskirts of a large coastal village of the Ga people. On the edge of the village the Portuguese had built a trading fort. Like Kisa's people, the Ga were pleased at first to trade their goods for European products. But when the Portuguese began asking for, and then demanding slaves, many of the Ga people developed a healthy dislike for the pale skinned foreigners.

Kisa stopped her band outside the village to survey the land. 'Let's camp here for the night,' Kojo suggested, and Afia nodded in agreement. 'We can make plans.'

'You must go into the village as a man, sister,' Afia said. 'These people have chiefs and follow men, not women.'

Kojo agreed. 'Go as a man, love of my life. I will follow you gladly into battle, Kaapo.' And smiling, he gave her a male name whose meaning was the gods' bravest man.

'That is a bold name, my love. I will have to live up to it. Kaapo,' she said it slowly as if tasting it. 'Yes, I will become Kaapo.'

Kisa went away and, with the help of Afia, came back dressed and disguised as a man. Amador recognised her immediately but some of the other men took a minute to see through the disguise. Some were taken aback but Kojo explained and defended her as s/he stood silently staring at them. Amador backed Kojo and slowly the others came around. They were seeing a new side to the woman who had led the mutiny and it deepened both their fear and awe of her. Fela looked at her differently now. Lust was being replaced by respect for this versatile woman.

Around a small fire and a smaller portion of traveller's porridge, they discussed how to carry out this new plan to throw out the Portuguese and take the fort. The consensus was that others would follow.

'We must spread out tomorrow.' Kisa turned to the practical, the way to get it done. 'Afia, I want you to go to the markets with Kojo. Among these people the women do the trading. Talk to them. Find out if they will encourage their men to fight.'

She turned to the others. 'Go to the places where men gather. You must find angry men, who hate the traders and soldiers in the fort. Tell them an army is forming. Stay away from those who are profiting from this madness. Find all who will join us and tell them to meet us here in three days.'

'I am going into the fort,' she continued. 'I will find out how many there are and what defences they have. I will meet you back here when I have finished. Bring me the names of those who will fight with us.'

After the others lay down to sleep, Afia helped Kisa with her makeup. She was already dressed as a fighting man. She used cloth to bind her breasts tight to her chest and then Afia applied makeup: dark black stubble for an unshaven face and a scar on the cheek. Afia shaved her head and fitted a man's cap over her skull. Kisa watched sadly as her beautiful braids fell to the ground, then steeled herself. *This is what I must do. Hair is nothing.*

In the dawn time, they set out across the Ga village. Kisa touched foreheads with Kojo and Afia before leaving them at the market. The new man, Kaapo, strode off towards the fort. He sauntered up to the gates and declared to the guards that he had gold to sell. The guards were suspicious, but he showed them the gold glittering in his pouch – what looked to be a substantial amount too, their minds, twisted by suggestion, thought. The gate swung open and Kaapo strode in.

To his surprise, the fort was nothing much inside. It looked more impressive on the outside because of the height of the wooden walls, but inside it was rough and unfinished. There were a small number of white men in uniform and even fewer better-dressed Portuguese officials. The man at the trading table bought the fake gold without a second look because the thought arose in his mind that he could tell it was real by the weight and the colour. Kaapo took payment in seashells and walked around in a great circle at the base of the wooden barricades.

It was poorly built, and the gates had only one wooden bar holding them shut. Most important, there were no cannons. The Portuguese soldiers were armed but their muskets looked old and worn. Few had swords to use when there was no time to reload. Kaapo walked back out of the fort and then turned and watched the wooden gates close. He heard the bar slam in place and thought: *If we bring a log, our men can smash that gate. The bar behind will not hold.*

Back in camp some of the men were optimistic while others were sceptical. Some had met villagers who were willing to join them, others had not.

'There is much profit from this fort for the traders. They like it too much,' was the general belief.

Kisa had washed her face but otherwise was still dressed as a man. *I'll just have to get used to it,* Kojo thought as he watched her squat by the fire to discuss the day's findings.

'What did you learn?' Kisa addressed Afia.

'Much,' she answered. 'The women hate the fort and the white men. They call them devils here too. Convince them that you can win, and they will tell their men to fight!'

Kisa turned to the others. 'The Portuguese have no cannons and few soldiers inside their fort. There is only one wooden bar holding the gate shut. If I can get back in disguised as a soldier, I can open the gates as you attack. Tomorrow and the next day take me to meet all who wish to fight. We don't need an army to take this fort. Just an angry mob!'

It was agreed and the next day Kaapo was introduced to those in the village who wished the foreigners gone. Through oratory and suggestion, Kaapo heightened their anger and convinced them to take the fort.

'In two days, at dawn time, we will attack,' were his final words to each. 'Bring your weapons and your friends. We will throw them into the sea!'

On the final morning before the attack, Afia took Kaapo to meet the women. It was an easy job for such a slim but strong looking man with deadly swords to convince them that the attack would work. They all agreed to send their men to the fort the next morning.

That afternoon they made their preparations. Kojo and their band were to meet the villagers in the pre-dawn gloom and attack at first light. Kaapo then went back to the fort, this time disguised as a soldier of fortune eager to fight for the Portuguese. Mental suggestions got him through the gates and into a safe hiding place for the night.

Just before dawn, as the villagers and Kisa's band formed up outside with torches and began shouting at the gates, Kaapo attacked the two guards. The other soldiers were asleep and only slowly roused to the danger. By that time, it was too late. Two guards lay dead by the now open gates and the mob outside was rushing in, led by Kojo, Amador, Fela, and the freed slaves from the Goede Fortuin. Within the hour the soldiers were dead, and the fort taken.

The villagers lit a bonfire, drums began to beat, and everyone danced, celebrating the victory. Word spread like a wildfire across the village: the fort has fallen! It is ours!

By afternoon it seemed that the entire village was inside the walls, looting the rooms and dancing around the fire in celebration. Kaapo was elated. The first battle won! The first fort fallen!

Then the elders arrived. They walked up to the fire where the locals introduced them to Kaapo and his band.

'You have done a great thing, and we thank you,' the chief of the elders said to Kaapo. 'But this is our country, and this fort is now Ga business. You are welcome to stay in our village, but we will take charge now.'

Kisa and the others were used to the authority of elders and did not think anything of this. They bowed to their authority and withdrew to their camp on the edge of the village. Kisa was sure that many of the villagers, elated as they were by the ease of taking this fort, would join the band. She imagined one fort after another falling until they reached Elmina with a mighty force and then it too would fall. She slept well that night.

Over the next few days, they celebrated with the villagers, unaware of what the elders were doing. The first hint came when a new ship sailed into the harbour. They were flying the flags that now flew over Elmina Castle too, the flags of the Dutch nation and the Dutch West India Company. A longboat was rowed ashore. In it were officials of the company and a guard of well-armed soldiers.

Kisa watched as they were escorted into the fort. *Why are they here?* She thought. The answer came too soon. When the gates of the fort opened near sunset, the Dutch did not leave. Instead, it was a group of elders, all clutching bags of some sort, who came out.

Kaapo approached the chief of the elders. 'What does this mean?' he demanded to know.

'It is not your business, but we sold the fort to the Dutch for many gold coins and seashells,' the chief replied.

'No! You cannot do that!' Kaapo started to pull out his sword, but Kojo stopped him.

'We can and we have. This is not your land. Go home. We do not want you here. We have made our decision.'

The crowd looked ugly. They did not approve of this stranger confronting and disagreeing with their elders. Suddenly the man they knew as Kaapo revealed her true identity. A change came over him and they realised they were looking at a woman and a sorceress. She drew herself up tall and strong and lifted her hands into the air, speaking with the voice of prophecy: 'You will be cursed for this! Cursed!'

Kojo pulled Kisa back. Amador and Fela and the band surrounded their leader with weapons drawn, as they retreated to their camp. The crowd, fearful of the power of sorcery, did not follow. Kisa took off the rest of the disguise. She sat beside the fire; her head bowed in despair. Afia tried to comfort her and offered her a bowl of porridge, but she pushed it away.

'How could they do that?' she cried out to Kojo as he walked up. Wordlessly he sat down next to her and put his arm around her shoulder. 'They don't know what they are doing,' she continued. 'The Dutch are no better than the Portuguese and they have more guns, more cannons. The elders sold us out - for what? Seashells and a few pieces of gold?' She stopped as the awful truth sank in. There would be no victorious army marching north.

'I want to go home,' she said quietly and laid her head on Kojo's shoulder.

***

That evening, Kisa and Kojo called a meeting of all those who had fled the slave ship with them plus the few Ga people who hadn't followed the elders but wanted to fight with the strange sorceress instead.

Kojo built the fire and invited people from the more than thirty tribal groups to sit around it with them. He had acquired a small drum in the Ga village to replace his Kidi drum that he had left hidden in the forest beyond Elmina castle all those months ago when this adventure had started. He opened the meeting with ceremonial drumming to set the mood.

Then Kisa stood up. 'It is a great disappointment that the elders chose to sell the fort to the Dutch. But we took it! And we can take others. I march now back to my village. But I will continue this fight in the north. Come with me! Fight with me!'

'Somunye!' shouted Fela and others took up the chant. There was no doubt. Her followers believed in her.

***

The next day, Kisa and her small band began the long walk home. It took them a few weeks to get there. They passed through the country of the Fante, and it was there that the three ravens reappeared, circled Kisa and then flew in front of the band on their journey. At night, the

98

more observant of the party noticed that wherever Kisa rested, there was an owl in the tree above her. It was a small fishing owl, but it had a fierce look.

After the Ga village, the small band accompanying Kisa grew by one as they passed through each village, but these were not human followers. As Kisa left the Ga village, a large handsome dog, the obvious alpha male of the pack of pariah dogs that lived around the village, approached her.

Kisa stopped and stared at him. To the astonishment of all but Kojo, the dog stretched out his front legs into a bow before her. Then he fell in beside her as she began walking north. The villagers and her followers were surprised because these dogs were not pets, but 'pariah' dogs, children of the oldest dogs in Africa, who had been following humans but not living with them for tens of thousands of years.

They ate the refuse of the village, but they were not skulking parasites. They were strong, healthy animals who provided protection for the village as well as being the clean-up crew, along with other wilder animals such as ravens and vultures, who benefitted from human society. The dogs were respectful to humans but did not normally obey or stay with them. This yellow dog was different. For the rest of the journey, he walked beside Kisa and slept near her. She rewarded him by feeding him.

And from each village that they went by, another dog joined them. A few females at first and then a younger male. The new dogs bowed to Kisa and then as was more normal for pariah dogs, followed behind the humans in Kisa's party. Kisa's dog was the chieftain and they submitted to his authority. They ignored the other humans, but their golden eyes followed Kisa whenever she moved around the camp. And they followed Kisa's band faithfully, cleaning up the rubbish behind them and providing a rear guard from anyone who wanted to sneak up on them.

***

They journeyed north through the lands of the Ashanti, and it was here that Kisa had to prove her leadership in the first serious challenge to her authority, but certainly not the last.

The problem with being a beautiful young woman was that the men who were following, almost thirty now, could see and feel her sexuality. A man who took a sorceress for his wife would be powerful and most could not resist dreaming about her and what it would be like to lie with her. Kojo and she were obviously mates but they had not yet been able to consummate their relationship and perhaps instinctively the other men sensed her virginity.

One man decided to act – Amador, son of the king of the Sao Tome fishermen. Lust had been part of his feelings for her from the moment he laid eyes on her and he felt contempt for Kojo, a smaller and younger man. *She needs a real man beside her,* he thought, *and I am the only man here worthy of her.* Presenting herself as a man in the Ga village had only inflamed his passion further. He wanted to tame her, dominate her, and he convinced himself that she wanted that too.

He waited until she was drinking alone at a small stream. As she rose, he seized her by her shoulders with his strong hands, swung her around and kissed her hard. He felt her go slightly limp and emboldened, he forced his tongue into her mouth. She bit down hard, half severing his tongue. His mouth filled with blood and pain. He let go and grabbed his mouth as a precisely placed groin kick brought him to his knees. She stood over him as he crouched, waves of pain from his mouth and groin washing through him, struggling to breathe as his mouth filled with blood.

'You will never touch me again,' she hissed. 'You will worship me, serve me, fight with me die for me, but you will never touch me!'

Kojo appeared out of nowhere. He drew his sword and held it to Amador's throat.

'Swear allegiance to her now or I will end it.'

Amador spit blood, then swallowed more. 'I swear,' he mumbled thickly.

'And all who follow you,' as the blade bit into his skin.

'I swear for myself and my followers. We will serve the sorceress or die.'

Satisfied, Kojo stood back, sheathing his sword.

'Go!' Kisa commanded.

Amador went.

The word soon spread about what had happened. Kojo saw that even Fela was looking at Kisa with new respect. It made the journey north less tense.

'Kojo, we have to bind these people together.' Kisa lay in Kojo's arms on the thin traveller's sleeping mat that they shared under the stars each night. Kojo was holding her close under their shared woven ponchos which acted as their blankets at night. He wanted to cuddle and smooch and explore her body with his tongue more than he wanted to talk but for her it was cuddle only and talk.

'They are my little army, Kojo,' she continued while he nuzzled and listened. 'But they speak different languages, worship different gods, their skins are different colours, and they think of each other as us and them. They haven't really understood 'Somunye' yet.'

Kojo grunted his agreement to this assertion, sighed and lay back to talk, but he pulled her close so they could whisper in each other's ears. Since the days after the mutiny, when they could be together all the time, this was their alone time when they could discuss their plans. For most young people this would have been about where they were going to build a hut and how and when they were going to start a family, what to grow in the gardens, issues with livestock and neighbours and other family members. Not so Kisa and her Kojo. They were starting a war and they were still very young. They had won a battle, led a mutiny and taken a fort and they had a large group of people who were following them to an unknown future.

They talked about what Grandmother would say to do and how their teacher, Yasuki the Black Samurai would handle the situation. They remembered how he came to their tribe, taught them how to fight then fought with them when the slavers came. What would he do with these people?

'We must continue to train them, continue to insist that they speak Kiswahili, but most of all, Kisa, they must always respect you. You must be more than a girl to them. You must always be the Sorceress.'

Kisa nodded and they fell asleep at last.

***

Kisa led them back via Elmina Castle. They visited the old campsite and Kisa dug up her spear and sword. She stood before her people and showed them the great black spear.

'This is the symbol of my power. It was created in a great storm when the tree that guards our village was struck by lightning. I climbed the tree and cut it down myself.'

As she lifted it high, Kojo cried out, 'Behold the sorceress!'

Then she showed them the sword, now strapped to her waist. It had a golden dragon on the sheath and when she pulled it out and held it up, they could see that it was different from the short, curved blades of their peoples. As she lifted it up, the sun shone on it and overhead Udele the vulture screamed her welcome to Kisa. Her soldiers were awestruck. There was a moment of silence and then she called out.

'Somunye!'

They answered her. 'Somunye!' And at that moment they truly understood – she was their sorceress. She had saved them, she fought with them. She had a great cause and she needed them to fulfil it. Suddenly they knew their own purpose too. All doubts fell away before the sorceress, the spear, and the shining sword.

'Somunye!'

Chapter 10

Afia's Wedding

Finally, Kisa and Kojo found their way to their forest and reached the village, hidden deep within the maze. Kisa put her hand on the Sentinel Tree. It felt so good to be home. When they walked into the village, everyone was amazed, taking them for ghosts at first. Only Grandmother and Yasuki were not surprised. Captives had escaped before, of course, but no one had ever returned once inside the slave castle.

Grandmother assured the villagers that they were real. Kisa and Kojo introduced Amador, Fela, Sule, Okocha and Ugochi and all the other freed captives to the villagers. Chief Abrafo welcomed them, and everyone was thrilled to see Afia was with them. She was greeted with laughter and tears. The newcomers were taken to huts and provided with food, drink, and water to wash themselves. Then Grandmother took Kisa, Kojo and Afia to her hut for the news of their journey. Yasuki was already there. Kisa told them everything that had happened and what she learned.

She told them how she and Kojo had gotten themselves into the castle and then onto the slave ship. There was the story of the mutiny and then the journey by land. Kisa related how they had captured the fort in the Ga village, but how the elders betrayed them.

'I thought I would have an army behind me to take the forts all along the coast. But too many people are making profits from the white devils. I will have to raise an army another way. I will have to take the fight to the slave masters myself. We need a plan to make this happen!'

'Be patient, Kisa,' Grandmother counselled. 'First the village wants to celebrate your return. Afia's betrothed did not believe he would see her again. There will be a wedding before you leave. All things in their time.'

Kojo could see that Kisa wanted to argue, so he changed the subject. 'Tell Grandmother about the ravens and the owl.'

Grandmother raised her eyebrows at Kisa. 'I saw them when you entered the village. They are waiting in the trees for you. I have seen their eyes, tell me their stories.'

Kisa nodded. 'They joined me the day we left here. They made themselves known to me at the first water stop we made. They bowed to me and have served me since.' She paused, thinking. 'The ravens kept watch by day and the owl at night wherever we were camped or hiding. The ravens followed me on the journey to the slave ship. We did not see them again until we left the Ga village.'

Kojo continued when Kisa stopped. 'But they have been with us since and there are dogs following us too. Each village we entered; the animals were attracted to her. They see her power. A brave true dog has left each village. There is now a pack behind us. They have bowed to the sorceress. The rest of us, they ignore. But if anyone comes behind us, they bark and they clean up after us. No one would know we have passed.'

Yasuki spoke. 'It is good that the animals recognise her power. They will help us in this war.'

Grandmother nodded. 'And the trees too. It shows that the gods favour you, my sorceress.' There was a moment of silent prayer as the mention of the gods, then they went back to practical matters. 'Kisa, you must now always look the part of the sorceress when you appear before your followers,' Grandmother said.

Kojo nodded. 'We have discussed that. We had problems with one who treated her like an unmarried girl. We put him in his place, but we saw the need for her to show her authority when she walks among them.'

'I have prepared this for you.' Grandmother stood up and pulled out a leopard skin and skull headdress from under a blanket. 'I have been making it for you since you left. Stand up!' Kisa rose and Grandmother fitted it on her head.

Yasuki handed her the black spear then stood back to admire her. 'You look the part now, Sorceress. Wear it in all ceremonies. Let them always see your power and not the young girl beneath. When you are as old as Grandmother, you will not need it, but for now, there must be no doubt in their minds who you really are.'

'It's beautiful,' Kojo gasped. 'You are beautiful, my love. And it shows your power and your mystery.'

'Thank you, Grandmother,' Kisa turned to her old mentor. 'You have always looked after me.'

'That is because you are our hope, Kisa. Without you, there is none.'

Kisa carefully removed the leopard skin, rolled it up and sat down again. They were silent, thinking of the future, and then Grandmother said, 'Chief Abrafo ordered the making of a new hut for you two. Go there now, rest, refresh yourselves. There is a time for war and a time for peace. Your sister will soon be married, Kojo. Let us focus on peace for perhaps the last time for a long time.'

Kojo smiled, bowed, and taking Kisa by the hand, led her to their new home. Their time there would be short. He was determined to make it memorable. They stopped out the front, admiring the weavings hanging over the door and the windows. Then Kojo took his wife by her hand, and suddenly shy, she let him lead her into the hut.

'Take the herbs,' he whispered.

When she had finished, he slowly took off her beads, armlets, and anklets. Then he undressed her. She stood watching him, wide-eyed and waiting. He lifted her up and she put her arms around him as he carried her to the bed.

***

Afia's wedding was special because it almost didn't happen. Nothing was spared in making it the happiest day of Afia's life. Adwin, her husband to be, was not a warrior, but a kind and gentle man. He had thought that Afia was lost to him and wanted to make up to her for not believing that Kisa could rescue her.

Adwin's parents provided the dowry and Adwin appeared at Esi's hut in his finest clothes to offer them the bride-price. When Esi, as Afia's foster mother, accepted, Afia was led out to him. Her girlfriends had decorated her with a fine new dress, bracelets, and necklaces to wear, and beautiful designs of henna on her hands and feet. Her hair was coloured blue-black with indigo and shone in the sunlight.

After the ceremonies, there was a feast and then dancing to the drums, for not one day but three. The villagers had a good harvest and much to celebrate with the return of Afia, Kisa and Kojo. Kojo enjoyed the chance to play his drum with Addy and the drummers again. He didn't get to spend the whole evening drumming though. Afia and Shani made sure that Kisa was beautifully made up as a woman, not a warrior, for the night. Kisa enticed Kojo away from his drum and they danced together for hours. Finally, when it was all over and many were suffering from hangovers from too much palm wine, Kisa and Kojo went to their Sensei and Grandmother and asked them to help them plan their war.

Kisa's twin sister and brother, Shani and Kwame, wanted to join them. Kisa disagreed. 'I think you should stay home and train for another year. You are so young!' She practically raised them when Ama, their mother was so sick and weak after their birth. She had no fears for herself but the thought of the twins fighting and perhaps dying was daunting.

Then Yasuki sided with the twins. 'They are well trained and eager to help you. You cannot protect them from their destiny. And you cannot succeed without help. Let Kojo, Shani and Kwame be your lieutenants. Others will join you until you have an army. A long journey begins with the first steps.'

Kisa wanted to argue but Kojo and Grandmother both spoke up, agreeing with Yasuki.

'They have trained as long as us,' Kojo pointed out.

'Shani has skills as a sorceress and Kwame can shape change better than anyone but you, Kisa.' Grandmother's arms were crossed in her best 'I'm the Obeah and intend to be obeyed' stance. Kwame let out a whoop of triumph and Shani practically danced with happiness.

Kisa sighed and gave in. 'This war has only begun. Taking the slave ship and freeing a few people changed nothing. To the south we took a Portuguese fort, but the locals handed it to the Dutch. I will not go back that way.'

'There are many slave raiders coming from the north, bringing captives, and capturing more on their way to the forts of the white men. I want to take the war to them. Kojo and I travelled north to Salaga and Tamale on our first journey last year and saw the slave markets. It is on the roads leading to the markets where I propose to start the war.'

Yasuki agreed. 'When I came from the east, I followed the slave masters in order to find Kisa. The lands to the north and east are much drier than here. Most of the land is flat and open, covered only in grasses, but there are patches of trees, acacias and great baobabs that can survive the dry times. The slave masters travel during the wet season because there are few rivers in that flat dry country, and they do not carry water for their captives. They must be able to drink at puddles and streams after rains or they will die, and the long journey will be in vain for their captors.

'The wet season extends from the middle of the year to its end, and that is when we should fight our war. After that the hot wind from the desert blows frequently, keeping the slave masters away.' Yasuki went on.

'The slave masters travel west as far as a great line of rocky hills, where the land suddenly rises. If they turn south before this, they are cut off from the coast by a great river. But when they reach this escarpment, which will offer us ample hiding places, they turn south and begin the last part of their evil journey... through the forests to these villages and on at last to the white men's castles. It is there, on the edge of those hills, where we can start our war.' Kisa was pleased to hear him say 'our war'.

Yasuki continued. 'I think that Kisa and Kojo should go north with me first. Once we reach the open country, we can go by horseback. We will find the hills and the trails used by the slavers, look for places where we can hide and set up ambushes. From there, we can go a day's ride away to Tamale. We can use it as our base and buy supplies from the Dagomba people.'

Grandmother nodded. 'There is good hunting too. When I travelled through that country years ago, I saw elephants, hippos, buffalo and warthogs, and many antelope too. Baboons live on the plains and monkeys are found in the trees. Hyenas, lions, and leopards can lead you to kills.' Grandmother looked at Kisa. 'The eagle and the vulture hunt there also.'

Kojo stood up. 'I agree with Sensei. The three of us should go to this place and learn as much as we can.'

Kwame interrupted. 'But Shani and I want to come too!'

Kisa stood up. 'Later you can, but for now we need you to choose and train our army. Choose the village children most capable in hunting and fighting. Talk to the

111

men and women we rescued on our journey. Who wants to stay here and farm? And who wants to hunt with us?'

Kwame looked disappointed and pleased at the same time. Being given such authority made up for having to wait for adventure. His time would come. Of that, he was sure.

Yasuki agreed. 'You will stay here. This is for the elders to decide our course of action.'

Together the three of them went to the Chief and a village meeting was called. It included the new men and women who had come back with Kisa. It was decided that most should stay in the village and train in the fighting techniques of Yasuki. But Kisa turned to Amador and Fela and said, 'I want you two to come with us. You are already warriors, and you will be commanders in my army.' Amador was pleased at this sign that Kisa had forgiven him for his indiscretion. He saluted her. Fela also was pleased at the promotion.

That night, Grandmother held a ceremony and threw the sacred bones to determine the most auspicious time for them to set out. Three days later Kisa and Kojo left with Yasuki, Amador and Fela. Their plan was to walk north to the open country where they could buy horses. Then they would ride north and east, to look for the paths of the slaving parties and a place suitable for a camp.

As soon as they entered the maze, three ravens flew beside them. High above, a vulture cried. Behind them came the pariah dog, with his large upright ears, curled tail held proudly over his back, and yellow coat gleaming in the sunlight. He too looked like a warrior. Ahead of them, a small owl was asleep at the site of their first camp, a day's walk away. He would be awake and waiting when they arrived.

Chapter 11

Journey North

After leaving the maze, Kisa and her companions took the road that ran north towards the village of Goaso. The country was forested, with people living in huts along the road. When they reached Goaso, they went to the small marketplace where they found food and news. It was mostly about the petty doings of the village, but there was also talk about a recent raid by slavers. The village was mourning the loss of several good men.

The travellers continued north to the village of Kintampo. Kisa and Kojo went to the farmer who was caring for the horses they had acquired on their previous journey, Amara and Ayo. Then they went looking for horses to buy for the others to ride, plus a donkey to carry supplies. Yasuki picked a quiet mare while Fela chose a spirited young stallion. Amador was not interested. He crossed his burly fisherman's arms and stoutly refused to ride a horse.

'I am a man of the sea, and I will walk,' he insisted.

Kisa smiled. 'You can lead the donkey then.'

Amador snorted and took the animal's rope. He looked at the animal with some misgivings, but the patient donkey just sighed and allowed himself to be led.

Kisa was thrilled to be mounted on Amara again, who was excited to be out of the pasture and on the road. She snorted and pranced beside Kojo's patient Ayo and

Yasuki's calm mount, Laila. Kisa's dog was not impressed and fell back to the rear next to Amador and the donkey.

'What shall we call your dog, sorceress?' Amador asked.

'He told me that his name is Chaga,' Kisa answered.

'Chaga. A good name, sorceress.'

On the road north from Kintampo, it was easy to find signs of the raiders. The paths were littered with broken chains and the bones of those that had died along the way. Both sights drove Kisa into a rage. She said nothing, but Yasuki and Kojo could read the signs. Her body grew stiff, her eyes hardened, and her fists clenched.

She pointed her black spear towards the bones. They could hear her whisper: 'I will avenge you,' before she turned and rode on.

That night they camped by a stream. Kisa fell asleep in Kojo's arms and for the first time in a long time, the dream came back. She had almost forgotten it in the events since the mutiny.

In the dream, she was fighting Sefu the slave master, in a battle to save her village. But the village was empty, she was alone. All her weapons were gone, her feet and head were bare. Only a thin smock covered her. Sefu loomed above her on his big black horse, his sword raised, the look of the evil dead in his eyes. She knew he was already dead, but it made him the more dangerous because she was sure that he could still kill her. He rode up, the hard hooves and the fierce teeth of the horse of the dead striking at her. All she had were her head, her hands, her feet. She danced out of the way of hooves and teeth, struck the rock-hard temple of the horse with one fist, only to have it bounce off as Sefu's sword cut down towards her head.

She danced aside as her partner, the heavy war horse, was guided by the spurs of his master. Sefu swung great sweeps with his sword with his strong right arm while his left hand roughly steered the horse to trip or trample her. Kisa woke with a yell, sitting up in a pool of sweat and waking Kojo beside her. She was shaking so bad that she could not speak. Kojo held her. Yasuki walked into their tent, took Kisa's chin in his hand, and looked deep into her eyes.

'The dead stalk you,' he said, and it was not a question. She tried to nod yes but he held her firm. 'It is a test. Is your sword in the dream?'

'No,' Kisa sighed as the grip of the dream on her soul loosened. 'I am alone, with no weapons. He comes on a horse of the dead with eyes of fire and hooves of steel. Sefu. He comes back from the dead to kill me.' A sob escaped her.

'You need no weapons, Sorceress. You are the weapon. Defeat him with your bare hands. Stare him down with the eyes of the leopard. Will the horse to disappear beneath him. Send it back to the land of the dead. Then send him back too. It is a test.'

Yasuki smiled as he released her chin and stepped back out into the night. Kisa sank back into Kojo's arms and was almost instantly asleep.

***

116

It took two weeks to come at last to the hills, but once they were out of the forests and on the savannah, they picked up speed and covered greater distances each day. Everywhere they saw new animals: tall giraffes and large savannah elephants and many kinds of antelope, large and small, with strangely shaped horns and beautifully marked coats.

Always they kept watch for slavers and made friends with any farmers that they met or villages they passed through. Most were half empty, with little to protect them from the attacks of the slave masters. Areas once rich with crops were lying fallow and untended.

The next town was Larabanga, a typical village of that country with round huts that were capped with peaked, thatched roofs. In the middle of the town was an ancient mosque, to let the slave masters know that the people were followers of the desert prophet, Mohammed. This gave them some protection since the Arab slave masters were also followers of the prophet and generally left other Muslim communities alone. The exception to this rule was a willingness to buy any criminals the village had. Selling criminals into slavery was a good way to get rid of troublemakers and eliminated the need for jails.

***

After acquiring supplies, they continued the ride north. Every thirty to fifty kilometres, they came to another village. At each village the dog, Chaga, waited on the outskirts, only joining them again when they took to the road again. Overhead flew the ravens. Whenever they were ready to camp, the little owl appeared before them, sitting in a tree at the most suitable campsite.

Kisa sat on her horse languidly, draped over her rough saddle, thinking about the future. Her training was over. What she had to do now looked like a huge task without an end.

'First, I must find Badru and kill him,' she muttered, searching for a starting place. *But how will you find him?* Her mind answered. She looked around at the country, steadily becoming more open with wider spaces between the trees than in the jungle-forests of her homeland.

Yasuki rode up level with Amara. 'What is troubling you?'

'I am wondering how to find Badru, the man who took Afia,' she began.

'He is not important.'

'Yes, he is!' Kisa couldn't help but argue. 'I hate him so much! What he did to Afia - what he wants to do to all the others.'

'You are not seeing clearly,' Yasuki interrupted impatiently. 'He is a pawn. He is nothing. You will kill him, but it will solve nothing. Did it solve anything to kill the other one? Sefu? Slavers are like cockroaches. You kill one and another appears. And they are all the pawns of the true slave masters. You will never see them on the roads.'

Kisa disagreed with him but did not argue further with her teacher. 'Who are the true slave masters then?'

'They are not seen. They hide in cities. Their riches protect them. They live in walled compounds and send men like Badru and Sefu to do their dirty business. They are rich but their hands are never soiled, just like the white slave masters in their castles on the coast. They are protected, rich, impossible to reach, but it is they who must die to end this.'

'Then why do we fight?'

'Because we must.'

***

They came to a country where the language spoken was different from their own. They had entered the country of the Dagomba tribes and the newer Gonja people. Another fifty kilometres of open savannah woodland brought them to the village of Techiman, an important market on the north-south road. After another quick stop for supplies, they rode on and at last in the distance, they could see the rocky Konkari escarpment rising above them. They rode till they came to the bottom of the ridge. They tethered the horses and continued climbing on foot, where they could see the savannah plains stretching out in all directions.

The five companions climbed to the top of the tallest hill, with Chaga scouting the easiest way up in front of them. At the top was an outcrop of sandstone rock that took them to the highest point on the entire western savannah. To the east they could see the village of Dagoba and beyond, the town of Tamale. To the west stretched savannah country through which sparkling blue rivers ran. Looking north, they could just make out heat waves rising off the distant desert.

Yasuki moved up beside her and stood facing north. He put his arms out to mark west and east. 'The slave masters come from the lands to the north, east and west. They travel on roads that run from east,' and he motioned with his right hand. 'And to the west, from one ocean to the other. I came over that one.' He faced east and bowed to his long dead Japanese master. 'It is called the Ind Ocean, for the land that lies there.' He turned back to the north and motioned with his left hand. 'To the northwest is the trading city of Wa and beyond that the other ocean.'

He motioned with the right, 'To the east, the crossroads where north south routes cross these east-west pathways, at the town they call Tamale. All roads pass through Tamale, north to south and west to east. The caravans have been coming south with salt and gold since time began. Everyone wants something they do not have. Our main camp will be down there,' and he pointed to the west side of the line of rocky hills. 'Tomorrow we will look for the best site.'

Kisa was only half listening as she looked up and saw the circling vulture high above her. 'First let me fly, Sensei!' Kisa was eager to mount on the wings of Udele and see the country from high above.

'Not yet,' he answered. 'We must discuss this journey of yours first. You have to use this time to see everything and memorise it. For now, let us look for a campsite. You must be well-rested for this journey.'

They made their way down and found a sheltered spot. Amador gathered firewood, started a fire, and made dinner while Kojo and Fela looked after the horses and the donkey. Kisa was standing, with the dog at her feet, looking at distant vultures in the sky. Yasuki sat down and was soon in a state of tranquil meditation. After the evening meal, they discussed their plans for creating a camp suitable for an army.

'We will need shelter from the winds, a good water supply, trees to hide us from any who venture on to the hills,' Yasuki said.

'Yes,' Kisa agreed. 'We can set a guard at the top of Konkari to keep watch and send messages.'

Kojo nodded. 'There is plenty of game and we will only be a day's walk west from Daboya and Tamale, where we can get supplies.'

'Why are there so few people living in this land?' Amador asked. 'It is rich.'

'The slave masters,' Kisa hissed. 'Our sworn enemies have already emptied this land.'

In their explorations, they confirmed this. They found the remains of a village, burnt to the ground, and the bones of many who died.

'None must have escaped because there was no one to bury them,' Fela noted sadly.

They found a cave on the side of the escarpment as well. It was deep and well-hidden, but the little owl sat before it and hooted, until they searched and found the entrance. They looked inside and found signs that it had been inhabited, but nothing permanent.

'Perhaps some of the local people hid here during the raids,' Kojo mused.

'It will be useful to us. We can store supplies here,' Amador pointed out.

The next day they explored the river valleys and woodlands to the west of the escarpment. Three days of exploring led them to the perfect camp site. Situated on the edge of a gently flowing stream in a grove of dawadawa trees, there was a small clearing, hidden from view and flat enough for bark and thatched shelters. There were no villages within two days ride. The isolation was perfect.

Yasuki spoke. 'This is a good place for a permanent camp - where the army can remain undiscovered between attacks. From there they can go east over the hills and down the valleys to the road that runs from Tamale to the slave markets of Salaga.'

Kojo and Kisa nodded. They had visited Salaga. Almost all the captives from the north were brought there to be sold to intermediaries who would deliver them, after resting, bathing, and feeding, to the European slave castles on the coast.

Yasuki continued. 'Or our fighters can move south from here to the roads used to bring captives from the trading city of Wa. Horses would be best there for the distances are greater.'

'Yes! Horses with warriors riding them!' Kisa could see her vision coming to life – she had seen it the first time she looked in Amara's eyes. She saw herself riding Amara in front of many horses, all with strange, red-skinned men on their backs - swords drawn and wild cries echoing in her mind.

'It will be so,' Yasuki agreed.

***

Later, Yasuki took Kisa aside while the others prepared for the night's sleep.

'We must talk about your flight tomorrow. You must learn as much as you can as quickly. You must see beyond what our eyes see here. Look down first. See the strength in these rocky hills. They are the bones of the earth mother. Then follow the waters – circle, circle, see them flowing down both sides from where we stand, down into rivers. Choose one and follow it for they meet up southeast of here and then the one big river goes all the way to the sea. Take her there. Come back up the coast to the castle – she will know the way... then follow the roads back north to us waiting for you. Be ready to draw us a map when you return. You will see so much more than I could learn on foot so long ago!'

He turned to the East and bowed again. 'My master told me that you must know the way of the land you are fighting for, its hills and valleys, rivers, roads, and villages. You do not have time to learn it any other way. Fly with your bird and see it all. But be prepared to draw that map for us!'

Then he left her to sleep. She did not, lying instead half the night, watching the stars arc over above her from east to west. Kojo kept her warm, asleep beside her, but her eyes were on the heavens in anticipation of the journey she was about to take. When at last she could stay awake no longer, she slept, and the dream came back.

Sefu was racing towards her on the horse of the dead. She was alone and without weapons once more, standing it seemed on the clouds themselves high above the

123

earth. She dodged the horse again as he attacked her, but this time she was looking hard. How could she bring it down with nothing but her hands and feet? She heard Grandmother's voice first: 'Call on the leopard!' Then the voice of Yasuki spoke inside her head:

'Use your hands as knives. Drive the points in deep!'

She danced around the horse, staying out of reach of the sword, moving in on Sefu's unarmed left side, looking for a point vulnerable enough to penetrate with a small knife.

'Aim for the eye!'

She leaped in, screamed a wild cry and scratched the horse's eye with fingers turned to the claws of the leopard. They ripped through the eye and the red firelight went out as blood spurted forth. Kisa was already leaping sideways and backwards in two long strides as the hellish horse screamed, reared, and turned with bared teeth for her. Kisa's eyes glowed yellow as she dodged, feinted, and moved in again.

She hit the horse with a second blow to its other eye, this time using her fingers like the point of a knife, driving in deep. The second red fire went out in a spurt of blood. Blinded, the horse reared, fell over and disappeared in a cloud of black smoke. Sefu rolled to the ground and jumped up. With a roar, he lunged at Kisa. She danced back and forth, staying out of reach and then moved in. She used her foot, with a knife-like edge, and hit Sefu's knee. It snapped backwards, and broke. Sefu toppled over with a cry of pain.

Leopard eyes glowing, Kisa cut behind him, grabbed his hair, pulled his head back and hit him hard in the throat with the side of her hand. It was a blow hard enough to break his windpipe, but it did more. Her hand went straight through his throat and decapitated him. She was left holding his head, blood pouring out, staining the clouds beneath her a deep red. Sefu disappeared, and Kisa woke up with a yell. She looked into Kojo's eyes.

'I had the dream. I was fighting Sefu! I had no weapons, but I defeated him!'

Yasuki jumped up at the sound of her yell and came to them.

Kisa jumped up. 'I sent Sefu back to the world of the dead!' she cried out in triumph.

'It is good, sorceress. I do not think he will trouble you again,' Yasuki said and bowed to her. 'Now sleep without dreams. You have earned it,' and he returned to his own blankets.

The next day they returned to the highest point on the escarpment. Kisa saw vultures in the sky and felt the yearning to join them. Suddenly she was looking out of the great vulture's eyes. Before, she had to use Grandmother's potion to make the leap. Today it seemed as easy as mounting her horse.

Kisa was welcomed by Udele. She looked out of Udele's eyes at the world spread out below her. She circled and called out to Kojo and Yasuki to let them know where she was. Her ravens flew around her, calling. Amador and Fela were startled by Kisa falling to the ground in a trance. Kojo caught her as she fell and lowered Kisa's unconscious body to the ground. Kojo and Yasuki looked up at the vulture circling and crying overhead and understood.

Yasuki explained. 'The sorceress flies with the vulture. She sees much that we cannot see from here. She will return soon.' Fela and Amador looked with amazement at this further proof of the power of the sorceress.

On the great wings of Udele, Kisa soared high above the Konkari escarpment.

The warm air currents lifted her up. Circling circling she rose higher and higher. Higher and higher she rose circling. Then the wind of the world whipped her sideways.

She looked at the bare rocks, felt their strength, their great age. She saw tiny waterfalls, rivulets, streams, flowing off both sides of the rocks, down into the valleys and, east and west, she saw the rivers that Yasuki had spoken of and the towns that nestled beside them.

She followed the river on the eastern side and Udele, with a scream, turned in her chosen direction and flew south. The forests grew thicker again, the waters grew wider as more and more small streams flowed in from Konkari. Far to the south she found the place where the east and west rivers came together to create the mighty Volta River.

She swung around, looking for the road on which she had journeyed. With Udele's keen eyes, she spotted the great road running in a zigzag path back north to the Konkari. She came to where it crossed another road, coming from the northwest. On it she saw a caravan, a long line of donkeys, chained to human slaves and all loaded with wrapped goods on their backs or heads. She let loose the vulture's scream as she circled above the slave masters, then she turned back to the heights of Konkari. Soon she was circling in a small circle directly over Yasuki and Kojo. She closed her eyes.

When she opened them again, she found herself nestled in Kojo's arms. She gave him a breathless, bright-eyed hug and then stood up and stretched. She picked up a stick and drew a rough map in the dirt of what she had seen.

'I found Udele so easily. We flew all round and even down the great river before turning back north to Konkari. On another road from the northwest, I saw a caravan, like the one I saw the last time we were here! But I could not tell what the donkeys and the slaves carried.'

'Salt,' Yasuki answered. 'They bring salt from across the desert. They carry many other things too: Cloth, gold, and silver, all the goods of the north in exchange for all that is produced to the south. We will see many caravans on the roads. Only some will have captives for sale. Those are the ones we will attack – not salt caravans.'

'But we could free the other slaves who carry the salt,' Amador began.

'There are not enough of us yet,' Kojo interjected, then Yasuki continued.

'We must choose our battles carefully. Our army is still small, and most will be fighting on foot. Large caravans are too well guarded and the traders in salt are not our enemies. We must focus on the slave masters.'

Kisa nodded in agreement. 'I also flew over the town to the east. Tamale. I think we should go there tomorrow. It is close. Perhaps we can find recruits for our army there.'

Kojo stared hard at the drawing in the sand. He memorised the drawing as he imagined the view from above. A plan formed in his mind.

Chapter 12

Crossroads

Tamale was the biggest town between Kumasi, the capital of the Ashanti people, and Timbuktu, the far and fabled capital of the late Songhai Empire. Tamale was located at the crossroads of north-south road with the biggest east - west trade route from the Atlantic to the Indian Ocean. Travel across the continent was only possible through the Sahel country of open grasslands. To the north was the desert and to the south, impenetrable jungles.

Only the Tuareg crossed the great Sahara Desert. It was very profitable to do so, and they guarded the routes jealously with their swords. The caravans from the Mediterranean brought the riches of the north to Timbuktu on the edge of the river Niger. Then goods were taken by river or by the southern road to Tamale, where the east-west trading roads passed through.

The people in Tamale were followers of the Arab prophet, Muhammad. They had built a great mudbrick mosque for their prayers, and it was much larger than the impressive one in Larabanga. The people of Tamale were part of the Dagomba nation. Kisa practised using their language, Dagbani, which Grandmother taught her many years earlier. Kisa sometimes dressed as a man, as she had in the Ga village, to gather information about the slave trade. The best sources were the public houses where men gathered to discuss the weather, crops, and politics. In the marketplace however, she dressed as a woman and mingled with the local ladies to find out how they viewed the slave trade. They found that Tamale was, as Yasuki had said, located on the crossing of three ancient trade routes so it had grown into a commercial centre for the northern region centuries ago.

The north-south road from Timbuktu to the Salaga markets had raiders passing through, whilst other merchants brought their goods too. Gold came from Timbuktu and salt came from Daboya, to the north-west of Tamale, and then both goods were taken on the eastern road that ran to Yendi and beyond all the way to the Indian Ocean.

A third road ran west to the capital of the new Gonja kingdom, Damongo, and to Wa, a major trading town. The central market of Tamale, and the palace of the leader of the Dagomba, the Gulkpe Naa, marked the junctions of the three roads, all of which were being used by the slave masters.

Kojo thought about the map that Kisa had drawn in the sand as he listened to the stories of the various roads running in and out of Tamale. He spent time in the marketplace, where he bought some small containers of paint, a brush and a piece of supple leather suitable for a scroll. When Kisa asked him what he wanted with these things, he answered cryptically: 'I am going to put your sand drawings on it.'

Slavery had long had its uses in Tamale. There was no jail or prison of any sort. If the crime was serious enough, the punishment was death. For lesser crimes, the criminals were simply traded to the slave masters, who earned a good profit if the criminals were strong enough to survive the journey to the coast. Still, these criminals had relatives, some of whom felt that their family members were badly treated and did not agree with the custom of selling them into slavery. Like so many others, the community was divided between those who profited from the business and those who hated it.

In addition to the ancient tradition, there was the new market for slaves, to grow sugar in the land across the sea. With the demand growing, the slave masters were no longer confining themselves to criminals, but were raiding the surrounding villages. Survivors moved to Tamale for protection. They also brought with them a hatred for slavery. Kojo befriended a young man named Majeed, who was vocal about his anti-slavery feelings.

When Kojo introduced him to Kisa and Yasuki, Majeed told them about a great slave camp to the north on the road to a town called Bolgatanga. 'The desert dwellers bring salt and slaves down that road. They camp at a place called Pikworo.'

'What does that mean?' Kojo asked.

'The hills of fear.' Majeed said, brushing a fly from his face as he continued. 'The place is surrounded by outcrops of rock on which the slavers place guards. The captives are held there until there are enough to take south to the markets. They come through Tamale and then head down to Salaga where they are sold to those who will take them to the coast and sell them again to the white men in the castles.

'Pikworo is the home of the most terrible slave masters in the north: Samore and Babatu Sato are their names. They built that evil place. They buy captives from the north there, then they sell them on to other men, mostly the Gonja horsemen, who take them to their town of Salaga. It is the most important slave market north of the slave castles on the coast. Salaga is on the banks of the Volta river and is as far as horses can go, because of the sleeping sickness. On the other side, even the slave masters must walk.'

Kisa interrupted. 'Tell us more about the Gonja horsemen. We met many Gonja men when we were in Salaga. Where do they come from and where do they get their captives?'

'They live to the west of here and they are newcomers to this land. They came when their empire, the Songhai, fell to the Moors. The first Gonja to come here were cavalrymen sent by their emperor to defeat the Akan peoples and stop them from selling their gold to the north, because it was making the gold price go down. But while the Emperor's cavalry was crossing this land, his kingdom was attacked by the Moorish Sultan from the far north. His army was much smaller but they had guns and cannons. They sacked the great city of Timbuktu and laid waste to the Songhai Empire.

'The horsemen could not return to their homes, so they raided villages, captured women, and started their own towns to the west: Wa and Buipe. They call themselves the Ngbanye, which means brave men. They cannot range too far south because their horses would die, but all the tribes of the savannah country from here to the far western ocean are game to those who want to sell them for profit.

132

'The Gonja men say they are followers of the desert prophet, but they still believe in the old ways. They have fetish priests and Obeah women too. They believe they will be born again if they die in battle, so they are fearsome warriors. Many of them are honourable men but be careful of those you meet on the road. They are the bad ones who will sell you to the slave masters.' Majeed looked doubtful as he said it, seeing the fitness of the two young people before him and the man he took to be their father, who looked deadlier than either of his children.

'They fight a lot with the Konkomba, and the Anumba tribes, and we Dagomba people too, for we all speak sister tongues and were here long before the Ngbanye came. Sometimes they raid our villages and steal our women and children. Sometimes they trade with us. We need their salt but have little that they need. They grow their own maize and millet, yams and cassava. So, we let them and the other traders, slave or otherwise, use our roads. The traders bring great riches through our land: salt and spices, gold, ivory, and rare and precious woods. But now it is mostly captives for the slave markets.

'We too follow the old ways in our hearts, but we have our mosque now as a sign to those who come that we are under the protection of the Prophet. If we did not make these travellers welcome, they could destroy us. We are caught in the middle. And I hate them,' Majeed said softly. 'They took my older brother when I was a child. They swept through our village and took many. The rest of us had to flee, then we came here and settled. My family farms near here even now. But I cannot grow yams while so many are being taken from their families and sold to some terrible fate that we do not understand. Some say they are eaten by those white devils.'

'No', Kisa interjected. 'We have seen them. We have been in their great fort and on one of their ships. If they only ate their captives, it at least would be a quick death for our people. They take them far across the sea and then work them till they die.'

'You have been across the sea?' Majeed looked at her with awe growing in his eyes.

'We have been on their ship. We took it and destroyed it before it could cross the middle passage to the land that they call the New World - the one that we once just called the far land. We heard from the sailors, before we killed them, what would happen to our sisters and brothers in the hold. Some of them have joined us. We are going to come here as a band and fight the slave masters. We will kill them and free their captives!'

Kisa half rose to her feet and her voice began to rise in excitement. Kojo put his hand on her arm in warning and she sat back down with a smile. One look at Majeed told her he would join them.

Yasuki spoke: 'Tell us more about the lives of your people, Majeed.'

'We are farmers. We grow yams and many other crops and raise sheep, goats, cattle, and chickens. We even have bees to make our own honey. Many of us are craftsmen too. My uncle's family makes brooms, baskets and mats. We have great weavers and makers of beautiful pottery. We make a potent brew of beer too, but we must never drink it in sight of the mosque now. We make our own soaps, shea butter, and groundnut oils. And you see my smock?' He pointed to his brightly coloured shirt. 'My mother made it herself. She is a clever seamstress.'

The companions smiled and agreed, then Kisa got to the point. 'Join us!' She whispered urgently. 'Help us kill the slave masters, to save your family!'

Majeed looked in the eyes of the intense young woman in front of him. 'Yes!'

***

Over the next few days, Majeed introduced Kisa and Kojo to other young men and women who hated slavery. None of them knew how to fight the ancient trade that was robbing the land of so many good people. Kisa and Kojo offered the bravest the chance to fight back.

Kisa and Kojo met individually with Majeed's friends and then proposed to those who wanted to join to come to a meeting at their camp site on the edge of town on Kwa, the free day of the week. Ten men and one woman came with Majeed and his brother Mahamadu on the day. Kisa and Kojo greeted their new friends and invited them to share a meal with them. Amador and Fela, who had stayed in the camp because they did not speak the language, served tea and porridge to their guests. After eating, Yasuki watched as Kisa disappeared into a tent while Kojo rose to his feet to explain their plan.

'We are going to build an army to fight the slave masters!' As he said this Kisa stepped out in her leopard skin headdress. She lifted her black spear high in her left hand, then she set the butt of the spear in the soil with a thump and raised her empty right hand into a fist. Their guests stopped drinking their tea and gazed in astonishment as she opened her fist and a bright white flame leaped upward as high as the trees.

'I am a sorceress and a warrior!' she said, drawing her strangely shaped sword from a sheath emblazoned with a golden fiery dragon. 'I will kill the slave masters!' She pointed the sword toward Yasuki. 'This man is the master who has taught us how to fight.' Yasuki rose fluidly to his feet and bowed to the guests.

Kojo stepped forward and began to speak as Kisa sheathed her sword and then stood in imposing silence with the great black spear from the Sentinel tree and the leopard headdress giving her total authority. 'We have trained all our lives for this,' Kojo continued, 'and we will train you. We have many fighters from our village to join us when we are ready. And we have the power of the sorceress!'

He pointed to Kisa, who raised her right hand again and this time a red flame rose up from the sword tip. In it they saw the shape of a slave master, burning.

Majeed jumped to his feet. 'I will serve you, sorceress!' His brother jumped up too, followed by their friends.

'Fight!' shouted Kojo. 'Fight for the sorceress!' Majeed and Mahamadu took up the cry, followed by their friends.

'We fight! We fight for the sorceress!'

Kojo began drumming, pounding out the rhythm on the little Kidi drum that was his constant companion. The Dagomba men danced around the fire in rhythm with their words and the drum. Amador and Fela joined them while Yasuki watched with approval. Kisa stepped backwards to allow them room to celebrate their decision. Kojo tempered the drumming, making it slower and softer and then stopped. The Dagomba men sat down again, but their tea was forgotten. They stared at the sorceress as Kisa stepped forward once more.

'We will go west now, beyond Daboya to the hills of Konkari. We have set up a camp there from which we can attack the slavers using these roads. Soon we will go south to our country and bring back all our good fighters. Then we will give the slave masters something to think about besides money!'

Kisa turned to the one woman present, who had stood with the others, but remained silent and had not danced. She was clearly older than the young men she had come with. 'Why are you here, sister? Do you have no children to protect?' Kisa asked her gently.

'My name is Niena. My people lived to the east,' she said, pointing. 'But they are gone, my children, my parents, my sisters and brothers.' Niena choked back tears. 'My husband is a cruel man. I do not wish to stay here. I have a thousand reasons to die and none to live. Teach me how to fight and I will join with you, Sorceress.'

Kisa sheathed her sword and made a fist of her right hand. She stretched it out and Niena walked forward, touching it gently with her own fist. Then Kisa turned to the others, fist outstretched and, in turn Majeed and each of the others touched their fists to hers.

'I will teach you a word,' Kisa said. 'Somunye. It means we are one. We are brothers and sisters in this war. No matter where we come from, what gods we worship. Somunye – we are one. The fighters I bring from the south speak many languages, come from many different tribes. But we are one. Somunye!' She cried out and raised her fist high.

And for the first time, her new Dagomba fighters answered her. 'Somunye!'

When silence fell at last, Kojo spoke again as Kisa took her silent but powerful stance with her spear. 'Come with us now and see our camp beyond Konkari.' He said as he pointed to the escarpment.

'We are going to build a village where an army can safely hide. You can help us do that or come back and find more recruits. When the camp is made, we will bring back our warriors. Look for us again when three moons have passed. We will come back at the start of the rainy season, when the slavers begin moving their captives. We will teach you how to fight and then start our attacks.'

Majeed answered in an excited voice. 'We will go to your camp with you. Then while you are away, we will look for more people who want to fight! We will gather weapons and be ready to follow you in three moons!' His companions cheered in agreement.

Niena stepped forward and went down on one knee before Kisa. 'Take me with you now, sorceress, that I may serve you!'

'Yes,' Kisa answered and offered her a hand up. Niena rose, kissed Kisa's hand, and then stepped behind her. She suddenly knew what her task in life was to be: to make sure that Kisa had all her personal needs met. It was as if Asase Ya had sent Kisa another mother.

The next morning the companions packed up their campsite and waited for Majeed and his friends to arrive. As they marched, the newcomers saw three ravens circling over Kisa's head. Overhead a great vulture circled and cried. A great yellow dog with savage eyes paced beside Kisa's horse.

'She commands the animals too,' Majeed whispered to the others. They nodded, seeing further proof of her power.

They returned to the campsite that they had chosen. Majeed and the other Dagomba youths came from much drier country, and they gasped at the fertility of this land. It was rich with wildlife: deer and wildebeest, zebras, giraffes, and elephants. There were crocodiles and hippos in the rivers and marshes, and noisy, brightly coloured birds in the trees. Around the campfire that night, Kisa explained her plan to the Dagomba men.

'I must journey south now, back to our village, to collect the rest of our army. I want you to start a permanent camp here for us while we are gone. When we return, we

139

will need huts, gardens, corrals – a village where we can plan our campaigns and come back to when we need rest. It is the place where we will bring the captives that we free so that they may join us, either by helping in the village or by fighting with us. Will you do this?'

Majeed stood up. 'I speak for us all. We will build you a village while you are gone. We will train and be ready to fight when you return.' His friends raised their fists in support and raised a cheer.

'Except for me.' Niena stood up. 'Let me serve you on the journey, sorceress.'

Kisa nodded. 'I accept your service. You will be a great help to me.'

Fela spoke up. 'I will stay here, sorceress, to help build your village and train these men.'

'That is good, Fela,' Kisa answered. 'Look for us again when the full moon has come and gone three times. There will be an army at our back. Be ready! We leave tomorrow.

The next day Kisa, Kojo and Yasuki set off for home, with Amador and Niena beside them, to collect the rest of their little army. High overhead, Udele circled. The ravens flew before them, the dog Chaga paced beside them, and the little owl met them at their campsite each night.

The Vulture Circles

Chapter 13
Kisa's Raiders March

On the ride home, Yasuki discussed how they should fight the war, using his extensive knowledge of warfare from his years in Japan. 'We cannot meet them face to face, like an army. They are armed and although their victims are innocent villagers, they can fight. Some may even have guns. We must practice stealth. Hide when they are looking. Attack when they are sleeping. Fighting fair is not an option. They have no morals. We will not show them mercy or give them warning.'

Kisa and Kojo agreed with their teacher. Kisa in particular had no intention of showing the slave masters any mercy. The memory of her lost father burned in her mind, as did her dreams of killing first Sefu and then Badru with her bare hands.

The travellers settled into easy routines that hastened the trip. Kisa led the way, with Chaga padding beside Amara. Yasuki and Kojo rode next to her when the road widened or fell back when the forest closed in. Niena followed on her newly purchased pony next to Amador, who as usual was leading the donkey with their supplies. The ravens circled above them, always watchful. Sometimes they cried messages, before flying ahead. When Kisa spotted her owl in the evening dusk time, she stopped at the campsite chosen by him.

Amador unloaded the donkey, who he had named Ayor after his braying call, and set up camp. Kojo unsaddled the riding animals and took them to find sweet grass to eat. Niena built a fire and cooked dinner while Yasuki sat down to meditate. Niena put a blanket down for him near the campfire, with his back to a tree for safety. Yasuki took off his sword, bowed, sat, closed his eyes. Later, Niena brought him water for washing.

Kisa stood aloof from the activities of the camp. Always her mind was somewhere else, thinking about the future, thinking about how to fight this war. She practiced her fighting moves to limber up from the day's riding. Chaga sat lion-like beside her, watching her every move.

When the food was ready, they gathered around the fire to eat and discuss the coming war before sleeping. When the first light appeared in the eastern sky, the owl hooted, and Kisa rose. She drank but wasted no time with food. The others raced to pack as she saddled Amara and then set off down the road. A single cry from the lead raven announced that the journey was continuing.

Niena was coming alive in her new life. She was free from the abusive relationships she had lived with before. As soon as Niena left Tamale behind, she felt a great weight lift. She was walking down a new road, one that had been denied to her for so long. Once she had cursed her lack of children; now she was glad that she was not so burdened. She found herself singing as they walked, and the others encouraged her because she had a beautiful voice. Kojo often played rhythms on his little kidi drum with her chants and soon Amador was adding in his deep baritone. Kisa smiled and listened.

Yasuki neither smiled nor chanted. He seemed more and more to be in a world of his own. As they walked, Yasuki watched Kisa and thought *I did not come to fight this war. I came to train a child. She is trained, honed, like her sword. There is bright steel in her. I see it in her eyes.*

We created this weapon, Grandmother and I, and now the arrow is flying. She no longer needs me as a teacher. That job is done. There will be a short time more as she learns the art of warfare and then I am done.

He found himself thinking often of the old woman who had called him to this task all those years ago. She was a sorceress, highly respected in the village, but still, she was a woman. He found himself thinking how nice it would be to feel the warmth of a woman's body on cold nights. He chuckled to himself for the thought, but it would not go away.

***

At last, they approached the village in the maze. Everyone turned out to greet them when they reached the outlying gardens. Afia ran ahead of the rest to tell Kojo breathlessly that she thought she was pregnant, even though it had only been a few weeks since she married. For answer Kisa closed her eyes and put her hands on Afia's womb.

'Yes. There is a child. I feel her, blessings on her and her parents.' Kisa smiled as she removed her gentle hands and in her mind was the feel of the twins when they came into her mother. She could touch the spirits of the unborn too. Afia hugged her brother and touched her forehead to his. He towered over her now but, for her, he was still the baby brother she had rescued all those years ago. Kojo looked into her eyes and understood with a shock that Afia had become his mother the day their real mother died. Blinking back tears, he took Afia by her hand and the two of them followed Kisa into the village in the maze.

Grandmother and Chief Abrafo were standing at the Sentinel Tree and on either side of them, lined up and armed, was Kisa's new fighting force. There were almost fifty of them, both men and women. Some were Nzema villagers and others were those who had joined Kisa on her journey to free Afia. Some were freed from the slave ship by the mutiny she and Kojo had led. Others, inspired by the taking of the fort in the Ga village, had joined them on the march north. Now they had been turned into a single fighting force by Shani and Kwame, who had worked tirelessly to train them in Yasuki's methods since their leaders went north.

Most had already seen battle, on the slave ship and in the Ga village, so all the twins had to do was show them how a group of samurai warriors would fight. The recruits saw the value of the training, and in addition they were inspired by their sorceress. They responded with eager willingness and were proud to show off what they had learned in a few short weeks.

They had to wait of course. There were discussions to be held with Chief Abrafo and Grandmother first and then food and a brief rest. Kisa, Kojo and Yasuki joined them in Grandmother's hut, where she served them a rich stew of bush meat and yams. Grandmother looked tenderly on Yasuki as she handed him his bowl. His hand brushed hers as he took it and he noted that she did not pull away. Perhaps there was hope.

After eating, Chief Abrafo spoke. 'While you were away, your fighters trained hard every day. I think you will be pleased at their progress.'

'They look ready,' Kisa answered. 'We look forward to seeing them perform. We found a place for our camp and we found more fighters in the local towns who want to join us. They will need training in our way of fighting so Sensei Yasuki will return north with us.'

Yasuki was watching Grandmother as Kisa said this. He noted a look of fleeting disappointment on her face and he was surprised to feel his old heart pounding. 'But I will return soon,' he said. 'This war is for the young ones. My duties are almost finished. I came here to train an army, not fight a war.'

Grandmother nodded. 'My part also is finished. This is a war for the young.'

'Then let us inspect your troops,' Chief Abrafo finished. 'They are eager to show their skills.

Kisa put on her leopard headdress and took up her sword and spear. When she, Yasuki and Kojo emerged refreshed from the hut, they found Shani and Kwame waiting to put the new fighters through their paces. The result was impressive because the different factions in the new army were competing with each other.

The Nzema villagers had trained the longest and, although they were still young, they wanted to prove they were the best against these newcomers. But the Sao Tome fishermen, big burly men, were also seasoned fighters and had no intention of coming second to a bunch of farmers.

Some of the captives that Kisa and Kojo had freed on the slave ship were from far flung places like the jungles around the Niger and Congo rivers. They were also good fighters and had come together under the leadership of Okocha, the Ibo warrior. They were not as big as the Sao Tome fishermen, but they were quick and lithe, with wiry strength. They were also older than the Nzema village teenagers and they didn't want to come in second either.

Kisa and Kojo drew their weapons and tested their sparring skills. Yasuki nodded approval as the fighters showed their mettle. All performed well, each in the style of their tribes, but honed by Shani and Kwame in the techniques of the black samurai.

'You are ready to fight,' Yasuki declared when they finished. They threw their weapons in the air and cheered. Kisa cheered the loudest. Her troops were ready for battle!

***

That night there was feasting, drumming, and dancing until dawn. Then there were prayers and offerings to the gods for the success of their mission. Grandmother made sure that all the gods from the earth mother to the sky god knew of their plans and were properly approached for their support. At last, Kisa and Kojo gathered their troops together to explain their plans, while Yasuki watched. As usual, Kisa appeared as the silent sorceress, with spear, sword, and headdress, while Kojo addressed their troops.

'We have found a good camp site. It is hidden but close to the roads used by the slave masters. There are high hills nearby where we can watch the roads. We have new recruits from among the Dagomba people there, building our first huts. Our numbers are still small, but enough that we can make the slave masters lives difficult. We will concentrate on the road that runs south out of Tamale to the Salaga slave markets. There are places along the way where we can watch and attack when the slavers stop to let their captives drink.

When we have freed the captives, we will take them back to our main camp. There they can be trained and so our army will grow. We will leave here after the new year when the rainy season nears. It will take ten days of hard walking to get there. We will set up our camp, show you the countryside, and then we will strike!'

The fighters cheered again. They were eager to begin, but preparations had to be made. They gathered their gear and food together, but the most important chore was to marry the girls who were going as soldiers. Even though they were going to fight, in the eyes of the tribe, they still had to have husbands to look after them. It was an important aspect of tribal life. Family was everything and even though trained to fight, these girls were to be protected for their equally important role as mothers in the future.

Families were consulted and parents had the final say. The newcomers were closely inspected before they were allowed to marry any of the girls, to make sure they were not the dreaded hyena men of legend. Hyena men were handsome but had mouths on the backs of their necks, covered by hair. A girl unlucky enough to marry one was killed and eaten by her husband, who could then turn into a hyena and disappear in the wilderness. It was a fate no parent wanted for their child and for this reason, girls had to have their parent's approval before marrying. Some of the young already knew who they wanted to marry, having been living and training together for years. Others, more adventurous, were drawn to the newcomers who had come with Kisa from the south.

All the women saved by Kisa on the slave ship had stayed with her. Only one, Okocho's wife Ugochi, was married. Some wanted to fight while others were content to be camp workers. Building fires, cooking and helping with packing and unpacking were important chores and valued by Kisa. Kisa was not only their rescuer and their leader but now the head of their family and she was eager to see them married, for their own happiness as well as the contentment of her band of fighters. She wanted no intrigues and sexual problems to arise. Even with everybody safely married, there could still be problems, of course, but having a large group of unmarried men and women seemed a much larger problem.

So, for the time before the march to war, there was much flirting and dancing, getting to know one other and testing out relationships. On the auspicious day chosen by Grandmother and under the stern eyes of their Chief Abrafo and their beloved sorceress, the men and women fighters were married, so that peace would prevail within their ranks while war was being waged.

Except Shani. Shani refused to pick a suitor even though there were many, both villagers and newcomers.

'I don't love any of them!' she complained to Kisa. 'Besides, I am a sorceress like you Kisa. Not as powerful, but I have been training with Grandmother and Yasuki too. Perhaps it is not my fate to be married. Anyway,' she continued when she could see Kisa was going to argue with her. 'My brother Kwame is still unmarried too and he will look after me. You know that!'

There was no changing her mind. Kwame made it clear that he was prepared to die to defend Shani, so reluctantly an exception was made, and Shani remained unwed.

Niena chose Amador. She had ignored him for the journey south but once in the village, she looked at him with new eyes. He was strong and brave, a seasoned warrior and handsome too. She found her loins burning at the thought of marrying him. Amador saw her new interest and happily courted her, for he wanted a wife. After the humiliation by Kisa, he needed to reassure himself of his manhood. Niena was no virgin, but he didn't need that. Niena worshiped and served Kisa with all her heart and deep down, Amador wanted to do the same, but he also needed to show that he was not a weak man because he served a woman.

Kisa approved the match. It would calm Amador and make him an excellent lieutenant when his passions were sated with a bride. And who better to guard her faithful Niena? Just as Kisa needed Kojo to protect her back, so Niena would need someone to protect her.

Yes... Amador... perfect... Kisa thought and blessed the match.

Each of the couples was provided with a hut for the three nights following the wedding, before they marched to war. They were given privacy in a safe, sweet environment, a clean hut with fresh blankets and bedding for the short honeymoons. Some would undoubtedly make babies. Kisa and Kojo had discussed it one night as they cuddled together, enjoying what was really their honeymoon too.

'The camp will become a village. Some of the women are destined to be warriors of course - like Shani,' Kisa mused. 'But some will be mothers and become grandmothers and keep the children safe while we fight.'

'I agree, my love,' Kojo murmured as he pulled her close. 'Enough talk now!' She smiled and snuggled into his arms.

Meanwhile, In Grandmother's hut, another discussion was occurring.

'Nonsense! I will not marry you!' Grandmother was laughing at Yasuki's' proposal. The old man sat calmly, unperturbed by her response. 'Marriage is for young people. Do you think I can give you a child?'

Yasuki did not respond to that. The old woman shook her head, but Yasuki continued. 'Marriage is about love. I love you. It is as simple as that. Think about it while I am gone. I do not intend to fight this war. That is for Kisa to do. I go to train an army. When they are trained, I will return. Think about me when I am gone and answer me when I return. That is all I ask.' Yasuki rose in a fluid motion that belied his age. He bowed to Grandmother, who, for once in a very long time, could think of nothing to say. Pleased with himself for having the last word, Yasuki took his leave.

***

On a bright morning, before the rains came, Kisa, dressed as the sorceress, with Kojo and Yasuki by her side, called her raiders together on the edge of the village. Chief Abrafo and the villagers gathered behind them. A ceremonial fire was lit, and Grandmother performed the rituals for the success of the group. Then she threw the bones and, on inspecting them, pronounced that all was auspicious for their coming journey. She finished the ceremony by blessing the fighters.

Kisa's troops were gathered in the groups who would fight together. Amador led his Sao Tome fishermen along with Sule and the sailors. Beside them were Okocha and his wife, leading the other men and women freed from the slave ship. They had become a tight group through the shared sorrows of captivity and the joy of fighting together for their freedom.

Kwame led all the other newcomers who had come from Ga or other villages along the way home and was working to bind them together as a fighting unit. Shani lead the Nzema fighters, along with their new spouses. And behind the three sets of troops, there was a fourth troop: the pariah dogs, now a well-disciplined unit under their leader, Kisa's dog, Chaga. They spread out behind the humans, guarding their rear. This did not seem so important now, when they were still among friends, but the dogs would be vital in the future. Kisa and Kojo inspected them and made sure that all was in readiness for the journey.

Then Kisa spoke. 'All of you have suffered because of the slave masters. Now we will fight back! Follow me to victory!'

When the cheering stopped, she turned and strode forward, the black spear of the Sentinel Tree lifted high for them to follow. Yasuki and Kojo marched behind her, and her troops followed in their disciplined groups. Before her flew three ravens. Above them Udele the vulture wheeled and cried out. The villagers followed them to the edge of the gardens and then with waves and drums, wished them success on their journey as they disappeared into the maze.

Chapter 14

On the Wings of Udele

Each night on the march north, the fighting groups divided again into married couples. No intimacy was allowed but they could sleep together for warmth and protection. They found that four couples fit nicely around each campfire for eating and sleeping. Groups formed around friendships and Kisa and Kojo saw that this was strengthening their band. The little army walked for several days until they reached Kintampo, where the leaders picked up their horses and the donkey.

Kojo told them. 'We do not have enough horses for all of you to ride – yet! Or enough donkeys to carry our supplies. But when we return home, it will be different. Many of you will be mounted and we will have so much of the slave masters' gold that we will need ten donkeys to carry it!'

The army laughed and continued to march north but now behind mounted leaders, which made it all seem more real to them - that they were part of an army, who were going to have revenge for the evil done to them. Seeing Kisa, Kojo and Yasuki mounted encouraged the others. Each one thought, *some day that will be me!* The little army skirted the village of Larabanga and marched north into the river valley below the Konkari escarpment. Kisa used the markers they had left to take them to their new home.

They reached the hidden village behind the escarpment on a warm and sunny day. Storm clouds were gathering in the distance, marking the approaching wet season, but all was bright and cheerful as they marched into the camp. Introductions were made between the Dagomba men and women and the troops from the south. The Dagomba were impressed by the number of trained warriors who had come and how many different tribes were represented among the new troops.

The Dagomba prepared a feast while the newcomers set up camp and washed off the dust of travel. Then they all came together to eat, drink palm wine, and talk in their shared language, Kiswahili.

Kisa and Kojo were pleased to see that everyone was eager to get to know one another. Kojo took out his drum and soon the people were dancing. Fires were lit and the celebrations went on into the night until at last, the Dagomba returned to their huts and the newcomers to their bedrolls.

The next day the work began. The different groups chose where they wanted to be based and discussed plans for huts and storehouses. Fela and Majeed were eager to show Kisa the progress that had been made. Several large huts had been built for storage of food and other supplies and corrals had been made from brush for both the horses and farm animals. Already the Dagomba villagers had brought chickens and goats so that milk and eggs were available as well as bush meat. The Dagomba had also built themselves smaller huts for their accommodation. Since most were unmarried, there was a sleeping hut for the men and a second hut for the women. Kisa approved the work that had been done and laid out her plans for the new army.

'Most of my troops are married couples. We will let them choose areas and build huts for themselves. Then we will allocate chores to those who are most able: building, farming, animal husbandry, preparing weapons and getting ready for fighting. Yasuki will organize training. All troops must continue to train with him!'

***

Kisa approached Kojo and Yasuki and said, 'I want to fly again. I must use Udele to see far, far away - to the west and to the north and to the east. To see what the vultures see, and we cannot.'

Yasuki agreed. 'This will be a long voyage. Let Niena nurse you. That frees Kojo to guard you. We must have supplies up there. Water for you and food for your guards. It must be comfortable for them, for we do not know how long you will be away. Today we prepare. Tomorrow you will fly, my sorceress – and you will go much further this time than these old eyes have seen. Bring us a picture of all the land around us.'

'And I will turn it into a map!' Kojo finished eagerly.

When all was ready, they climbed back to the highest point on the escarpment. Kojo prepared a place for Kisa and Niena sat down to wait with her. Kisa laid her head in Niena's lap and let her mind make the leap. She closed her eyes and when she opened them again, she was in Udele.

First, she flew north, high above the land, higher than any other bird. She left the savannah behind and flew over the great northern desert. There she saw the caravans from the north with their blue robed Tuareg camel masters. She watched them high above the fabled city of gold, Timbuktu on the great river Niger, where the desert ended. She circled high over the city that was built on trade and turned into a centre of learning as well. She saw the great mosques, the compounds, the earthen walls, and buildings. And she saw the camels coming in with their loads of salt and slaves.

Some of the goods were being loaded into boats that floated down a canal to the Niger river. Some took the goods across the river to continue their journey south to Tamale while others went upstream and downstream. Upstream led to Djenne and then into the foothills of the coastal mountains that fed the river and hid the gold.

She followed the road back south and began to spot the parties of slave masters marching their captives down the road or ravaging the countryside with their raids. She followed them south to the slave camp of Pickworo where she saw them chaining the weeping captives to the rocks below.

Her anger rose and she called out with Udele's voice. She wanted to say: 'I will free you' but they did not understand the call of the vulture and quailed in fear.

Her vulture nostrils widened at the smell of death and despair in that place. She watched them sitting chained together in the hot sun without protection. They ate their food from shallow holes in the granite rocks on which they sat, waiting, until chained together and sent south with whatever trader had bought them for the next part of their hopeless journey.

She saw them look up at her, wheeling high on a thermal over the camp. A man, chained out in the sun to a rock with no protection looked up for his last time. She felt his spirit leave the broken chained body on the punishment rock as she watched, and she cried out in Udele's voice her anguish and anger at those who had killed him. Several slavers looked up at the sound. One laughed and said, 'It wants to feast. Unchain the body and tie it to the vulture's tree. She will feed well tonight!' The others laughed with him before doing his bidding.

Kisa cried out again and was answered this time by drumming. Below her, captives began rhythmically chanting and hitting the rocks with their chains and smaller rocks lying within reach. Tap, tap, tap, then louder, as they hit the rocks over and over in a poly-rhythmic pattern that grew from the first tappers until the slavers silenced them with whips. Kisa could bear to watch no longer. She gave one more cry and flew on.

She turned Udele west, caught the thermals, and rose higher and higher until she could see much of West Africa below her. She rose and rose and rose again on the thermals so high that the air became thin and cold. Then she used Udele's strong wings to fly up the Niger all the way to its source in hills, beyond which lay the ocean. She saw the little creeks in the hillsides that flowed down to create the river. Nestled among the hills were men digging in the earth for the gold that made the region so rich.

Over the hills she found the sea. She smelled salt in the air as she approached it and saw the blue-grey waves beating on the shore. A sudden urge sent her flying south high above the coastline. The winds blew the great vulture all the way to her home in the forest. That she could not see, but the European forts and castles along the coast assaulted her eyes. springing up like mushrooms along the coast Axim, Elmina, and others that she could not name.

At last, across from the island of Sao Tome, she saw where the Niger river entered the sea. She circled high above the giant forested estuary spreading out below her. Turning north, she flew till it was one great river again. Then she followed it north for thousands of miles until the jungles ceased and she came at last to Gao, the other great trading city, hundreds of miles downstream of Timbuktu.

She flew far lower than she had been for all the long circular journey from the upper Niger to the sea, to the lower Niger and then back up to the capital of the old Songhai Empire. She circled slowly over Gao. In the river were the same thin, double-prow pirogues she had seen to the west. On the shores there was a market, with hide covered sheds covering the goods as they waited to be loaded or sold.

The city was dominated by its mosques and the tomb of their beloved Songhai Emperor, Askia the Great. Most of the buildings were made of mud brick and dotted with green trees, but the landscape was dry beyond the reach of the river. It had been the centre of the Songhai Empire a hundred years earlier but now it was dying back into a quiet town on a backwater of the river. Kisa saw little of interest and was almost ready to return to the high hills above Tamale, when she spotted a road that led east out of Gao and ran through the stony desert all the way to the city of Agadez.

Agadez. She had heard the name mentioned many times as a centre of the age-old Arab slave trade. Agadez -

the most likely home of her hated enemy, half-brother of Sefu, the one-eared slaver, Badru. She had one last journey to make. Flying higher, she sped east. Rising higher on the thermals, she saw Agadez in the distance. It was just another mud brick city with a mosque. It looked so ordinary, but she could see caravans coming in and a large slave market in the town. Among those buildings were the slave masters. She cried out but though they may have felt unknown shivers of fear, her voice could not reach them.

Higher still she rose, circling, till she could see another ocean - the Ind Ocean that Yasuki had crossed all those years earlier to find her. She felt no desire to fly any further. It was time to go back. She had seen all she needed, and she couldn't kill the slave masters from the body of a vulture, so she headed east and south.

She flew back to the Niger River, this time to a town south of Gao, Niamey. Here she saw slave markets, filled with captives from the east, bound west and south to the new European slave castles. From Niamey she flew to the next big town of Ouagadougou and once again saw more slave markets. Turning south she flew over Bolgatanga and then in the hills south of that town, she saw the largest slave market yet – Pikworo, the Hills of Fear. At last, she returned to the high hill where Kojo and Niena waited for her while they protected her physical body.

'I have seen so much,' she gasped as she sat up. 'How can I show you? You will need a larger map, Kojo!'

She didn't continue, but instead got to her feet and went straight to camp so that the others could also hear about her travels. She took a stick and drew a map in the sandy soil. She placed a small stone for the camp, a bigger

160

stone for Tamale, and a thick double line between to represent the Konkari escarpment. She added lines for roads, and X's for caravans that she had seen. Then she drew a wavy line out in a great semicircle.

'This is the great river they call Niger.'

She used rocks to mark the trading cities she had flown over - Djenne, Timbuktu, Gao, Niamey.

'This is where it all happens, all the goods that come from the north then go south on the river or by land, everything happening in the south starts there. I followed the river west to the sea. I followed the coast all the way home and beyond.'

She added wavy lines for the oceans. She showed the Atlantic coast and marked the forts and castles with rocks. 'See how many of them there are!'

She drew a circle in the ocean to show Sao Tome. 'Where Amador comes from, you remember it, Kojo! From there I saw where the great river comes into the sea. I followed it back north so that I came in a great circle, back to the third city. This one. The one that Majeed called Gao.

I felt the need to go further east. There was a road that led all the way to the slave masters' city... the one they call Agadez. Agadez. It is the gate of the desert... all the camels from the northeast come that way and then to the river.' Kisa continued to draw her map. She showed the roads from Agadez, through Niamey on the Niger to Ouagadougou directly to the north. She drew the road south from Ouagadougou to Bolgatanga and then she made some humps to show the Hills of Fear.

'There were more slaves there than any place I have seen north of the Salaga Markets. It is a barren place where the captives are chained to the rocks and fed in holes carved into the rocks. Everyone from the north must come through there… and after that … Tamale.' She brought her stick back to her starting point. 'I need food and rest now, Sensei. Then we can talk.'

Kojo held back, studying Kisa's sand map, committing the names of the dots to his memory, imagining the lands that Kisa had seen and planning to redraw it on a new, larger scroll. Niena used the fire to cook yams for their dinner. Then, over a wholesome meal by the campfire, they discussed the future.

'I see how the caravans travel,' Kisa began. 'All trade goes by the same roads. Of most importance to us is that road that comes south from the Hills of Fear to Tamale and then on to the Salaga markets. Most of the slaves are taken to the Hills of Fear. Then they are marched south to Salaga. But there is a great east-west road that also goes through Tamale. It is used to bring goods all the way to and from the eastern ocean where you came from, Sensei.'

Yasuki nodded. 'I travelled that road and then turned south from Tamale to find you.'

'Yes!' Kisa continued with excitement and fire in her eyes. 'And I saw it all with Udele's eyes. I will find the slave masters, and my army will destroy them!'

Kojo raised his fist. 'Somunye. We are with you. We will do this.'

Niena stared hypnotised at Kisa. Yasuki nodded his agreement and rose his fist also.

Chapter 15
Preparing for War

The four went back to the village and called a meeting to explain what would happen next. Kisa spoke first.

'Kojo will go to Tamale with Majeed and Mahamadu to bring back any more of the Dagomba people who wish to join us. Kwame, I want you to organise work crews here. We need more huts built. There is a village nearby which was destroyed by slavers. We can use what is left there to build our own village. Shani, I want you to organise the planting of our first gardens. And our best hunters should start bringing in meat. These plains are rich in game. We can buy some food from Tamale but for safety and secrecy's sake we should be as self-sufficient as we can. It is good that your people have built storage huts, Majeed. Our fighters need more training too of course. I leave that to you, Sensei.' Kisa bowed to her teacher, then continued.

'I want all to know how to fight, with or without weapons! Soon Kojo and I will lead our first raiding party against the slave masters. Everybody must be prepared.'

There was much cheering at this announcement and then arguments broke out about who should be in the first raiding party.

'Silence!' Kojo demanded. 'You will get your turn! But your leaders must learn what works. Kisa and I have decided who shall do battle with the slave masters first. We have all fought battles before, but these raids must be our best effort. We must protect the captives while slaying the slave masters and those who serve them.'

'All of them,' Kisa emphasized. 'We want no tellers of tales. We must keep ourselves hidden for as long as possible. Kwame and Shani will go with us. Choose others to take care of your duties here. Amador, I wish you to accompany us, Niena will attend to me as always.'

Then Kojo continued. 'Majeed of the Dagomba, Fela of the Ashanti, Okocho of the Ibo, as leaders you should come with us also,' and they nodded their agreement.

'What about you, Sensei?' Kojo asked as he turned to Yasuki.

'I will come with you this time.' Yasuki replied. 'I wish to see how you fight. But I will watch only. It is you who must fight, not me.'

'So,' Kisa was counting in her head, 'Kojo and I, Kwame and Shani, Amador, Fela and Okocha – seven fighters. Who else is ready to fight do you think?'

Amador spoke first. 'My fishermen are already good fighters. They were blooded in the mutiny on the slave ship and when we took the fort from the Ga village. Your Nzema and Dagomba youth are not blooded. I think they should wait.'

Kojo nodded. 'Sule and his two sailor mates can come if they wish. And I believe that Majeed and his brother, Mahamadu should come as representatives of the Dagomba nation on whose lands we fight. They are not blooded yet.'

'That is a good-sized band,' Kisa agreed. 'Majeed and Mahamadu still have to prove themselves in battle, but I do not think they will be found wanting. I would prefer Niena do camp duties rather than fight. What about your wife, Okocha?'

Okocha's dark skin turned reddish as his cheeks filled with blood from embarrassment. 'Ugochi cannot fight, Sorceress, she is pregnant.'

Kisa laughed. 'That is good. Congratulations, Okocha. That is a good omen for our success.' She turned back to the others. 'Those who remain here will train. In a few months some of them can join us by which time we will know the terrain and the routine, if there is one, for each attack. We, with the support of our beloved teacher, Yasuki, will start the northern war.'

After it was decided and all went to prepare, Kisa turned to Kojo. 'I will fly with Udele again. I want to find the best place to launch our attacks. I am going to the Salaga Road.'

Kojo nodded. 'I think it will be our best hunting ground too. Whether they come from east, north or west, the quickest way from Tamale to the coast is through Salaga. And the slave markets are there.'

'Yes, I will find out where the parties are and how fast they are moving. When I return, we will march.' Kisa could not hide the excitement in her voice.

Kisa went to the place that Niena had prepared for her and launched herself into Udele. She flew straight and true to the road leading south out of Tamale. She saw a slave party leaving the city gates. Further south she saw the road from Yendi come into the Salaga Road and here she saw a second party with a fat slave master on a donkey at its head. Some apparently turned off before Tamale to shorten the distance. Further down the Salaga Road, halfway to Salaga, she saw a large party of slave masters returning north from the sales. They were all mounted, with clinking bags of coins in saddlebags. They were well-dressed and singing loudly, drunk on the profits of their business.

Kisa circled above them. Her ravens had followed her and they too circled the slave masters. The four birds cried in mournful unison and the word death echoed in the minds of the slavers. They felt suddenly chilled and looked with superstitious apprehension at the birds above them. Then their leader, a man with a scarred face and missing one ear looked up before calling to his companions to forget the birds and ride faster.

Kisa screamed a vulture scream when she recognised her foe. In the time that she had been gathering her army, he had gone home, been given a raiding party by his father, and captured enough people to make a visit to Salaga. She wanted to swoop down and kill him but knew it

167

was useless with all the armed men around him. Seething with hatred, she turned and flew back to Kojo.

'He was there! Badru! A successful slave master, returning from the markets. He uses that road now. It is there we must hunt. I saw slaving parties leaving Tamale and more coming in from the road from Yendi. The hunting will be good. And next time that devil comes south, I will have my revenge. Let the northern war begin!'

Badru was frightened by the vulture. He remembered the vulture that had flown above him as he fled from the cursed sorceress and her village. He tried to shake it off but that night he had the dream again. The sorceress stood before him with leopard eyes glaring at him. He drew his sword and tried to strike but she countered every blow with her bare hands. At last he fell and as he lay before her, she turned into the vulture and pecked his eyes out as he lay screaming. He awoke in a sweat, trembling with fear.

'I will go home,' he muttered. 'I will be safe in Agadez.'

Chapter 16

On the Salaga Road

The vulture circled lazily in the warm updrafts over the savannah. Kisa looked through Udele's eyes at the land below, scanning for her prey. To the south of the savannah, where a wooded stream cut across the road between two low hills, Kisa's body was being protected by Niena, Kojo and Chaga.

When Kisa's soul soared out of her body to Udele, she always left her body in the protection position: seated, legs bent at knees, hands wrapped around legs and head folded in for maximum protection. Niena tended to her every need while she slept and Kojo was always on guard beside her, willing to give his life if necessary, to keep her waiting body safe until she returned. Beside them sat the yellow dog, always on alert and ready to fight for his mistress.

The raiders below paid no attention to the vulture. They were used to vultures following their deadly trail, as they killed the weak and left their bodies for the aerial clean-up crews. But this was no ordinary vulture that was circling downwards to get a better view. The small party of men were driving a weary line of captives, chained and yoked together. Kisa counted six slavers and about twenty captives. The captain was on a dark brown donkey and was not Badru, but she felt the same upwelling of hatred and anger towards this unknown slave master as she did towards Badru.

The slave master led the way. Behind him came his lieutenant on a donkey, which also carried the food supplies for the slavers. There was no food for the captives. All they could hope for were regular streams or puddles where they could slake their thirst. Each wore a wooden collar that had heavy metal chains running between captives. There were a few women and children at the head of the line, followed by a number of young men, the white men's favourite prey, destined for short and brutal lives on the sugar plantations of the new world. But first they had to get there.

On each side of the captives walked two guards, each equipped with sharp knives and stinging leather whips, which they used to drive them on, trying to cover as much ground as possible each day. Women and children who fell and could not get up were handed to the men to carry until they were strong enough to walk again. If they showed no improvement, they were run through with knives and left for the vultures.

Kisa felt the anger rise till it threatened her ability to think clearly. She heard her teachers whispering their advice and support, breathed deeply and then sent her spirit back to her human form. She looked down at the seemingly sleeping form of her younger brother, Kwame. He was astral travelling through his own spirit animals, the insects. His sister was sitting protectively next to him, just as Niena was crouched by Kisa. Kojo stood over all four, stoic in his stillness.

Kwame had been taught by Grandmother to leave his body and meet his spirit animals. Kojo and Shani had spirit animals too but found it hard to make the leap to another body. Kwame, on the other hand, had shown great promise in the art and Kisa was putting it to the test now.

170

'There are not many slavers,' she said as she unfolded herself and stretched stiff muscles. 'I see Kwame has not returned yet. I want to know what he saw, but I only counted one slave master with five underlings. There were many more captives.' She flexed her fingers three times to indicate around thirty. At that moment, Kwame's eyes opened, and he sat up with no sign of sleepiness.

'I did it!' He crowed. 'You were right, Kisa. I did not need Grandmother's potion. I pictured locust and I was there, flying fast. I found them on the road just a half day's walk from us. I landed on the donkey that carries food for the slave master and listened to their talk. They spoke Kiswahili so I could follow it. They were discussing the need to find water soon. They will have to come to the third crossing to find it. And I saw Udele above me!'

Kisa smiled at his excitement. 'Yes. We are spies such as they cannot imagine. Just don't get yourself swatted!'

Kwame laughed. 'I am too fast for them.'

'We can take them when they stop for water at the stream,' Kisa continued. 'They will have to stop. The trail is dry, the captives have not had water for more than a day at least. When they are down and drinking, we will strike.' Her anger rose in her voice. 'Kill the slavers, all of them! One is young, he will beg for mercy but if he escapes, he will turn on us. Understand me well. We cannot let any of them live.'

She stared hard at Shani as she said this. Shani was barely twelve and had a girl's deep love of all creatures, especially babies. Her natural instinct was mercy, but that was a hindrance out here. She had to steel herself. Kisa

171

turned to Kwame. 'Stand by her. Fight with her. If she hesitates, kill her opponent.'

Kwame nodded gravely. He was the same age as his twin of course, but in this matter, he was more mature. He had trained with the best since he was barely old enough to walk. He was a warrior to his core. He saved mercy for his own tribe, no one else, and he would gladly die to save his beloved sister. They were twin souls and there was a part of Kwame that would always love his twin more than any other woman in his life.

Kisa turned to Kojo. 'Call a meeting with your drum. We march.'

The troops gathered. All the leaders were there: Amador, the Sao Tome fisherman, Fela the Ashanti warrior, Okocha of the Ibo; Majeed of the Dagomba, and other fighters chosen for their leadership abilities. Kisa explained her plan and they set out to find hiding places within striking distance of the stream.

The three ravens sat in a tree on the last rise before the drop to the stream. They cawed loudly when the slave master on his donkey came into sight in the distance. Behind him was a line of weary captives and their guards.

Kisa was directly across the creek, with Chaga at her side. Her sword was unsheathed in her right hand, in her left was the tall black spear and over her shoulders lay the leopard skin cloak. Overhead, the three ravens circled and cried. Higher overhead, a great vulture circled lazily, watching the action below.

The raiders waited in silence and at last were rewarded with the sounds of the slaving party - the crack of the whips, the chains clanking and the shouted orders of the slave master. As they approached the tiny creek, the thirst-crazed prisoners broke into a half-running shuffle to reach the water. They threw themselves down in it, scooping up water with their hands. The guards' eyes were turned towards them.

Kisa stepped out of the shadows and stared at the slave master, who stopped shouting and stared back, stunned at the sight of the tall armed woman and the great dog. A drum was heard. Kisa charged in with her great black spear - the hardened wood of the Sentinel Tree - in her right hand pointed towards the slave master. She wore greaves to protect her shins and the tops of her feet. Her feet could be used with deadly accuracy. Her blows with them were always hard enough to stun her opponents in countless practice fights.

She went for the slave master and brought his donkey to its knees with a sharp crack to its head with the spear. Her enemy was thrown to the ground. She stepped into range for a head blow from the side of her heavy spear that left the man senseless. Stepping over him, she aimed for the second in command as her troops swarmed over and around her.

She swung the stick around as her sensei taught her, using it to strike hard enough to the side or top of head to fell them. One after another, she struck and then leapt over that man, leaving him for her followers to finish off. And they did so, swarming behind and around her, using their short swords, knives, and spears to kill the band of slavers and their master. The guards were cracking their whips and tried vainly to draw their knives and swords but too slowly.

They were cut down where they stood. Kisa watched as she stood over the slave master's body.

Let them do the killing, she thought. *They need the practice.*

Just as Kisa had foreseen, Shani hesitated over a fallen slaver. But Kwame pushed past her and killed the wounded man in front of her. None were left to tell the tale of the new raiders on the road from Tamale. Udele and her family would take care of the bodies.

The captives were stunned. They stared at their saviours, not sure if these people had come to save them or merely capture them for themselves. To their relief, Kojo found the keys to the chains on the dead slave master and the others cut through the ropes to free the captives. They stood huddled in a group for a few minutes, rubbing their limbs, and then they went back to drinking. It took long minutes to satisfy their thirst. In that time, Kisa's fighters dragged the bodies into the scrub away from the road.

The freed captives approached Kisa, who was standing proud and motionless watching them, while her band cleaned up. They whispered among themselves in several languages which were strange to Kisa. She showed them by gestures and a bit of Kiswahili that they were to be taken to safety and, more importantly, fed.

The captives were guided to a camp that Kisa's followers had established in the wooded hills behind the Salaga Road. They were given dinner and haltingly they found common words and told their rescuers where they were from. One man, Kakande, had more words of the language Kiswahili than others.

'We are from a land far to the east, many days walk from here, called Buganda. Our country is green and rich but the slavers have been stealing our people for as long as we can remember. I was taken while defending my village. These others are mostly my kin though some died on the road.' Tears welled up in Kakande's eyes, but he blinked them back angrily.

'You can go home if you wish,' Kisa told him. 'You are free. But it is a long way, and your companions are weak. We can offer them safety in a camp to the north and west of here. If you wish to avenge your people, join us! We can use your strength.'

Kakande turned to his companions and explained Kisa's offer to them. There was not much discussion before he turned back to Kisa. 'We will come with you. I will gladly fight with you, as will my friend, Mulondo.' He pointed to Mulondo who nodded to Kisa. 'His wife and child died on the road. He too wants revenge.'

Yasuki had waited in the camp during the fight. He came up to Kisa. 'You have fought well.' he said, 'but this first fight was almost too easy. It is because we are still unknown. We must keep the secret as long as we can. I am going to leave the fighting to you now, Sorceress. You need to test your wings as a leader. You will learn faster if I am not here.'

Kisa started to protest, but Yasuki held up his hand. 'I will take the captives back to the main camp. There, I will train new warriors for you, while you fight this war, my Queen.'

Kisa bowed formally to her teacher and agreed. Kojo smiled. He was now married to a Queen. *My Bandit Queen,* he thought.

***

In the camp, whispers began. Kisa's soldiers talked among themselves, noting how not a single scratch had been sustained by anyone in the raiding party.

'It is only the first fight,' some said.

'Or perhaps it is because we fight for a sorceress,' said others.

'We shall see,' was the consensus.

Yasuki left soon after with the freed captives, except Kakande, who was eager to fight even though untrained. Yasuki took Sule with him because Sule had shown promise as a guide.

'My years at sea have taught me how to navigate by the sun and stars. It is not so different here.' Sule explained to Kisa. 'I can go back to the warrior's camp now and bring the young fighters to you when they are trained, sorceress.'

Kisa nodded. There were no trails between the hidden camp behind the escarpment and her camp on the Salaga Road and she wanted to keep it that way. Let Sule lead them back and forth instead. It was a good use for Sule's skills.

'I will walk this time with the others,' Yasuki said unexpectedly as he turned to Shani. 'You must learn to ride. I give my horse Laila to you.'

Shani jumped up in surprise. 'But Sensei, I am the gazelle. I run! Not ride!' She had never argued with him before, but it did not anger her teacher.

'On the horse, you will surpass the fastest gazelle. Learn to ride, little sorceress, and great glory will come to you, I promise.'

Yasuki walked to his beautiful grey Arab mare, gently laid a hand on her halter and led her to Shani. 'You have served me well, Laila. You were always slow and steady for this old man. I give you now to your true master. Love her. Serve her. Carry her into battle and bring her back safely.' He handed the rope to Shani.

Shani looked deep into Laila's eyes and placed her forehead gently against the mare's forehead. The two stood silent, motionless for a moment and bonded to the depths of their souls.

'We are one,' Shani said in wonder.

All who watched saw the mare in the eyes of the woman and the woman in the eyes of the mare. Kisa thought of her bond with Udele. It was the same. Something great would come of this, she was sure.

After they left, Kisa called her small band together to discuss what to do until Yasuki sent the first trained warriors back.

'We have had our first success. Now we must plan how to win all our battles. Many slavers are already in Salaga, and they will be heading north soon. There will be no slaves to free, but something better. We can kill the slave masters before they have a chance to start new ventures and we can relieve them of their horses and wealth, which can be used to purchase food and weapons.'

Kojo spoke up. 'They will be well armed, and their guards will be travelling with them. We are still few so we must pick and choose. If one slave master is travelling alone with a few guards, that might be possible. The group you described to me was large and with no captives to hamper them, they would be able to fight better.'

Kisa saw the point of this. 'I think we must judge each fight on its merits. And I think we are too small to stop all the slave parties. We will be able to do more when the others join us. I will fly tomorrow and tell you what I find. Then Kwame can use his skills to judge further whether it is a party that we can take.'

The next day she flew both north and south. Another party was a day's walk away and moving very slowly, for the captives were weak and sick. To the south no one could be seen leaving Salaga.

'We go north,' she told Kojo when she returned. 'This slave master is younger, leaner, and harder than the first. He rides a horse instead of a donkey. There are twice as many slaves and so twice as many guards. It will not be as easy as the first time. The guards have whips and knives. Kwame, I want you to infiltrate their camp tonight. Find out more.'

Kisa decided to use the same crossing for the attack. She debated what to do with Shani, who was shaken by the events of the first raid and decided to leave her behind at the camp. Shani was shamed by this but was also happy not to go. She needed time to get to know Laila and work out her role in future battles.

Kisa's raiders returned to the stream they had used on the first raid but this time Kisa and Kojo brought their horses, Amara and Aya.

'This crossing worked for us once. It will work again. Its waters are clean and strong. It has a magic about it.' Kisa spoke quietly to the others. 'Because the slave master and his lieutenant are mounted, Kojo and I will also be mounted. It takes away that advantage. We will engage them and that will leave you free to kill the guards.'

They chose their positions carefully, spreading themselves out so they could attack the rear of this larger force as well as front. Once their plans were made, they retreated to a sheltered space in the forest to rest for the night. All except Kwame, who left his body for that of a cricket in the camp of the slave master.

He hopped towards the fire where the slavers were noisily eating and drinking. A little way off, the captives were huddled miserably in the cold air, chained together and with nothing to slake their thirst or fill their bellies. The slavers were laughing and talking about what they would do with the money they got when the captives reached Salaga. It was uninformative, being mostly boasts about the amount of alcohol they would consume and the number of whores they planned to visit, so Kwame counted them. Besides the slave master there were eighteen guards. It was a big group, more than Kisa's raiders. It was impossible to count the captives in the darkness.

Kwame returned to his body and confirmed with Kisa the size of the slaving party. 'Perhaps we should let this one pass,' Kwame finished.

'No!' was Kisa's sharp answer. 'I will fight the slave master. The rest of you strike hard and fast. I did not come here to hide in the bushes. As soon as I attack, hit them from all sides. Kwame, as soon as I kill the slave master, grab the keys, and release the prisoners. They will help to create confusion.'

***

Early the next morning, Kisa's raiders spread out in their chosen positions. Kojo and Kisa brought their horses close to the stream, ready to begin the attack when the slave master and the first group of slaves reached it. Kwame was close behind, ready to do his part. So was Chaga, who crouched next to Amara. The horse was trembling with excitement as she sensed the coming battle.

Time passed slowly but at last in the distance, Kisa and the others could hear the shouts of the slavers and the crack of whips. The slave master on his horse rounded the corner and was followed by the first of the captives. They quickened their pace as they saw the stream ahead.

The slave master stopped as the first captives knelt to drink. The others jostled in desperation behind them, but the whips of the guards and their chains held them back. At that moment all hell broke loose as Kisa and Kojo, swords drawn, swept out of the forest on their horses.

'Somunye!' The battle cry echoed through the hills as Kisa reached the slave master. He reacted quickly, drawing his sword and he managed to parry her first stroke with the spear. Kojo cut down the second mounted man as the rest of Kisa's raiders raced screaming on to the road. Amador's curved sword took out a guard before he had time to raise his whip. The other guards milled in confusion, struggling to drop their whips and get their knives out. Fela killed a guard and so did Majeed in quick succession. The captives were milling about in confusion. One or two saw what was happening and used their chains to trip their captors, making it easier for Kisa's raiders to kill them.

Kisa dropped the spear, pulled out her sword and attacked the slave master again. He was an expert swordsman. It was the hardest fight of her young life, as the man repeatedly stabbed at her. She had no time to strike, only able to stave off the blows that he was aiming at her. Kojo had his hands full with the guards, who still outnumbered Kisa's raiders. She could not use her martial arts from the back of the horse. All she could do was hold the much bigger and stronger man back.

Then Chaga acted. With a savage growl he launched himself at the slave master's horse, grabbing its neck in his strong jaws. The horse reared and the slave master was unseated, falling heavily into the rocky stream bed. Kisa leaped off Amara and ran to meet him, slashing down hard on his sword arm as he struggled to get to his feet. The man screamed but it was cut short as her sword cut through his throat. Several of the guards saw their leader fall and turned to run away. Kwame leaped forward to get the keys to the chains off the dying man. Then he ran to the nearest captives and began to release them.

'Fight with us!' Kisa yelled. 'Freedom! Somunye!'

The battle turned into a rout. The slavers fell one by one. Some died swiftly by the sword. Others were beaten to death by the angry captives. The three that ran away were quickly overtaken by Kisa and Kojo on their horses and cut down.

Kisa rode back to the stream. Blood was dripping from her upraised sword. 'Somunye!' she cried, and it was echoed by all, even the captives who did not know the meaning.

Overhead the ravens circled, crying. The second battle was won.

***

The clean-up took longer than the battle. Once the chains were removed, the captives drank from the stream and then sacked the slavers' food stores from the packs on the donkeys. Kisa watched them from the back of Amara and then turned to Kojo and Kwame.

'Have the men drag the slavers' bodies deep into the forest. Find an open space where Udele and her family can feast on them. Then find someone who can speak to these men. Ask Kakande if he understands any of them. Their language is strange to me. Make them understand who we are and why we have freed them. Explain that we will take them to a safe place where they can rest.'

Kojo and Kwame nodded and set about their tasks. Kisa dismounted and approached Chaga. She put her hand on his head. 'You were a great help to me today, Chaga. That man was a good sword fighter.' Chaga grinned, showing his teeth, as Kisa said, 'You are a war dog now, my friend.'

By evening the job was done. The slave master and his guards were relieved of all their earthly possessions and their bodies left a long way from the road where the vultures could feast in peace. No travellers would know what had happened to them. The freed captives were taken back to the camp, where they were allowed to rest and recuperate.

Kisa approached Kakande. 'You fought well today, even without training. I am proud of you. You are a blooded warrior now.'

Kakande turned to the other warriors and cried out: 'Somunye! I am a warrior now!'

The others took up the cry and then they spent the evening dancing to Kojo's drum and drinking the last of the slave master's palm wine. It was a victory worth celebrating.

The whispers circulated again. 'It is our second fight. No one was wounded. Not even a scratch! It is the power of the sorceress!'

There were fewer naysayers this time.

***

That night, Kisa dreamed. Badru came for her and she was unarmed. She spun and kicked, dodged and feinted, leading him on in a deadly dance. Blow after blow landed on him while he was unable to touch her. She woke elated and shook Kojo out of a deep sleep.

'Sefu is gone. It is Badru who comes to kill me, but I am getting better,' she said. 'Still, I have to practice more. We must have more training in between each battle. I am being shown this in my dreams. I must learn to fight without weapons. We all must!'

'Do we have to train now, my love?' Kojo reached up and pulled her down to him. She pretended to struggle before sinking into his arms.

'Tonight, we make love, not war,' she sighed.

***

A few days later, Sule arrived with the first reinforcements for Kisa's raiders. 'Sensei Yasuki sends his greetings. These men are eager to fight for you.'

Kisa inspected them. Mulondo was among them. 'I thought you would train longer,' Kisa said to him.

'I know enough to kill,' Mulondo responded. 'And I have my family to avenge.'

'Then show Kakande what you have learned. He has already killed in battle, but he can still learn our fighting techniques,' Kisa told him.

Mulondo nodded and went to find Kakande. Kisa turned to Kojo. 'We have enough fighters now to form two parties. Divide the new men among the old so that each new man has someone more experienced to help him. I will take some to the north, along the road to Yendi. You keep the rest here. I will attack those who are coming from Yendi and leave those who come from Tamale for you. What do you think?'

'How will we communicate?' Kojo asked.

'Keep Kwame with you. You can send him to me on insect wings if we need to speak. I will fly with Udele and circle you if I need you.'

'That should work. I think that the traders of Salaga will have a lean season.'

***

The two groups settled into a pattern that allowed them to cover the two roads from Yendi and Tamale to Salaga. Shani rode with Kisa while Kwame worked with Kojo. Kisa's group camped on a secluded river and attacked on horseback because the road from Yendi was longer. Once contact was made, Kisa preferred to dismount so that she could use her martial arts as well as her sword to kill her enemies. Always her mind went back to her recurring dreams when she had no weapons.

I must never become dependent on sword and spear, she thought. *I must be ready to fight with my hands alone if necessary.*

Between raids, Kisa pushed the raiders to train with her. Formal training happened every day that they were in camp. Kisa flew regularly with Udele to find slaving parties. Once discovered, Kwame infiltrated their camps on the wings of a locust and listened to the slavers' plans. On returning to the army, he passed on vital information that was used to plan their ambushes.

Shani was developing her own style when they fought. She was becoming more and more confident on the back of Laila. She learned to grip with her knees so that her hands were free. She still did not want to kill. Instead, she carried a flaming torch and sang a fierce battle song in a clear voice that struck fear in the slave masters before her.

Kisa rode beside Shani with sword held high, an avenging angel of death. The slavers were struck

185

motionless at the sight of the two women and helpless to defend themselves. Kisa's sword swung and heads flew as Amara leaped over the cowering captives, leaving them unharmed. When they reached the other side, they watched as their warriors finished the job. In no time at all, a slave master and his underlings lay dead, Shani ended her song and the job of freeing the captives began.

Meanwhile on the road from Tamale, Kojo and his raiders were busy too and business was drying up in Salaga but as yet no one knew why. And still no one in either raiding party was wounded or killed. It seemed that they were protected by the gods themselves. The warriors became bolder, took more chances, but none suffered so much as a scratch at the hands of their enemies. The rumours ran thick now. 'The sorceress protects us! The gods love her, and they will not let the evil ones touch us.'

Kojo heard the rumours and felt some discomfort. He tried to caution his fighters. 'Take no chances! No one knows the will of the gods.' But his words went unheeded.

More and more, Kisa's raiders were convinced that as long as they fought for the sorceress, they were protected. Kojo had to admit that they fought all the braver for it, so he gave up trying to convince them otherwise. By hiding in the scrubby hills, both hunting parties succeeded in keeping their presence hidden from the unsuspecting slave buyers in Salaga. Party after party ended their journey on the road. Without exception, the slave masters were killed, and their bodies stripped and hidden in the hills for the vultures and the hyenas.

Captives were freed and sent with Sule to the main camp to rest and then train to join the army. If they didn't want to fight, they were welcome to help with the building and gardening work of their new home. A few chose to leave and try to find their way home, but they were sworn to keep the secret of how they had escaped.

Down in Salaga, suspicions rose when the slaving parties ceased to arrive. Finally, they sent someone north to Tamale to find out what was going on. No one in Tamale had any idea. 'The parties left', they said. 'But they never arrived,' was the answer. No one knew why.

Kisa rode south to have a meeting and a night with Kojo as often as she could. She was lying in her beloved's arms, when Kojo suggested it was time to send a message to both towns.

'Send one of the freed captives to Tamale and tell them there is a sorceress making war against the slavers on the southern roads. When they ask for your name, have him say he does not know. He only knows you are called the Bandit Queen.'

Kisa laughed. 'What a strange name! Where did you come up with that?'

'I don't know, maybe it came from the ancestors.' Kojo was serious about this. 'The market traders know something is happening. We will start more than a rumour. We will start a legend. They must see you as a powerful force... a queen!'

Kisa nodded. 'Perhaps you are right, my love. The Bandit Queen.... Why not? I think Grandmother would approve.' And the matter was settled.

Another slaving party was attacked and overcome. This time, a captive was chosen, and a message sent to Tamale. There was a Bandit Queen on the southern road.

Chapter 17

Warrior's Village

After several months of fighting, Kisa and Kojo decided their little army needed a rest and a chance to celebrate their successes. The first rainy season was ending and so was their first hunting season. They took the newly freed captives to the main camp. Kisa and Kojo had not been back for a while and were amazed at the changes that had occurred while they were at war. There were many more huts and gardens to be seen now. Several of the women were pregnant.

'It's a village, not a camp anymore.' Kisa said.

'A village of warriors,' Kojo answered, noting the new troops practicing the teachings of Sensei Yasuki on level ground near the huts.

'That is what we will call it,' Kisa mused. 'Warrior's Village. A good name, Kojo. Where else would a Bandit Queen live?'

'I wonder if the white devils have heard of you yet. When the markets dry up, they will know. What will they do about you? My guess is that the Bandit Queen will soon have a price on her head.'

'Let them come here after me,' Kisa replied with a grin, 'and I will have their heads instead.'

***

The traditions begun on the journey north continued. All spoke Kiswahili and the newcomers were taught this common tongue. Each night the villagers gathered around campfires to tell stories from their past lives. The results could be seen in the general friendliness and camaraderie that existed between peoples who otherwise would never have met or perhaps even been enemies in their old lives.

Kisa stayed aloof from these gatherings to maintain her mystique. She attended the nightly gatherings but did not take part, sitting instead on a chief's stool at the head of the fire, holding her spear, wearing her headdress, and listening. When there were disagreements, people discussed these at the evening campfires. The sorceress had the last say but in fact in all the small issues of village life, she let everyone have their say and then vote on the solution. All she had to do was give her blessing on the decision at that point.

Only at night, alone in her hut with Kojo, could she let the mask slip and be herself again. Kojo could see that it was a strain to always have to keep up the sorceress persona.

One night he said to her, 'Don't you think that it is time to have some fun? Majeed has told me that they have a celebration in Tamale this time of year. It is called Damaba – the Festival of Light. We should go.'

They called a village meeting to discuss the idea and most of the young people wanted to go. Kisa threw the sacred bones to see if it was auspicious. The message she got back was that they should disguise themselves for safety. So, they dressed as Mossi people from a village far to the west, coming to see the great fire festival for which Tamale was renowned. Kisa dressed as a Mossi chieftess to maintain her position of authority but otherwise was determined to join in the festivities.

When they arrived, they found the town decorated gaily and crowded with visitors. It was easy to blend in and raise no suspicions as long as they avoided the few Mossi people who had actually made that long journey. At the festival, they ate the local delicacy, saaham, a flour mix floating in a hot soup, and watched as the townspeople danced around the homes of the chiefs. The men dressed in new smocks while the women wore colourful skirts and elaborate head dresses. The chiefs could be identified by their round woollen hats. Some of the men also carried sticks with feathers tied to them to show their status as chiefs or sub-chiefs.

On the last night of the celebrations, a special ceremony occurred which Kisa and Kojo had never seen before, nor had anyone of the other tribal groups in her band. It was unique to the Dagomba people and was called the Bugum Chugu, or Fire Ceremony. It began when the head chief came out at dusk time and held up a lit torch. The call went out and all the townspeople gathered, carrying unlit torches. One by one they came forward and lit their torches from the chief's torch, before heading out through the town and the lands beyond, calling and looking as if for someone lost.

'What does it mean?' Kojo asked Majeed.

'Long ago, our first head chief, the father of our people, lost his son. The boy wandered off and fell asleep under a tree. No one noticed that he was missing until the

191

night. The chief was beside himself with fear for his son. He grabbed a torch and went running everywhere, calling for his son. All the people took up torches and went to look with him. At the dawn time, they found him safe. He grew up to be a great and wise chief. In honour of his father's love, we re-enact this scene to mark the beginning of the new year. It brings us good luck.'

Majeed smiled. 'May it bring us good luck in the hunt this year too.'

After the celebrations they returned to the Warrior's Village where the leaders met to discuss how to begin their second hunting season.

'We have had important successes on the roads to Salaga,' Kisa began. 'We have freed many captives and our numbers are growing. Many of these people are trained and ready to join us. It is time to cover more ground and stop more slave masters. We will form a third raiding party to go north of Tamale and patrol the road coming from Bolgatanga. Amador, take Fela and Okocha together with their fighters with you and your fishermen.'

Amador smiled and nodded acceptance as Kisa continued. 'I want Kwame to lead the Yendi party. Take Mulondo and Kakande with you. Kojo will hold the Salaga Road.'

Kojo spoke up. 'It is good that we have enough fighters, but if we are going to be so widely spread then we need a way to communicate with one another. We need to develop a better code so that when you fly with Udele, you can tell me by signals where the slaving parties are.'

He stopped to think. 'You could tilt Udele's wings to show me which direction to go. And use her voice – have one call for each of our bands and other calls for the slavers.'

'This idea has merit,' Yasuki said. 'Let the sorceress fly from the hills in all directions. She can find the slavers and then fly above each band to let them know where to find them. There will be nowhere for them to hide!'

'Yes! I will fly with Udele and signal you when slave masters are near. I will stay here and fly from Konkari.' She looked with regret at Kojo who also realised it meant separation from his beloved wife. They both cherished the nights they had together. Now there would be fewer of them.

Shani interrupted. 'What about me? I want to lead a group that can patrol along the Wa Road to Larabanga. Because it is a longer road, the slave masters use horses. If we can capture more horses and train men to ride them, we can have a cavalry. And I want to lead them!'

To her relief, her older sister agreed, at least about the cavalry. 'We need a unit of mounted fighters. That is certain. We can cover more ground and attack larger slaving parties if more of us are mounted. I will think on how to do this. Our first task will be to get more mounted fighters for Shani to use on the road from Wa to Larabanga. Then we will have four fighting bands and I on Udele can unite them.'

The others agreed and the meeting ended. They went back to their huts in silence, each thinking about the parts they had to play in the coming hunting season. Kisa and Kojo held hands as they went to their hut, something they seldom did, but Kisa was feeling the weight of their coming separation.

Kojo was feeling it too. 'I wish you could be closer to me. At least when you were fighting on the Yendi road, we could meet often.'

'Don't worry,' she whispered to him as she sat down on their sleeping mat. 'When the dry season comes and we are here together again, I will make up for it.'

'I will make up for it now,' he answered as he pulled her to him in the darkness.

Chapter 18

The Gonja Horsemen

The next morning, Yasuki looked up at the circling vultures in the updrafts above the rocky escarpment, as the sun warmed the land. 'Join Udele today,' he said to Kisa. 'Go south to the road from Wa to Larabanga. I sense something important will happen there.'

Kojo prepared a place for her where he and Niena could guard her waiting body. Chaga sighed and lay down beside her. Kisa put herself into a trance and sent her mind out to find the birds. Suddenly the transition was made, and she was soaring high above the escarpment, looking through the eyes of Udele.

She set off in ever widening circles, following the roads south and west of the escarpment. She saw a slaving party making their slow way towards Larabanga. Anger rose in her, but she fought the emotion, concentrating instead on assessing the party. There were almost twenty slavers with over forty chained captives. Then in the far west, her keen eyesight caught the sight of dust rising. Flapping her great wings, she headed towards it. Below her she could see nine men on horseback, riding east along the same road as the slaving party at a slow canter. Their skin was a reddish shade of brown, much lighter than her own and she could see that they were tall, slim but muscled, and well-armed.

Kisa returned to her body, stretched, and grinned. 'I have seen a slaving party on the southern road and in front of them come a group of mounted warriors. I propose we meet them and see on which side they fight. If they will join us, we could take those slavers!'

Yasuki nodded, but Kojo shook his head. 'How do you know these warriors will not just kill us instead?'

'We are not barefoot farmers, Kojo. We are mounted and armed.'

'Disguise yourself as a man,' Yasuki said, ending the discussion. 'I will ride with you.'

They set off down the hill to the plains. Shani saw them coming and mounted Laila to join them. She was so connected to Laila that she no longer needed saddle or reins. Once in the open, they raced towards the men that Kisa had seen from the air. When they were in sight of the horsemen, Kisa stopped. The others drew up behind her. When she was sure the horsemen could see her, she raised her sword high in the air.

The leader of the horsemen saw the four strangers and stopped. His eight companions pulled up next to him and they stared at the strange sight. Three black men, much darker than the men of this country, stared at them silently. All looked dangerous and the one in front held a long sword upwards. Behind them was the most beautiful woman they had ever seen, mounted bareback on a grey Arab mare but looking as grim as her companions.

Before they could speak, the young man at the front sheathed his sword and rode forward, right hand raised in the sign of friendship and parlay. His companions followed him and they stopped an arrow-length away.

'Akwaaba,' he said, as if welcoming them to his land.

The leader of the horsemen urged his horse forward a step and spoke in the Dagomba language. 'This is our land now, so it is I who should be welcoming you. Where do you come from, strangers? My name is Bolley, and these are my brothers. We are the NgBanye, but the Dagomba call us Gonja, for our skin is the colour of red kola nuts.' He grinned. His skin was indeed a lovely shade of reddish brown.

Bolley assessed them as he spoke. He saw a young man flanked by two other men, one old and strangely dressed in black padded clothing marked with unknown symbols. All three were well armed and looked comfortable with those weapons. He did not think they would be easy prey, even for nine armed horsemen. Besides, he liked the look of them, especially the woman waiting behind them. He met their leader's eyes. 'Who are you?'

'My name is Kaapo,' Kisa answered as she lowered her raised hand. She could see this man wanted to talk, not fight. These are my brothers, Kojo and Yasuki, and my sister Shani. We are travellers from the south, near the lands of the Ashanti peoples. We are hunting the slave masters. Are you friend or foe to those who trade in human lives?'

'Foes! All of us have lost family to those hyenas.' Bolley spat out the last word.

'Then join us! There is a slaving party coming down this road even now. It has only twenty raiders and one fat slave master. We intend to kill them all and set their captives free!'

Bolley was speechless for a moment. He had not expected to be invited on a raid. And his mind was distracted by the sight of the woman bareback on the grey mare.

She looks barely old enough to menstruate. Who is she? She looks like a young queen. And no saddle! No bridle! How does she control that mare?

'I will have to discuss this with my brothers,' he said at last and turned his horse. The nine men rode out of earshot and talked earnestly among themselves.

'They are crazy men,' was the general view, but these were young warriors spoiling for a good fight. Three men and one girl and they were going to take on a slave master? Some had thought to make sport with these strangers, but they now voted to ride with them. Making sport of the slavers instead, who would be on foot and hampered by their captives, could be more profitable. Afterwards they could decide what to do about these crazy men. As for the girl-child, all of them could picture taking her as a new 'wife'.

'We will join you,' Bolley reported back.

'Good,' was Kaapo's answer. 'We would have killed you if you had tried to stop us.'

Kaapo abruptly turned Amara and galloped off with Yasuki and Kojo close behind. Shani, robe flowing, raced in front of them all. The horses of the Ngbanye stretched out to keep up and the miles flew beneath their feet. They roared out of the west like a bleak desert wind and hit the slavers hard. A torch appeared in Shani's right hand and blazed into a fiery bright white light to blind the slave masters and light the way for the warriors.

The slave master saw them coming and ordered his men to gather in a circle around the captives. Then he hid inside the circle. The slavers were hampered by being on foot. Their captives, though tired and thirsty, saw an unexpected opportunity to gain their freedom.

Kaapo let out a wild war cry as they closed the distance, and this was picked up by all. 'Kill!'

Swords flashed as horses charged. Several slavers fell in bloody heaps and several more panicked and ran. The fat man had already turned and fled. Kaapo and the other two strangers charged past the captives and chased the slavers down, slaughtering them as they ran. The fat man's horse was foundering as they circled him, closing in. He threw himself on the ground, blubbering, 'Please, by the prophet, spare me!' but his words and head were cut short by Kisa's sword.

Shani stopped at the captives and held her blazing torch high. 'Freedom!' she cried. The captives raised their fists and cried back, 'Freedom!'

When the slaughter of the slave masters was finished, Kaapo and Kojo circled back to join Shani and Yasuki in the midst of the captives. Kojo leaped down from Ayo and strode forward with the keys to the chains and an axe to break the wooden halters.

'Free yourselves!' Kaapo cried from the back of Amara, who reared high and neighed an accompaniment.

Overhead, Bolley noticed a great vulture circling and crying out.

Bolley sent two men to help Kojo and soon the captives were free. They stood rubbing sore arms and shoulders and gazing with astonishment at Shani.

'A goddess has come to earth to free us!' A man whispered and the whisper spread throughout the group. He knelt and the others followed him.

Bolley and his men were also thunderstruck by Shani's part in the battle. They had never seen a woman do anything like this before – ride unprotected on an unbridled horse, while carrying a blazing torch?

'A sorceress rides with the crazy men!' The whisper rippled through the Gonja horsemen.

Kaapo moved Amara forward and spoke to the captives in a deep, masculine voice. 'You are free. Eat and drink from the supplies of the slave masters. Use their donkeys and go back to your homes. Tell them a new force is rising in the south that will throw the slave masters into the sea.'

Shani raised her torch and all the captives except one moved away, following the orders they had been given. The last man, the man who had called her a goddess, stepped up to Shani and bent one knee.

'My name is Yao. I have no home to return to. I want to fight with you!'

Bolley and his men laughed at him. Shani glared at them, then said to Yao. 'I accept your service if you can ride.'

Kojo walked up to Yao with the slave master's horse. Luckily it was a quiet animal. Yao took the reins and swung up on a horse for the first time in his life. Gingerly he pulled on the reins and the animal moved behind Shani and Laila.

Kaapo rode over to the Gonja horsemen and spoke to Bolley. 'I thank you for your help. You and your brothers are good fighters. Let us find a place to camp and we can share our stories.'

Bolley liked this young man and admired the way he had attacked and killed, showing no mercy to the slavers. His admiration for Shani was even greater. She was clearly powerful as well as beautiful. Her brave use of the torch had impressed him beyond measure. He had no intention of leaving these people any time soon.

'We will share food with you,' he agreed.

They rode back towards the hills and found a small stream with flat ground nearby for camping and good grass for the horses. Kisa and her companions made one campfire and tethered their horses close by.

'Are you going to tell them who you really are?' Kojo asked.

'Not yet. I think they will challenge us tonight,' she answered thoughtfully.

Yasuki nodded his agreement. 'I see it in their eyes. They think they are better fighters. We will have to prove ourselves their equals, at least, before you can reveal yourself, Kisa.'

They roasted some yams and took them to the Gonja campfire, along with a flask of wine.

'Share our food with us, friends,' Kaapo said. 'And our good palm wine.'

Bolley motioned them to sit, and they ate in silence. Most of the Gonja eyes were focussed on Shani, who ignored them with dignity.

When the meal was finished, Bolley spoke. 'We enjoyed the fight today, but your words must be answered. You said that you would have killed us if we had not joined you. Three men against nine? And we are warriors! You will have to prove yourselves now. Show us that you can fight us, not just some fat slave master.'

'One on one. Hands and feet only. No knives,' Kaapo said, to set the rules.

Bolley nodded agreement. 'You first then. Against me.' Kaapo stood up, taking off his weapons. The Gonja horsemen made a rough circle as their chief shed his weapons and stepped into the middle. Kaapo approached him and he attacked, fists swinging. Kaapo dodged each blow, dancing around Bolley, never letting a strike land. After a few minutes, Kaapo started dodging in close and striking small blows to Bolley's face and torso, then dancing maddeningly out of his reach.

For long minutes the fight continued, Bolley attacking, Kaapo dodging and striking back. None of Bolley's punches connected. None of his opponent's missed. The Gonja horsemen were impressed. This young man, though smaller than Bolley, was a better fighter.

At last, winded, Bolley stopped and bowed. 'I cede,' he said with admiration in his voice. 'Perhaps you could have killed me today after all. But what of your companions? Are they as good? Have each fight one of the best of my men. Show us what they can do.'

For answer, Kojo walked into the ring as Kaapo stepped back. The tallest Gonja man moved in to face Kojo. His arms were much longer than Kojo's, but it gave him no advantage. Kojo danced in and out, never letting his opponent touch him. After a few minutes, Kojo 's foot swept out and the man went down heavily on his back with a grunt. His brothers laughed and cheered. The second fight was over.

Yasuki stepped into the ring next, against the beefiest Gonja man. He wasn't fat but he was big, solid, and very well-muscled.

'Take him, Jinapor!' his companions yelled. 'Show him what you can do!'

Jinapor charged in like a bull. Yasuki waited till the last second, stepped aside and with one blow, knocked him out. The circle went silent. The three companions had proven themselves. No one asked Shani to fight.

***

The next morning, over the local favourite hot drink, cocoa, Bolley asked Kaapo what he and the others meant to do next.

'We will wage a war against the slave masters. You should join us.'

Bolley laughed. Secretly he wanted to do just that. Not because of the slave masters, but because of Shani. 'You must prove to us the worth of your war. What's in it for us, if we cannot resell the captives?'

For answer, Kaapo said, 'Let us feast together this night. My brother Kojo will drum for you. Then we will talk. I will show you how you can profit from the trade. And I have a surprise for you as a reward for fighting with us.' The Gonja horseman was intrigued and agreed to stay. It fit Bolley's plan to follow Shani, which was rapidly becoming an obsession. Kaapo continued. 'Kojo and I will hunt now to provide meat for the feast. Join us.'

Bolley agreed and the three saddled their horses. They rode out across the savannah until they found a small herd of antelope. All three were armed with short hunting bows as well as their knives. Bolley went around one side and with whoops and hollers herded the startled animals towards the two men. Arrows flew and two antelope fell – a doe and her yearling fawn. The three hunters dismounted and ran in to finish the kills with knives. They gutted their prey and draped the carcasses over their horses for the journey back. Amara was too skittish to carry such a load. The smell of blood upset her, but Kojo's and Bolley's mounts were quieter and carried the meat back to camp.

Fires were built and the meat hung over the smoke and flames to cook. Yams were buried in the coals. As the smells of the cooking meat drifted around the camp, Kojo began to drum. Gradually the horsemen gathered around, and all sat in companionable silence while Kojo entertained them with complicated rhythms, as their dinner cooked. Over the meal, they traded funny stories. Kojo started by telling them a story about the spider known as Kwaku

Ananse, who was the sun god's youngest child and a clever trickster.

The Gonja horsemen knew about the sun god's child, but in their stories, he was a rabbit. They traded stories back and forth about the spider and the rabbit and found that many were similar. The rabbit trickster of the Gonja men was always escaping from foxes, hyenas, and lions by cleverness rather than strength, much as Kwaku Ananse, the spider/man escaped from his enemies in Kojo's stories. While they talked, the night darkened, and the moon rose. The man the Gonja knew as Kaapo got up and quietly walked back to his camp. A few minutes later, he came back, dressed now in a cape and a leopard skin headdress that covered his face. He walked to the centre of the circle of men and lifted a fist high, while tossing something into the fire with the other hand. Blinding flames leapt up in a roar and in the flames the men saw a fierce and savage leopard.

Kojo cried out: 'Behold the sorceress!'

Kisa answered. 'See me! I am the spirit of the leopard!' Kisa stepped into the firelight, throwing off her cape and revealing herself in her true form. 'See me! I am the sorceress!' The leopard-skin headdress remained, and her eyes glittered like the leopard to the astonished men. She pulled out the long, strangely shaped samurai sword and lifted it high. 'I come to make war!'

She spun to face Bolley. 'I will drive the slave masters from this land!'

She turned to the other Gonja horsemen, looking each fiercely in the eye. They felt suddenly as if they were looking into the eyes of a great vulture – set in the head of the leopard - and around both, the body of a sorceress unlike any they had ever met. Shani had seemed amazing to them. Kisa overwhelmed them. She drove them to their knees, and they bowed their heads before her power.

'Join me and bring honour to your people!'

The Gonja horsemen knelt in open-mouthed wonder. They had never expected this. They saw before them a sorceress, suddenly revealed as the holder of ancient powers from the old religion, before the coming of the Prophet Mohamed.

'We will have to discuss this.' Bolley said at last. He took his men aside. Bolley listened to all the arguments for and against the proposal to join the army of the sorceress. Some feared her. Some did not want to follow a woman. Then Bolley spoke, quietly but with conviction: 'I am for joining them. They are proven fighters, and she is a sorceress! So is her sister, though younger. With us behind them, nothing will stand in their way.' Some still shook their heads doubtfully. They knew the power of the slave masters.

'We hate the slave masters.' Bolley continued. 'Why not fight when we have a sorceress before us and an army beside us?' That made the odds sound better and several heads stopped shaking 'no'. 'If we win, our families will be protected. If we do not, the gods will honour us. It's better than sitting around doing nothing, isn't it?' His companions had to agree with that. In the end, to a man, they nodded 'yes'. They loved a good fight.

Bolley returned to the fire. 'We will fight with you.'

Chapter 19

The Making of a Cavalry

Bolley and his men were brought into the Warrior's Village and soon became a part of it. Their skill with horses was badly needed. Kisa and Kojo spoke with Bolley, explaining their plans.

'We have studied the land from the ground … and the sorceress studies it from the air.' Kojo motioned to Kisa as he said this.

Kisa spoke. 'I have seen the roads that the slave masters use. I intend to hunt them on all those roads. For this, I need cavalry. That is why I sought you out. I will divide my forces, send out parties to various roads to lie in ambush. But I also want mounted men who can ride hard and fast to intercept the slave masters when they least expect it.'

Bolley grinned. 'My men and horses are ready and willing for that task.'

Kisa also spoke with Yao. 'Do you want to become a fighter?' she asked him.

'No, sorceress. I am a farmer. I will help you by growing the best yams you have ever tasted here in the village!' Kisa was satisfied with this. Not all men were meant to be warriors.

After settling in the village and helping his men build huts for themselves, Bolley went looking for Shani. He couldn't get the beautiful woman who rode bareback and without a bridle out of his mind. He found her looking after her mare.

Bolley walked up to her and smiled. Shani pretended to ignore him, but she felt a bolt of electricity pass through her loins at the sight of him. She busied herself brushing Laila, but out of the side of one eye, she watched him approach. He was tall and lean with wiry muscles, some of which sported strange tattoos. His curly hair was held back by a band of leather that held a long eagle's feather, the right of a warrior to wear. His leggings were of soft leather, but his feet were bare. His chest was also bare, but he had a red cape over his shoulders. A broad belt held knives and a sword. Between belt and leggings were bright pants that matched his cape. His walk had the slightly bow-legged swing of a man who seldom leaves the saddle.

If he isn't on a horse, he is bedding a woman, Shani found herself thinking. Blood rose hotly to her face and turned it a red brown not unlike the natural colouring of the man approaching her.

He slowed to walk and went slower with each step. He gazed at her as if seeing a female form for the first time in his life. She stood a head shorter than he, but her back was as straight as one of his finest hunting arrows. She carried herself like a born queen. Her dress was skimpy compared to those of his people. In the warm jungles of the south, women who practiced the old religions wore less clothing than the Muslim-influenced garb of the women of north-western Africa. Her garments accentuated her figure instead of hiding it. She was young and he saw that her breasts were small and upright, as she reached up to comb her mare's raised neck.

The horse was staring at him hard. Where had this southern woman come across such a perfect grey Arab? Dished face, perked ears, wide intelligent eyes. Her conformation was as perfect as the woman who groomed her.

Bolley was falling in love so fast he felt like he was falling off a cliff. He was not inexperienced in the ways of women. He had a few that he visited in various villages, but he found himself thinking... *never again... If I can make this woman mine, I will never look elsewhere!*

Both of them had stopped breathing and now both took a deep breath and tried to regain control of their emotions. Laila stamped and snorted as Shani brushed too hard. Bolley remained frozen ten steps away - staring at Shani's hair, her hands, her arms, her feet. She wore light sandals, and the shape of her foot was perfect to Bolley's suddenly love-mad mind. He focussed on her foot instead of her eyes, which were now turned on him.

'What do you want? I am not a piece of meat for your dinner!' Shani's voice rose above her normal low pitch.

Bolley, for the first time in his life, was struck dumb before a woman, not knowing what to say. Abruptly he turned his back on her and stalked over to his own horse, a stallion called Adham- the black, who was tethered nearby and had his own eye on Shani's mare. Bolley laughed as he stroked the big Arab's arched neck.

'You feel the same do you not? We are in trouble, my friend. These are no ordinary women, neither Shani nor her mare!'

He watched her at the evening meal, so she hid behind her girl-friends. They noticed and giggled while sheltering her. They were all married women and thought this very funny. Shani was the only unmarried girl in the camp.

Bolley's men had already discovered this. Over their own meal at a separate campfire, they complained to their leader. 'The women here are all married. We will have to be allowed to bring our own women to this camp, if we are going to be part of this army.'

Bolley agreed to discuss this matter with Kisa. He approached the fire where Kisa, Kojo, Yasuki and Kwame were eating their evening meal. Shani slipped off to a friend's hut when she saw him coming.

Kojo stood up and greeted Bolley as a fellow warrior, offering his right hand. They took each other by the forearm briefly and then let go.

'I wish to speak to the Sorceress about my men,' Bolley began.

'Join us then. Niena, will you give our guest a cup of cocoa?' Kojo motioned Bolley to sit by the fire.

Bolley squatted and addressed Kisa, who was lounging comfortably on a woven mat and nursing a hot cup of cocoa. 'My men have wives at home. If we are to join you, they will need to bring their women here.'

'I understand,' she answered. 'I want this to be a village, not just a camp. All my warriors, men and women are married. It makes for a more peaceful life. The enemies are all around us. We must have peace here. Tell your men that they may bring their women and children, but you

210

must build your own shelters for them. How long do you think you will need to do this?'

'The moon will rise twice, and my men will be ready to fight. I have no wife as yet, so let me fight with you, sorceress, in the meantime.'

'Yes,' Kojo answered. 'Only a few of our soldiers have horses. Kisa and I have been riding ours for some time and are learning how to use them in battle, but we have so much still to learn!'

'You can teach us, Bolley, and we will be happy to learn,' Kisa added.

Bolley was surprised by this statement. He had expected the sorceress to act all-knowing. That had always been his experience with elders who claimed special knowledge. The most mysterious thing about this sorceress was that she was so young and yet had shown such power and strength in the first raid, when he had thought her a man. And he had seen her perform magic too – usually reserved for much older practitioners. But now she was showing that she didn't know everything, that she could learn from him. His respect for them both grew. He was going to enjoy fighting with them, of that, he was sure.

**

A few days later, Kisa invited Bolley to join her on a second raid. She informed him that on the other side of the hills, a small band of slavers was moving south with a few captives.

'I have sent some men on foot with Kojo leading them. They will reach a sheltered spot on the road ahead of the slavers. I want you to join Shani and I on horseback.

211

We will ride in front of the slavers after they have passed our hidden raiders. When the slavers' eyes are turned on us, Kojo will strike from behind.'

Early the next morning, Bolley, Shani, and Kisa left the camp. Bolley took the opportunity to speak to Shani. 'I have never seen anyone ride without saddle or bridle, young sorceress. How do you do it?'

Shani blushed and refused to look at Bolley but answered him softly. 'Our minds are one. She understands me and I understand her. There is no need for bridle or whip or saddle. She will not let me fall!'

Laila moved forward next to Kisa and Amara. Bolley followed in love-struck silence.

Riding fast, they soon cut across country to the road south of the slaving party and Kojo's hidden warriors. When she saw the slavers, Shani led the way, holding up her flaming torch to blind the slavers. Kisa was beside her, wielding a sword and letting out a blood-curdling cry. Bolley's stallion pounded after them.

The slave master screamed orders to his men behind him but out of the trees came Kojo and his men. Kisa cut down the slave master before he could hide behind his men. Bolley slashed his way through the forward guards. Behind them, Kojo and his raiders killed the other slavers, whose only weapons were whips and knives. Faced with armed men instead of cowering captives in chains, they were soon dispatched. None of the raiders suffered a scratch. The captives were freed and told that they could accompany Kojo back to the Warrior's Village if they so desired.

'Or find your own ways home,' Kisa informed them. 'You are free to make your own choices again.'

All were from villages far to the north and west, so they chose to follow Kojo and serve the sorceress. Kisa instructed her men to dispose of the slavers where no one would find the bodies. 'Bring the horses and donkeys back to you. You have earned them this day and any wealth that the slave master was carrying. Divide it evenly among yourselves.' She raised her sword and shouted, 'Somunye!' Her soldiers echoed it behind her as she, Shani and Bolley rode off.

On the way home, Kisa discussed the future with Bolley and how his raiders could benefit from this war. 'As you can see, we will take the weapons and the food, the pack animals, and the horses when we raid slaving parties to free the captives. But there is a more profitable way for your men to make money. Attack the slave masters on their ways back home, when they are laden with gold, bars of iron and copper, jewellery, and the other profits of their trade. It will be more dangerous. Their slave drivers will not be burdened with captives and so more able to fight back. But you and your men are mounted and that will give you the advantage. As we get more horses, you can train other soldiers to ride, and fight mounted. Sweep in fast, kill all, take their goods and be away again.

We can all become rich this way. You must share one third of your takings with the rest of my army. They will be freeing many slaves and they must be rewarded too. But the rest your men can keep because every slave master or guard who is killed is one less that we must deal with later. What do you think?'

Bolley's eyes were on Shani, riding as always in front, but he heard every word. *Everything I take will be given to Shani,* he thought. *She will be my wife!*

'I agree to your plan, sorceress,' he answered.

When they reached camp, the soldiers told the others that again, no one had been wounded. Bolley heard this and asked what it meant.

Majeed answered. 'In all the raids and fights, no one has been hurt, no one killed. We have fought many battles, and no one has had even a scratch. At first, we thought that perhaps it was because of our training. Or perhaps because the slave masters are not used to fighting free men. Their guards know only how to punish captives in chains.'

'But it is more than this!' Amador continued. 'We are protected by the power of the sorceress!' Around him the other warriors, nodded in agreement.

'The power of the sorceress!' The others repeated. 'No one can hurt us while we fight for her!'

***

A few weeks later, Bolley's men were back in the Village with their families, and all were busy constructing huts to live in and corrals for their livestock. Along with their women and children the Gonja had also brought several new recruits with them who also had their own horses. Several brought long horned cattle with them as well. At first Kisa and Kojo and the others thought these were for food, but Bolley explained another use for the animals.

'Our forefathers came south on the orders of the great Songhai Emperor. They were his best cavalrymen, and they were ordered to find the Ashanti people and punish them for selling gold. He saw the gold market as his own by divine right.'

Kisa nodded. She had heard this story from Majeed already, but she could see that Bolley knew far better the history of his tribe.

'Our forefathers came to this land to do that,' he continued. 'But back home, the Emperor was attacked by an army that came from the north. The enemy were outnumbered ten to one by the soldiers of the Emperor, but the invaders had guns and cannons. They sacked the cities. We were left stranded, so we settled here, unable to return home. But our forefathers taught us the ways of the Songhai cavalry and I will teach them to you.

'These cattle are a powerful weapon. We can drive them ahead of us through the lines of the enemy. They trample all before them and bring confusion to our foes. We can use them when we attack the slave masters as they return to their homes, when they have no captives to be hurt. The slave masters will fall before us like sheaves of wheat at the harvest.'

Kisa and Kojo were impressed. 'I see that we still have much to learn from you, Gonja horseman. I want to see this plan in action!' Kisa smiled as Kojo said this. Her dream of a cavalry was coming true.

Kisa called her leaders together and explained for Bolley's benefit how she could fly on the wings of the vulture and see through Udele's eyes.

'Our village is built. Our army is ready. We have a cavalry now. I propose to fly with Udele and find all the slave parties on the northern, southern, and eastern roads. I want our new cavalry to attack slave masters heading home with their profits. For the rest, I will divide you into groups. Kojo will lead one. Kwame another and Fela a third. I will come back and tell you where to go and where your prey will be waiting for you.'

Bolley was impressed. *This sorceress has powers beyond what I already knew,* he thought, *but what about Shani?*

As if she heard his thoughts, she spoke up. 'I wish to ride with the cavalry! I am mounted. It is my place to lead them into battle!'

Kisa looked at her and smiled. 'Yes, little sister. I think you have found your place.' She turned to Bolley. 'Will your men follow Shani?'

Bolley could not say yes fast enough. Shani was watching him with shining eyes. *She loves me too!* He thought in amazement.

'And take some of the cattle with you. I want to see how this works. I will be watching you through Udele's eyes.'

That settled, Kisa and Kojo turned to the other leaders. They selected their men and went to inform them of their roles in the coming battles.

The next morning, Kisa rose high on the sun-warmed updrafts. The three ravens flew with Udele and the four of them searched the roads. On the southern road from Wa two slaving parties were spotted. On the northern road from Bolgatanga to Tamale a third party was seen. And on the road from Salaga, a party of rich slave masters, leading donkeys piled high with the profits of slavery was beginning the journey north to Yendi. Kisa returned to the mountain, satisfied. The pickings would be rich.

Down in camp the leaders met with Kisa and Kojo. Kojo was to take two groups, one under Amador and one under Kwame, to attack the two slaving parties on the Wa road. Amador and Majeed led a much larger group of men north to attack the large party coming south from Bolgatanga and the hills of fear.

The fourth fight was for Bolley and the horsemen. He could attack the slave masters on the way home from the Salaga markets and relieve them of their profits: bolts of cloth, bars of iron and copper, seashells and most important, horses and donkeys.

After the meeting, Kisa took Bolley aside and confided in him about her sister. 'She cannot kill. You must defend her with your life if need be!'

Bolley was quick to assure her that this would be so. Kisa saw the love in his eyes for her sister. After Bolley left, she turned to Kojo. 'Now I know why the gods did not want Shani to marry. This man will be her husband and love her as you love me.'

Kojo smiled and took her in his arms. 'No one can love anyone as much as I love you,' he whispered as he pulled her into their hut. 'But you are right. Those two will soon be one. I don't know if Shani realises it yet, but she will in time, I am sure.'

'Enough of them,' Kisa whispered as she pulled Kojo down onto their sleeping mat.

***

Shani led the way as the Gonja horsemen rode proudly out of the Village. Bolley was only an arm's length from her. Kisa flew over them to guide them to their prey. Two days later they intercepted the slavers halfway to Yendi. Bolley and Shani rode straight at the party. Bolley was yelling out a wild Gonja war cry and Shani had her torch held high.

The slave masters froze at the sight. As the slave masters struggled to get out their swords, Bolley's horsemen were among them, cutting them down with sharp swords and deadly spears. The warhorses reared and stamped as the slave masters fell. None lived to tell the tale.

And none of Bolley's men were wounded. He pointed this out to his followers and told them what he had learned from the other warriors. 'No one has been hurt since the sorceress began this fight. And we are doubly protected for we have our own sorceress leading us!' he said as he pointed to Shani. His men cheered. If the sorceresses were going to make them rich while protecting them from the swords of their enemies, they could ask for no more.

'Somunye!' Shani cried and lifted her torch high.

It was a new word to the Gonja horsemen, but they took it up willingly. 'Somunye!'

They took the profits back to the Village, shared the cloth and metal bars and seashells. Bolley's men were more than satisfied with what they are earning, but some of the villagers were envious. Kisa called them together. 'You can be part of Shani and Bolley's raiders too if you learn to ride well enough and fight from horseback. We are not risking unmounted men in those fights. The slave masters are at their strongest on the return journeys. They have all their guards with them. They travel in groups, so their numbers are large. If you can do this, you will be well rewarded. If you cannot, then be satisfied with the wealth that comes to the whole village. Remember- somunye... we are one and therefore we share.'

Several men decided to learn how to ride and join the cavalry. After all, where they not under the protection of their sorceress? All were convinced now that they could come to no harm. Kisa took the horses that had been captured in the raids. She lined up the men and gave them the horses. Then she turned to Bolley. 'Train these men for me. Show them how to ride into battle and how to fight from the back of a horse.'

Chapter 20

Kojo's Map

One night, Yasuki was sitting with Kisa and Kojo around the main campfire with the other leaders. They were all enjoying the evening meal together in companionable silence. After the meal, news of the day was shared. Tonight, Yasuki rose, stretched, and then addressed the group. This was something g he never usually did, leaving the discussions to the others. But tonight was different.

'The Sorceress sees all through the eyes of Udele, the vulture,' he began, conferring the primary power of leadership on Kisa. 'But it is her general's ability to understand and learn from her about what she sees that will matter to all of you and the warriors that fight for you. Kojo, stand up,' the old samurai ordered.

Kojo leaped to his feet in one smooth motion and bowed to his teacher.

'It is you who must be Sensei now.' Yasuki ordered him. 'There is still much that your leaders do not know, which you can teach them. Show them your map!'

Kojo turned to carry out the order. He made a flat smooth space in the sand next to the fire where the light would show it. The full moon lit it as well. The others gathered round and Kojo rolled out his leather map. The map that Kojo had drawn was straight from Kisa's mind through the eyes of Udele. Each time she came to earth and back to her human body, Kisa excitedly drew pictures in the sand to show Kojo and Yasuki. Kojo, it turned out, had a good memory for these drawings and could repeat them perfectly on his leather map.

Most of the fighters had little experience with maps, but slowly everyone watching came to an understanding that this picture on the leather scroll represented all the lands around them. First, Kojo pointed to an X that marked the location of the Warrior's Village. Then he showed them the long line that represented the road from Tamale that ran all the way to the Indian Ocean far to the east. It was a road so old that no one knew who first walked it thousands of years before and it was still the main east-west trade route across the open Sahel country that ran above the rainforests and below the desert. It was the Sahel that allowed for the continent-wide trading network to cross with relative ease from one ocean to the other.

In this way Kojo taught them about the country around them: the roads, the towns, the trade routes and most importantly the routes the slave masters took and how they got their captives to the coastal castles, controlled by the Portuguese, the Dutch and other European nations who wished to trade with Africa and preferred human flesh for payment for the goods produced by Europe that Africans craved: metals, cloth, spices, and ceramics.

Mahamadu, Majeed and the other Dagomba fighters already knew about the Tamale to Yendi section of the road. Bolley and his men knew the country around Wa. But the Nzema and other warriors who came from the southern forest country (Ashanti, Ga, and Ewe) knew nothing of the geography to the north of them. The Sao Tome Fishermen and the other freed captives from the slave ship Goede Fortuin knew even less.

Now they had a bigger picture of what was happening. On Kojo's map they saw the white men's forts and castles on the sea. They saw the slave masters' routes from distant slave cities like Zanzibar and Agadez and how they crossed the paths of the great traders from the north who brought goods across the desert from faraway lands. And they saw how all the roads met to the east of this village and how they could disrupt the trade in human souls. They looked with awe at the map and its maker and then up to their sorceress who wanted to make all this happen. They believed in them. They saw now how it could be done.

They cheered and took up her chant: 'Somunye! Somunye! Somunye!' It echoed against the cliffs above them, and the beat was picked up by Kojo's drum. The chant became a dance, the dance became a celebration of the battles they would soon fight. The celebrations went on long into the night.

***

Because the dry season was coming, a time when few slavers were travelling, more battles could not begin immediately. Most of the soldiers were happy to remain in the Warrior's Village but the Nzema warriors wanted to go home so they could spend time with their families. When Shani realised that Kisa was going home, she came to her sister.

'I want to stay here.'

'Why?'

Shani made excuses but Kisa was not fooled. 'You have fallen in love with that horseman, haven't you?'

Shani shuffled her feet, looked at the ground and did not answer.

'Do you think I am blind, little sister? But you must be careful. Perhaps that is why the gods did not give you a husband before. You must be married now if he is the man you want.'

Shani looked up, eyes glistening. 'He is! He is all I want in this world.'

'Then come home with us. I will invite him to join us. You will be married in the village as is proper.'

Kisa's people were bringing with them treasures undreamed of in the village before. The slavers liked to show their wealth in jewellery, weapons, and clothing. Many had horses and donkeys as well. Once dead, they had need of none of this. Kisa allowed her band to strip the dead slavers and then left them in hidden gullies for the vultures. There had been some debate about whether they should leave the remains on the roads as a warning to other slavers, but Yasuki vetoed this idea. 'Once they know about us, they will choose other routes and be harder to find. This year, surprise is our best weapon. It is enough that they have heard of the Bandit Queen. We will leave no other warnings for those who we miss this time!'

Kisa's only disappointment in that first season was that none of the fighters had found Badru. Through the eyes of Udele, she had searched for him, but no sign of him had been seen again.

The party going home to the village in the maze became a wedding party. Bolley brought his brother and his best friend with him. There was much joking between the men and the other soldiers about Bolley's impending wedding. Shani stayed apart, aloof, covering her head and face in a light scarf, riding Leila beyond Kojo and Kisa, Yasuki and Kwame, who protected her and kept her separated from her intended groom because this was what Shani wanted.

Bolley didn't understand and wanted to talk to her so Kojo took him aside and explained. 'Shani is a sorceress like her sister. She is still very young. You have had other women I am sure, but she is different. She will be your only wife and it may be that you will never have children. Her fate is tied to that of her sister and a woman finds it hard to be both warrior and mother. For some the choice must be to forego motherhood.'

Bolley looked at Kojo, knew he was speaking of Kisa as much as Shani. He longed to give Shani children, but he realised suddenly that Kojo, who must have the same longing, could not do this. His marriage was to a sorceress of great power who would bear no children. And he knew that Kojo was saying he should make the same commitment to Shani.

Kojo continued. 'We will not let you marry her unless you understand that you must protect and defend her to the death in this war. She loves you and will give all to you in that way but there will be no children. Do you understand now why we keep her separate and above you and your men until the ceremony? They are making jokes because it is all that they know - that women are for having children. But for those who follow the path of magic, other fates await them. Walk in with open eyes or walk away. That is your choice. And walk separately from her while thinking of this choice that you must make, so that on the day of your wedding, the way is clear, and you make your choice with open eyes.'

Kojo turned abruptly and rode back to Kisa and her sister. Bolley joined the others in silence and in silence he finished the journey south. The ribald jokes ceased under his silent glare, but nothing could dampen the spirits of the soldiers, marching back home triumphantly behind their beloved leaders and certain of a party to celebrate that would be all the bigger because of the impending marriage of Shani and Bolley.

The party did not disappoint. The village had ample warning of the return of their heroes – they saw Udele circling above, and then Kisa's three ravens arrived, calling in the sentinel tree. The harvests had been plentiful. Food was in abundance and the villagers immediately went about preparing a massive welcome home feast.

Yasuki, Grandmother and Chief Abrafo met them at the edge of the village and escorted them with honor. There was feasting and celebrating with drumming and dancing for three days and then Shani and Bolley were married. There was a beautiful ceremony with Shani prepared just as Kisa was for her wedding. She was dressed in new clothes. Her hair was hennaed and braided. Her neck, hands and feet were decorated with henna and jewellery. Then she was led out to her husband-to-be by the girls of the tribe.

Chief Abrafo acted in place of her father, who had been taken by the slavers years before. The chief gave the bride price to Kojo and Kisa, as the senior members of her family. Then Kojo presented her to Bolley who took her hand. Grandmother stood forward to carry out the ceremony. Their hands were tied together, and prayers were said. Offerings were made to the gods to bless their marriage and then they were declared husband and wife.

After the ceremony, they were led away to their specially prepared hut, while the villagers celebrated. Shani had taken the necessary herbs from grandmother to prevent pregnancy. Alone in the hut, they shyly undressed each other. Bolley, being more knowledgeable in these matters, laid her down on the sleeping mat, stroked her gently and then made long, slow, and passionate love to her. Later, as they lay together, they discussed the fact of not having children and to Bolley's delight, Shani said, 'I hope someday we can have everything - including children.' At last, they slept, while outside, the party raged on late into the night, to the sound of the drums.

After the feasting and partying, there was a time of rest and relaxation for the army. Finally, Kisa called them all together along with the new trainee warriors.

'It is time to go back north. It is time to continue this war.' Her warriors cheered. They were ready.

The

Vulture

Kills

Chapter 21

Journey of the Fon Warriors

The new season of the war started well for Kisa and her fighters. Many of Kisa's soldiers were mounted and all were blooded. None had been hurt in all the battles that they had fought. By now her men were sure that it was the power of the sorceress that protected them.

With Kisa organising them, four platoons patrolled the main roads that the slave masters were using. Bolley and Shani led the Gonja men along the Wa Road. Kojo hunted on the Tamale -Salaga road while Kwame and Fela guarded the road from Yendi. To the north, Amador and Okocha harried the slavers coming to Tamale from the Hills of Fear and Bolgatanga.

The word spread quickly that the Bandit Queen seemed to be everywhere at once these days. On the Wa road she was seen mounted on a white horse and shining a great torch which blinded her enemies. At the same time, she was seen on the road to Salaga, with a great black spear. How could she be two places at once? Rumors were rife that she was a great sorceress, like those from the old days before the coming of the Prophet. Those strong in their faith ridiculed the idea but others were not so sure.

In all the battles with slavers, whether they were marching captives towards the coast or travelling, well-armed and well paid, back to their homes in the north, no harm came to any of the raiders, even to the horses of the cavalry or the dogs that fought beside them too. There were none left among her followers who did not believe that all were protected by the power of the sorceress.

***

Far to the south, word reached the King of the Edo people in Dahomey of the attack on the Portuguese fort in the Ga country. He heard that the band of warriors who took the fort were led by a sorceress. He called the general of the women's division of his army to discuss this with her.

General Sung was a formidable woman, tall and slim but well-muscled, who carried her spear and sword with ease. She had fought many battles for her king, killed many men, and was willing to die for him.

'I have heard a story from the north which interests me,' the king began after the general made her obeisance and stood at attention in front of him. 'A fort of the white men was taken by the Ga people. Some say the leader of the attackers was a man, but others are saying that this man was a sorceress in disguise, a woman who could fight and kill as well as you do, my wife.'

Although virgins, his general and all her soldiers were considered to be married to their King. Any found to have committed adultery or worse, become pregnant, were immediately killed.

'The Ga are fools. They gave the fort to the Dutch. Then the sorceress revealed herself in her anger. She declared she was going north to fight against the slave masters, and many followed her. I would like to know more. Choose a party from the younger wives. I want them to find this sorceress and report back to me. Perhaps together we can rid our lands of this curse of the white men and their slave masters.'

General Sung bowed and left to fulfil her king's orders. She assembled fifty young women who had proven themselves in battle. With one hand on her spear and the other on her hip, she cried out to them: 'Your king has need of your service! Prove yourselves!' Twenty prisoners were brought from the barracoon and placed before them in a row. Heads bowed, they knelt before the soldiers.

'Kill them!' General Sung shouted the order. With an answering shout, her soldiers rushed forward. The twenty women who despatched the prisoners first were chosen. Nawi, the quickest and most bloodthirsty, took the head of her victim off with a single stroke. General Sung called to her. Still holding the bloody head, Nawi stepped forward and stood at attention.

'You will lead these women. You will take them to a land far to the north. You will find a warrior, a sorceress, who took a castle from the white devils and fights now against the slave masters.'

General Sung ordered Nawi to muster her new troops for inspection. Nawi threw the head in a waiting basket and hurried to the task. The chosen nineteen swiftly fell into place as General Sung walked up and down, looking at her soldiers. She stopped and addressed them. 'You have been given a noble task by your husband, the King. You are to find a sorceress who fought against the white men and took one of their forts. The people there betrayed her, but our King has heard that she is fighting a war. You will find her and fight with her!'

Nawi raised her arm and led her troops in a battle cry of assent.

General Sung raised her arm in response and continued. 'One of you will come back and report to us. Our King wants to throw the white men out of our land too. Their feet are a curse upon the breast of our Mother. We will continue the fight here and you will help this sorceress, if she is what she says she is. And may the Father God and our great Mother, Asase Ya, assist you!'

The soldiers cheered and threw the heads of their victims into the air. Blood spattered them as their wild cries echoed across the camp. The male soldiers shivered at the sound. They had great respect for the deadly abilities of the women they called Moni, 'our mothers'.

General Sung called them back to order. 'You captain is Nawi, she who is fastest to kill. Follow her, serve her as well as you would serve me. Come back victorious or die in battle… for our King!'

Again, bloody heads flew up in the air and the cries of the soldiers rang out. General Sung was satisfied.

***

The soldiers prepared for their journey. Nawi spent hours studying maps so that she could lead her troops to the Ga city. From there, she was on her own and must find this sorceress herself. At dawn time of the tenth day from her King's orders, Nawi assembled her warriors for inspection. Each carried a spear, a sword, and several knives. Their other possessions were on their backs, a drinking cup in a bag with other personal items plus a blanket. They would be able to travel light and fast.

'We set out today on a great task for the glory of our husband, the King,' she told them. 'Let none of you fail him or I will kill you myself. When I give you an order, it is as if the King himself were saying it. We will go to our deaths and glory singing his praises. Come with me now, my sisters, to serve him.'

There was no cheering this time. The soldiers, that the Europeans had nicknamed Amazons, marched silently after their captain, prepared to do whatever it took to fulfil their vows. To start with, that meant following her until they found this mysterious sorceress.

Chapter 22

Journey of the Dinka Herd Boys

Far to the west, near the White Nile River, the boys of the Dinka tribe were watching their cattle, as they did every day. The girls carried water and the boys watched the cattle. It was the traditional way. It was hot and the boys, Dut and his friends, Jok, Thon and Chol, were settled under the shade of the acacia trees, playing marbles with their piles of round slingshot stones. If one of the cattle strayed, a rock was fired into its side. That was usually enough to send it back to its companions, which left the boys with little to do but doze in the sun and play their games.

In the distance, the boys noticed a cloud of dust rising. It grew closer and in the heat waves they could make out the heads of men marching towards them. Who were they? At the head of the column was a man on a black horse. The boys didn't like the look of him, but they were not allowed to leave the precious cattle alone. The man stopped and stared at the boys. Suddenly he raised his hand and signalled the men behind him. The horseman's followers raced forward, spreading out across the plains, and heading towards the boys.

Some of the boys turned and ran. Dut and Jok picked up stones and slung them at their attackers. It did little good as the men overpowered the boys and, one by one, tied them together. Metal collars were put on their necks. The boys cried and tried to fight but it did no good. The men were bigger and stronger than the skinny youngsters. A chain ran from collar to collar and the boys were led away from the herd of cattle and into the unknown.

The Arab slave master looked with disgust at the boys he had captured. They were small and skinny. The whites wanted strong men or beautiful women. These children would fetch poor prices in the slave markets. Still, they were better than nothing. He had been wandering through the Dinka lands for days but found that the villages were too well guarded to be raided, with their fences of spiny acacia branches around them. He finally settled for the herd boys as the easiest prey. With the capture of Dut and the other boys, he had enough captives to make the trip profitable.

The four boys were chained together with others from different villages. The slavers lined them up and began driving them west. Day after day they walked. If they faltered, they were whipped. One boy fell ill and when he couldn't walk, the man on the black horse cut him down with his sword. The other slavers removed the dead boy's collar and left him on the side of the trail for the hyenas and vultures.

For Dut, Jok, Thon and Chol the journey was a nightmare of thirst, hunger, and exhaustion. At night they huddled together against the cold, for no blankets were provided and the fire was reserved for the slavers. They had to walk for hours with no water to drink. Only when they came to streams, were they allowed to drink. No jugs of water were available to them during the long walks between. Food was a handful of maize meal each morning before the day's journey began. At night there was nothing.

They travelled through the land of the Sara people, who were growers of maize. They lived in huts built of reeds and surrounded by reed fences, but these were no match for the slavers. Several Sara people were soon added to the slave caravan.

As the days dragged by, Dut did his best to look after his three friends. They were in the same age class, but he was the oldest. They had been a team, working together to protect their tribe's cattle since they were old enough to stop playing around their mothers' skirts. They had been equals at the time, but now, under the stress and hardship of the forced march, the younger and smaller boys instinctively turned to Dut for protection and leadership. Without him, they would not have survived. He fought to see that they got their fair share of the food. He pushed forward to make sure they had time to drink at the waterholes and streams. At night he made them huddle together so all could share his heat and on the long, hopeless march, he encouraged them and gave them hope.

The nightmare march continued until they reached the city of Kano. There the boys were sold in the markets to another slaver, a dark Nyamweri man. He and his men marched the captives for many more long days to the town of Niamey, where they were sold again in another market.

Badru bought the boys in Niamey and decided to take them to the Pikworo slave camp in the Hills of Fear. There he planned to sell them to the infamous slave masters Samori and Babatu Zato. The prices he would get were not as good as the prices in the white men's coastal forts, but his nights were still haunted by the dreams of the sorceress and the sight of vultures now twisted his guts with fear. He had to make money for his father, but he was too afraid to return to the coast.

The boys endured another long journey and at last they arrived in the Hills of Fear. As Dut walked down the hill into yet another prison, he saw three ravens circling over his head and higher still, a great vulture. Other vultures had filled him with dread on the long journey but somehow this one was different. She cried out and he heard the word 'hope' whistle down to him on the wind. The boys were taken to a large granite rock curiously carved with shallow depressions. In between were iron bars that had been hammered into the solid rock. Their chains were fastened to the iron bars and the boys sat down, exhausted.

A guard walked by with a bucket of water and slopped some into the depressions. Dut and his friends knelt and sucked the precious water into their dehydrated bodies. Later another guard slopped rancid gruel into the holes. They scooped it out and gobbled it down. There was no shade except for stunted acacia trees, which were too far away to help Dut and the boys. Instead, they spent several long days taking turns kneeling over each other to give them some shade. Dut started it and uncomplainingly, each boy took his turn being the human umbrella.

At last, they were led to a large flat rock and sold to another slave master. While the palaver was going on and prices agreed upon, Dut looked up. Curiously, the ravens and the vulture were back. Her cries seemed to upset the slave masters, who looked up and cursed as they shook their fists at her. But Dut heard again the word hope.

The slave masters were not normally disturbed by vultures, who were always hanging out around the edges of the camp. In fact, whenever a captive died or caused trouble or tried to escape, they were hung from the largest tree in the centre of the camp as an example to others. The local vultures sat there to take care of all who were hung there, dead or alive. But this vulture was different. Its cries were different, disturbing. And whenever it was overhead, ravens escorted it. This brought to their minds the disturbing news from the south.

Babatu Sato stood up at the slave auction and shook his fist at the vulture. He turned to the slave masters, sitting in ease beneath umbrellas as the captives were led onto the rocks to be sold. 'There is trouble on the roads south to the sea. There are raiders lead by someone they call the Bandit Queen. Her warriors are attacking slave parties. She is said to have the powers of sorcery. When you march south, I suggest you strengthen yourselves. Hire more guards. Carry more weapons.'

The slave masters were disturbed by this news and muttered among themselves. Badru was sure he knew who the Bandit Queen was but said nothing. He just wanted to get the best price he could and head home. The rest had no experience and did not fear enough. The profits to be made at the coast were too great. Most decided to hire a few more guards and keep going. This suited Babatu Sato. He had guards for hire and stood to make more profit because of it.

The next day the new owner of the Dinka herd boys hired two extra guards and marched his captives south, out of the Hills of Fear and down the road to Tamale. Their stay there was short, but stories of the Bandit Queen were everywhere. The slave master talked to another, and they decided to travel together for protection. Soon they were all walking down the road towards the slave markets of Salaga.

***

Kisa watched through the eyes of Udele as the large slave caravan left Tamale. In it were many of the skinny, dusky-skinned people of the east, their heads bowed over the yokes around their necks, their chained feet shuffling forward. She had noticed them before as she circled regularly above the Hills of Fear. She could see how young they were, just boys, how skinny, and how scared.

Soon you will be free, she thought. At that one of them looked up at her and her accompanying ravens. He raised his clenched fist to her. A guard noticed and hit him hard with his whip.

Kisa cried out in her vulture's voice as she flew on and thought, *He remembers seeing me at Pikworo.* Swiftly she flew south until she was circling over the roadside stream where her fighters were waiting.

'There is a party leaving Tamale. They will be here tomorrow.' She signalled to Kojo and then flew back to Konkari, satisfied that the boys she had seen would soon be freed.

Preparations were made and as the captives stopped to drink at the sparkling forest stream, Kojo stepped out in front of the slave master. 'Free these people now!' he demanded.

For answer the slave master laughed and lifted his own sword. Arrows rang out from his guards, who had been expecting this moment. For some reason they all flew wide of their targets and Kojo's men, shouting 'Somunye!' rushed in for the kill.

The fight was hard but the guards, though better armed than most, were no match for the Samurai- trained warriors. Soon, as in all previous battles, the two slave masters and their guards were dead. No mercy to any of them was shown.

Kojo signalled his men to release the prisoners. He walked among them as they shed their chains and drank from the stream. Most understood some Kiswahili, but a group of skinny boys spoke a language that Kojo had never heard before. 'Do you understand them, Mulondo?' He asked the man who had come from as far west as anybody.

'No Kojo. Their language is very different from mine. Perhaps when we get them back to the village, we can find someone who can speak with them.'

'Yes,' Kojo agreed. 'We must send them back with Sule anyway. They are far too weak to stay here. I think they have come from some very distant land, judging by their condition. They are so skinny that it is a wonder that they can even walk.'

After the fight, the freed captives were taken back to the Salaga camp to rest and eat. As soon as Sule arrived, Kojo sent them to the Warrior's Village. After they were settled in huts, a meeting was called to introduce them to the villagers and Kisa. Hopefully someone could talk to the boys. Everyone had a look but only one could understand them.

'Ah, those are Dinka children, cattle herders from a tribe who live next to a great river far to the east of my people, the Sara,' a tall woman with a scarred face named Akinyi spoke up. 'Their language is like mine. I think I can make them understand me.'

'They are cattle herders?' Bolley, who was visiting from the Wa Road with Shani, was clearly interested in this piece of news.

'They could be useful,' he said to Kisa. 'We have a small herd of cattle now to use in battle if they can be trained. Perhaps these boys could help us.'

Kisa agreed and the two of them took Akinyi over to the children, who were sitting a little way from the others.

'Tell them they are free now,' Kisa told Akinyi, 'but we could use their help if they want to fight the slave masters with us. Tell them we have some cattle they can care for.'

Dut, as the eldest of the group, stepped forward when they approached. Akinyi explained to him something of what was happening and told him that he and his companions could herd cattle here or go home. Dut talked to the others but there was no question about what they should do. There was no way they could find their way home again. Jok, Thon and Chol decided to stay with their young leader.

The four boys were taken in by Akinyi. They were given a hut next to hers and every day she made them food and taught them Kiswahili.

Every day they visited the Gonja horsemen in their compound. Soon the boys were strong enough to be introduced to the small herd of cattle that the Gonja had amassed and intended to use in battle. The boys quickly bonded with the cattle. Dut and the others made themselves slingshots and gathered piles of round stones for ammunition. The Gonja horsemen watched with bemusement as the boys used their slingshots to move the cattle around. The boys had long legs and could outrun the cattle and head them off if they went the wrong way. Then well-aimed stones convinced the cattle to change direction every time. The cattle learned to go where the boys wanted and they began taking the cattle out grazing each day just as they had done at home.

When they had learned enough Kiswahili, Bolley explained to the boys how they would be used. 'We will drive them through the camps of the slave masters when they are sleeping. We will follow the cattle on our horses and come in from the sides. We will cut down anyone who has not been trampled.'

Dut said, 'If that is what you want to do, you need cattle with bigger horns. Where we come from the horns are twice as long!'

Bolley laughed. 'You should have brought them with you.'

'And we can help you! We can use our slingshots to guide your cows. They will run when we tell them to," Chol added.

'But you are on foot and just boys,' Bolley smiled. 'Just teach us how to herd them and we men will do it.'

'Teach us how to ride,' Dut countered. 'We are small and could ride behind your men to the battle, then jump off when the cattle go in. Maybe we can keep our cows from running into the captives - see that they only trample the guards and the masters.' Bolley looked doubtful and Dut looked determined. 'And we can round them up again when the battle finished,' he concluded.

Kisa laughed and settled the matter. 'Train my cattle, Dut, and you can ride into battle with us.'

She turned to Bolley. 'It's a good idea,' she said. 'I think you should do it, Bolley. Your horses are strong, and these boys are so small. They would be like carrying a feather after being ridden by your brother Jinapor! '

Bolley couldn't argue with that, given how big his brother was. Kojo agreed with Kisa, and in the end, Bolley had to admit it was a better plan than learning to become a cattle herder himself. In his tribe only farmers herded cattle and were looked down on by soldiers.

So, Bolley took Dut and taught him how to hold on behind him when he raced his Arab stallion across the savannah. Soon, others of his band had Jok, Thon and Chol behind them and they quickly became adept at hanging on while galloping full tilt. It was better than sitting under an acacia tree playing games with rocks. They were small but they were beginning to feel like grown men in their new tribe, now that they had an important role to fill.

**

One day, Yasuki came to Kisa. 'We have trained the new recruits, ' he said. 'While Kojo works with Bolley to make this plan work with the cattle, you should take the

242

recruits to Kwame on the Yendi Road, Kisa. He has need of new troops I think.'

She agreed then she changed the subject: 'My men believe that they cannot be harmed. They think my... our ... magic protects us.' She drifted off as doubts about that assailed her.

'Do not tempt the gods,' Yasuki said sharply. 'If they are protecting you, acknowledge them or they will abandon you as quickly!'

'I meant the gods, not me,' Kisa made the sign of warding off the evil eye. Quickly she changed the subject. 'I think I will go south to Larabanga rather than over the hills to Tamale,' she said, surprising herself. 'I don't know why, but I feel I must go that way.'

Yasuki nodded. 'If something is telling you to go that way, do so. It is not good to ignore such a feeling. There must be a reason for it. The gods do walk with you, Kisa, because your cause is just, but do not tempt them with too much pride. You need their support.'

Kisa went out to see how Kojo was getting on. She found him with the Dinka herd boys. Dut was talking to Kojo excitedly about his coming part in the war. 'My people are peaceful cattle herders. I have never heard of using cattle to win battles before. Our cattle are our wealth. We would not risk them that way, but...'

Dut looked at the small herd of cattle, penned up by a fence of acacias. 'They are not as well-bred as my father's cattle. His cattle were bigger with much larger horns.' Dut held out his arms to show how big they were.

'But I can see that if these cattle were driven through a camp of sleeping men, they could do much damage.'

'Yes,' Kisa nodded. 'If you boys care for the cattle and get them to trust you, you can work with Bolley and his horsemen and ride horses into battle!'

All the boys were excited by this prospect. Their months on the road had hardened them. The ample food they had enjoyed since being freed was putting meat on their bones and making them stronger. And their hatred of the slavers was intense. They too wanted revenge.

Chapter 23
On the Horns of the Bull

After a day's rest, Kisa took a group of new foot soldiers out of camp. She was mounted on Amara with Chaga stalking beside her. Her new soldiers were walking behind them, their weapons untried, but all had a firm resolve to fight well. Above them three ravens flew and high above the black birds, the call of the vulture could be heard.

A day's march brought them to Larabanga, where they found the village in turmoil. Kisa was well known in this small town, and they were eager to tell her of the strange visitors who had come from the south and were looking for her.

'Two days ago, twenty women, all with spears and swords, marched into our village from the southern road! Very cruel they looked, like soldiers who have killed many in battle. They said they came from a land far to the south and they are looking for you. We think they wish to fight for you. We sent them to Tamale, not knowing where you were, sorceress.'

Kisa had her new soldiers set up camp outside the village and wait for her. Then she rode swiftly towards Tamale. Within half a day, she caught up with the strangest sight she had yet seen. Marching like the soldiers they undoubtedly were, she found twenty women armed to the teeth and dressed to fight. They were lean and hard like men, and they were striding forward with determination.

When they heard her riding up behind them, they turned and formed a half circle battle formation with spears pointed towards her. She pulled Amara up hard, causing the mare to rear. She lifted her fist in greeting and called out: 'Akwaaba, warriors! Who comes looking for the sorceress? Are you friend or foe!'

She drew her sword and lifted it high above her as if ready to kill them all if the response was the wrong one.

Their leader stepped forward and raised her own sword in answer. 'We come to fight with you! Our king has sent us to fight or die against the slave masters. I am Nawi, the captain of this small army. We are Fon people and we have been walking for three moons from the south to find you. Our King heard of you and wished you to know that he wants the white devils and the Arab slave masters dead and gone too. He is fighting in our kingdom of Dahomey, but he wishes to help you. We will serve you well, sorceress, in the name of our King!'

Nawi sheathed her sword and stepped forward; her palm extended in peace.

Kisa sheathed her own sword and jumped down from Amara. 'Akwaaba, you are welcome to join me, and your warriors. It is good to see women who can fight. We need more swords, for there are many enemies. Come with me now to my camp. You see that line of hills? It is on the other side. You have been long on the road so come and rest. I have an errand to the east but when I return, we will hunt together.'

Kisa took them to the Warrior's Village and introduced them to Shani. 'This is my sister and lieutenant,

Shani. She is also a sorceress and and has led many men into battle. Prepare yourselves and I will return soon.'

***

After Kisa left, Shani introduced them to the other women of the village, but the Fon women were dismissive of women who could not fight. 'We want an place of our own.' Nawi informed Shani.

An area was chosen, and the women were told they could build huts but Nawi informed Shani archly, 'We are warriors. We do not build our own huts!'

Shani found this annoying and told Bolley how she felt. He hadn't liked the looks of the Fon women, and this confirmed his dislike. Nonetheless, Shani arranged for the farmers to build several huts for the Fon women. Bolley told his men how he felt about the Fon warriors. Other than the sorceress, they were not used to seeing women fight. Shani led them into battle, but she did not fight. She only carried a torch. In any case, they preferred their women submissive, and these women were clearly anything but.

Nawi and her warriors quickly picked up the feeling of dislike coming from the Gonja warriors. They reacted with scorn and made a point of returning the dislike, making loud jokes about the Gonja men, and making rude gestures at them. The gestures and rude jokes were thrown back at them and the tensions in the village grew.

***

Meanwhile, Kisa went back to Larabanga and marched her men to the Salaga Road camp as fast as she could. There she found Kwame and Fela, resting after several hard battles.

'I have good news for you, Kwame,' Kisa said. 'We have other reinforcements who have come unexpectedly, and I want you to meet them. Will you come with me?' She explained to him about the Dinka herd boys, the Gonja method of using cattle in battle and how they would soon be able to use those cattle. She told him about the Fon warriors too. 'My army is coming together, little brother! Soon we will be able to attack bigger game!' Kisa finished excitedly.

'Of course, my sister. I want to meet your new recruits too!'

***

When she arrived, Kisa found out about the difficulties arising between the Gonja horsemen and the Fon warriors. Shani was eager to tell her big sister of all that had happened while Kisa was away.

Kisa walked around the village and found that the Gonja horsemen and the Fon women had settled into an uneasy truce in separate camps. The Gonja were camped to the west and the Fon to the east and no one was talking to anyone else. Clearly the Fon warriors intended to take orders only from Kisa in this war.

That night, Kisa discussed the matter with Kojo and Yasuki. Kojo liked the look of the women warriors, but he could already see that the Gonja men and many of the other male warriors were unsure of them.

'I am happy to have these new soldiers,' Kojo said, 'but somehow, they must learn to work with us. The horsemen are deadly fighters and I believe these women are too. They must learn to tolerate each other and fight together, men on one side on their horses, and the women on the other. Between them no slaver will stand a chance.'

Yasuki chuckled. 'It is so, Kojo. And if anyone can bring them together it is our sorceress.' He turned to Kisa. 'They all look to you for leadership.'

'I am going to take them north towards the Hills of Fear and take out a slave caravan coming from the Pikworo slave camp. We have not been active enough on that road yet. They will not be expecting us. By the time they realise what is happening, their heads will be separating from their bodies.' Kisa's hand clutched the hilt of her sword as she said this. 'In this way, I will bring the Fon and the Gonja together!'

She waited till all had eaten their evening meal and then she had a bonfire built in the center of the village. She sent Shani to bring the Gonja men to her while she went to invite the Fon warriors. She presented Bolley and Nawi with a jug each of palm wine. 'You are the wings of my new army,' she said to them. 'I need you both.'

To Nawi she said, 'I have been fighting for a long time with these horsemen. They are brave and true fighters and on horseback they are unstoppable. But the slavers are learning of us. They are arming themselves and fighting back, fighting for their miserable lives. If you fight with us, they will be overwhelmed with fear. They have never seen such women warriors as you before and they fear my magic. You were sent to fight with me, but I do not fight alone. Accept these men and fight with them!'

Nawi nodded as she took the wine. Kisa turned to Bolley. 'I know these women are strange to you and their language is not your language. But you see their weapons

249

and you see that they know how to use them. I want you to fight with them. For me.'

Bolley also took the wine and nodded his agreement. Kisa continued to both, 'It is important that your warriors all learn Kiswahili. We must be able to talk to each other. It is language that divides us. All must learn to speak our common language!'

Bolley and Nawi returned to their warriors with the wine and the two forces sat down at the fire together and began to drink. Soon both parties were laughing as the wine loosened their inhibitions. The two groups made jokes about each other in their own tongues. Only Kisa understood both languages and she translated the jokes to Shani.

'It will be alright now. I think they will fight together and after the first battle they will respect one another. I have not seen the women fight yet but Nawi assures me that all her soldiers have been blooded and will not hesitate to kill. I cannot wait to see them in action!'

Plans were made and Kisa threw the divination bones into the sacred circle to decide on the most propitious day to ride forward. When that day dawned the two groups lined up before their leader. Kisa looked at the men on their horses and her proud new female regiment standing at attention next to them.

Dut came running up to her. 'Sorceress!' He called out boldly. 'Let us come too! We have trained our cattle. We want to fight too!'

Kisa looked down at the boy with a smile on her face. 'Not this time, Dut. Your time will come soon, I promise you, but for now the fighting cattle are our secret. Keep training them while we are gone. I have big plans for you.' Dut was disappointed but stepped back.

Kisa turned to Bolley. 'Ride ahead of us. I will ride with the Fon. Cut across the plains to the northern road. Wait for us south of the Pikworo camp. We will only be a few days behind you. Scout out the camp and find a slave party readying to march south. We will take them on the road to Tamale and test our new warriors.'

Bolley saluted her and rode off with his men, who were eager to leave these strange aloof women behind until it came time to see them in battle.

Kisa motioned for the women to start marching and she fell in beside them on Amara. The women proved their endurance by marching all day without a rest. Another three days brought them to the Bolgatanga road, and another day saw them find Bolley and the Gonja horsemen. Bolley led them to their secret camp within striking distance of the slave party on the road from the Hills of Fear.

'We are in luck, sorceress. This is a big party. There are many captives and a small army protecting them. They seem very sure of themselves and do not expect trouble. We can surround them. You and the women can march in from the south. They will not believe what they see, and I think they will laugh at you, so few and all women.'

Bolley grinned. 'When you attack, they will regret their laughter! And when you are showing them what you can do, we will ride in from behind. They will be caught between the lions and the leopards, and they will feel our teeth.' Bolley looked over to the Fon warriors. 'Some of my men think the Fon will not fight well but I think they are wrong. I am looking forward to this battle!'

'So am I,' Kisa agreed. 'I cannot wait to watch them in action. They have a deadly feel about them.'

Nawi and the Fon women proved themselves the next day. They marched into the camp with spears and swords at the ready as the slave masters were lining up their captives to start the day's march. Kisa on horseback led the way. They stopped just out of spear range and the Fon warriors took up a bloodcurdling war cry. The slavers, who had gathered to watch them march forward and who had been making lewd suggestions at these strangely armed women, fell silent and the fear of death filled them for the first time.

'Kill!' shouted Kisa as she raised her sword and Amara reared. 'Kill them all!'

The Fon women raced forward, screaming 'kill!' in their own language. Their swords struck flesh and the swords of the slavers, and the battle was on. The slavers fell back or died on the swords of the raging women. But they couldn't fall back far because suddenly behind them were horsemen whose swords were also flashing in the sunlight.

Shani's torch flared bright, mirroring the brightness of the newly risen sun, and blinded the slavers. Trapped, the slavers tried to form a circle, but the horses leaped right over them, and the defence turned into a rout. The slavers ran for their lives but no matter which way they turned they met enemies. Kisa and Shani were on one side with bright steel and fire to blind them. Wild savage women were on another side, cutting them down like sheaves of wheat before the scythes. On all other sides, the Gonja came on their war-horses, trampling and stabbing until none of the slavers were left alive on the bloodied ground.

When it was over, the Fon and the Gonja faced each other in triumph. Their voices rose together in their different languages celebrating their victory and Kisa knew that the blood they had spilled had bonded them into a single fighting force that no slave master's party would be able to resist.

Chapter 24

Goodbyes

The next hunting season was the best ever. Kisa's army was well organized. Kisa flew on the wings of Udele to let her troops know where to intercept slave masters. No matter which road they took, the slavers were caught with no escape.

The army fought the slave masters for the rest of the wet season. Kisa now had over two hundred raiders. Because of this, they were able to split into four large groups: three out hunting at any one time and one resting and maintaining the camp. They had become so efficient that few slavers made it through.

Bolley took the Dinka herd boys to the Wa road, and they practiced their skills. Each raid began in the early morning just before dawn. Dut and his friends drove the cattle into the camp of the sleeping slavers, causing confusion. Then Shani with her torch held high raced in. Bolley and his horsemen stormed behind her, killing the slavers and freeing the captives. The cattle developed an uncanny sense of who to trample and who to avoid. After the first few stampedes, they never touched chained captives, only the guards and the slave masters felt their hard hooves.

None of the boys or Bolley's men was harmed. Even the horses and cattle suffered no injuries. 'It is the power of our sorceress and her sister,' Bolley confided to Dut and the others. 'Their magic protects us.'

Kisa and the foot soldiers held the roads to Salaga from Tamale and Yendi. They had no cattle and no horses, but it did not matter. The sight of the sorceress with her leopard headdress and black spear struck fear in the hearts of her enemies. Her soldiers cut through the slave masters and guards without harm to themselves and the captives were freed.

Meanwhile, bolstered by the Fon women, the Dagomba fighters harried anyone using the northern road that came from Bolgatanga and the slave camp at the Hills of Fear. The result of this was that no one was getting their captives through to the markets, which were suffering a recession due to the lack of business. Many slave masters, having heard of the Bandit Queen and her raiders, had decided on a longer route, or had given up altogether on the western roads.

So, the season ended on a high note. The raiders were happy because, once again, no one was harmed in all the battles they had fought. Their conviction grew that this was due to the mystical powers of their sorceress and not just their fighting abilities. In addition, the hunting season had been rich. As well as freeing captives, Kisa's army relieved the slave masters of their possessions. Some were sold or traded for supplies for the village. Others were given to loved ones as gifts along with the stories they had to tell.

Kisa pondered her progress on the ride south back to the village in the maze. Their successes meant fewer slavers were coming their way, but she knew that they were just changing their routes. As long as the European castles on the coast existed, the slavers would keep coming. She could not stop them this way. They were freeing some people and that was good, but in the end, she had to find a way to strike at the heart of the slave masters and then the white devils themselves.

Their return to the village in the maze was greeted with drumming and dancing and feasting for the victorious warriors. The celebrations lasted for several days, until all were affected by too much food and palm wine.

Then Grandmother made a shattering announcement. 'Yasuki and I are leaving.'

'What do you mean?' Kisa was startled but Kojo was smiling, as if he had suspected it all along.

'My work is finished here,' Grandmother started. 'And mine also,' Yasuki interjected, taking her hand.

'I am weary of my duties and have been looking for someone to succeed me' Grandmother continued. 'That person could have been you, Kisa - but your mission lies elsewhere. Shani could fill the role too, but she serves you to better advantage. Several of the young women have shown themselves to be adequate midwives and herbalists. That young man Adisa has a good head for stories and will do as the village historian. As for a sorceress? I do not think they have need of one right now.'

'And the young men and women are trained and able to defend the village,' Yasuki pointed out. 'We are free now to live our own lives.'

'But you are so old,'' Kisa objected without thinking.

Grandmother laughed. 'We are not dead yet! Our time together will be short and there will be no fruit in my womb, but we have the right to love one another, and we wish to do it without responsibilities. The gods know we have both had enough of duty. You don't need us anymore. You have an army. Let us retire gracefully.'

Kisa said nothing. She knew they were right. It was up to her now. The village was safe enough, not only without her but without Grandmother and Yasuki. And as for her, she was not in training anymore. She had been honed by the years of fighting on the plains, raiding the raiders. She realised that though she was the sorceress now, that Grandmother did not expect her to stay here. Her duty was to continue to fight this war with the army she had gathered. With the help of the gods, they would kill the slave masters and throw the white slave buyers into the sea.

Grandmother took her by the arm and touched the blackened spear of the Sentinel Tree, which Kisa always carried with her. 'You know the truth of that tree? He is linked to the Mother Tree of Africa. Trees are not like us, they carry both the male and the female in their bodies, and all are linked to the first tree, the Mother Tree. Your tree has always spoken to you as a male, but it is linked to the mother tree, as are all the trees.

'Someday you will leave Mother Africa and the forests of your home behind you. But I foresee a day when you will need the help of the trees. I have seen in my dreams that once that one land across the sea where you are going was one land connected with us but long before we were here as the people. The trees of that land too are distantly connected to the mother tree. When you need their help, use your amulet! Call out to your tree and through him to all the trees, the mother tree. The trees in the forest

257

where your feet will be walking will hear and then they will help you.'

'I will, Grandmother. I am going to miss you. I will wish I could still talk to you, see your face.' Kisa felt like a little girl again at the thought of Grandmother no longer being in her life.

'Shush, dear one. I will be there in spirit. You may talk to me through dreams. But you are the sorceress now. You won't need me as much as you think. Hold the amulet and talk to all the sorceresses down through the ages. It is your link to us as well as Mother Africa.' She reached out and put her hand on Kisa's which was clasping the amulet. Kisa closed her eyes and knew it was so.

Silence fell for a while as everyone pondered Grandmother's words. Then Kisa turned to Yasuki. 'Sensei tell me of your trip that brought you to me so long ago. I want to know all about it'

Yasuki stared hard into the fire, remembering.

'You have never spoken much of your journey to me,' Kisa spoke thoughtfully. 'Tell me what it was like for a lone man to travel so far and how did you find me? Even with Grandmother's dreams it must have been so hard to find us.'

'I had been taken to a country on the other side of the world by my master many years ago,' Yasuki began.

'You were a slave once?' Kojo asked, astonished.

Yasuki smiled. 'Yes, my name was Issufo back then. My first master was a Portuguese priest. He took me to the land of Japan. The trip took months by sea. When we walked down the gangplank to the shore, the people saw me and rioted because they had never seen a black giant before. The local warlord heard of the riot and ordered my master to bring me to him.' Yasuki chuckled. 'He made me scrub my skin to prove that I was not painted! Then he made my master give me to him. He had me trained in the way of the samurai and I fought for him for many years. After he died, I retired. I thought I would live my life out in comfort. Japan was my home. And then the dreams began.'

He looked at Grandmother and smiled. 'The journey back to Africa was much more comfortable. I travelled in my own cabin. I saw many strange countries – even the fabled land of Ind where they ride upon the backs of elephants. At last, I came back to my own country, far to the south and east of here. I only knew to go north and west to begin with,' Yasuki continued. 'I took a second ship north to the city of Dar Es Salaam. From there, I journeyed north for many days to reach a city called Nairobi. I passed a great mountain that the locals said was the highest in all of Mother Africa.

'My dreams kept telling me to go north, so I spent weeks riding to reach a city called Juba. The country is much drier there. And still I went north - the land became drier and drier with fewer trees until I reached a town called Ndjamera. There were many Arabs in that town dressed in long robes and turbans for the desert. And there I saw my first slave masters. Oh, they must have been raiding the lands I had come from but here they were far more obvious.

'From there the dreams told me to go west. I made for the city of Kano and from Kano, I finally found the Yendi road and thence to Tamale. There the dreams said turn south and became more specific, showing me the roads and then the trails. Each night I saw a landmark to look for the next day and by that way I came at last to you, Kisa.'

That was a very long speech for Yasuki. Kisa struggled to memorise the names of the cities he had seen along the way since she knew he would not repeat himself. The names were so unfamiliar.

'Why do you want to know all this now?' Yasuki finished.

Kisa stared into the fire thoughtfully. 'I have a plan. I want to find the city of the slave masters, Agadez. I want to try and find a way to stamp the slave masters out, like a nest of scorpions. That would cut off the supply of slaves from the east. Or at the least, I want to kill Badru and his father too for I think he is the real slave master and Badru is only his pawn, as Sefu was!'

Yasuki looked at her gravely. 'I think you will find that you cannot solve this problem there. But I know that you need revenge. You have never given up that idea. You must find out for yourself how vain it is. Go, but I am not wasting my strength on that journey. It is for you to take that path, not me.'

***

That night there was a great celebration with much food, drink, and partying. In the nature of small villages, there were no secrets. There was sadness as well. Yasuki had been in the village for almost twenty years and was a valued member of the community.

Chief Abrafo made a speech, telling everyone of Yasuki's many accomplishments and finished with: 'You will be missed my friend but know that you leave us so much better prepared than before you came. We can defend ourselves now.'

Then the Chief turned to Grandmother. 'You are a great Obeah woman,' he said softly. 'You will be much missed, but I know that Esi and Afia, Adisa and Ama will fulfil your many tasks to the best of their abilities. You deserve this time. May the gods and the great mother go with you always.'

Abrafo turned at last to Kisa and Kojo. 'Without you two, we would now be captives across the sea. You are our hope for the future. Fight this war and then return to us, triumphant.'

The villagers cheered and there was much touching of foreheads and clasping of hands between those who were going and those who were staying. Then the drums played, and people danced the night away.

In the morning, Yasuki and Grandmother took their leave first. They were joined hand to hand and in the other hand Grandmother carried her cane and Yasuki had his staff. Both walked tall and straight, unbent by their years.

Kisa stifled the urge to laugh. As they passed into the forest, they looked for all the world like Kwaku Ananse, the trickster, to her, moving on four human legs and two wooden ones. It was supposed to be a solemn occasion but forever in the future, whenever Kisa thought of her teachers, she remembered them as Kwaku Ananse, and it always lightened her mood and put a smile on her face. Somehow, she thought, Grandmother approved.

Chapter 25
The Road to Agadez

The troops reconvened at the Warrior's Village for the start of the new season, and the war continued. Kwame and Amador led the troops on the eastern roads from Tamale and Yendi to the chief slave market in Salaga. In the west, Shani and Bolley and their troops patrolled the road from Wa to Larabanga. And in the north, Nawi and her warriors, combined with the main force of Dagomba fighters, harassed the slave masters as they moved south from the Hills of Fear.

Kisa and Kojo camped together between the Yendi and Tamale roads and monitored the movements of all their troops, spreading the word by Kojo's drum and by Kisa from Udele. But each of the four groups of raiders had become more or less self-sufficient. Kisa was thinking beyond these four roads. It was time to extend the war.

She spoke to Kojo. 'Our troops can spare us for a while. The real slave masters live in the city of Agadez, the gates of the desert. If I could wipe them out somehow...' She stopped because she could see no way to do this

'Or at the least, you want to kill the slave master who spawned Mbwana Sefu, may his soul rot, or that evil, scarred half-brother of his!'

'Yes, Kojo, it is time we travelled east along the Yendi Road and see where it takes us. That is where the slave masters hide. It is beyond your map, but I have seen it from Udele. I want to strike the slave masters where they least expect it'

'I hope it will be so, my love,' Kojo said doubtfully as he remembered Sensei Yasuki's words on the matter. 'But I will go with you, you know that. And perhaps we can find a way to kill the scorpions and stop the traffic from the East.'

'Yes! We must choose a few of the best warriors to go with us. Take those who came from the East to help us find the way.'

Later Kisa talked to Kakande and Mulondo, who had come from the land of the Buganda, far to the east. They remembered some of the towns they had seen on their journey west. The biggest town in their country was called Kampala but they had never been there, being from small villages to the north. Their only contacts outside of those villages were the slavers. Their memories of the towns on their forced march were sketchy. They were held in slave quarters and saw little. It was the only time they could rest, so mostly they had slept.

Then Kisa called together all members of the band. 'I am taking a party of warriors east to learn more about the slave masters: where they live, when they travel, where they hunt. I am taking Kojo and Kwame with me as well as Kakande and Mulondo. The rest of you will stay here under the command of your generals, and hunt while the hunting is good. You may head home when the streams dry up. We may be back by that time, but I make no promises. There are tens of days walking between each village out there and we will need time to explore the towns when we come to them and learn the part that they play in the movement of captives west.'

Some of the soldiers were nervous about losing their sorceress but they had faith in Fela and Majeed and the other generals. Bolley and his men were happy because they had Shani with them.

Two days later, all mounted, they left Warrior's Village. Along with the five men who were accompanying Kisa - Kojo, Kwame, Kakande, Mulondo and Amador - was the ever-faithful Niena, who never left Kisa's side. Everyone, even Amador, was mounted on a strong, steady horse and two donkeys carried their food. As always, Chaga followed Kisa and overhead flew the three ravens. When Kisa wanted Udele, she too was soon flying overhead.

Reluctantly Kisa left the little owl behind. 'The trees become too thin where we are going. There will be a desert to cross. Stay here little friend.' In response, the little owl hooted, fluffed his feathers, and went to sleep in the tree.

Kisa felt ecstatic as they left. She was sure this road would lead her to Badru, wherever he was hiding. This was different than the route she had taken as Udele. There she had flown due east from Gao to Agadez and back again before turning south to Tamale and the escarpment. This time they were travelling the southern route to Agadez. They would pass through the city of the famed warrior Queen Amina, Kano, before turning north towards the desert.

The route from Gao to Agadez was shorter but harsher. It was stony desert country, with few animals except the poisonous kinds – vipers and scorpions – and the carrion eaters like Udele. So, Kisa decided to travel the route from Yendi to Kano, which passed through rich savannah country teeming with wildlife to hunt, and fish in the streams. They had the slavers' gold to buy most of their other needs in the villages they passed through. They planned to move as fast as possible over the two thousand kilometres they needed to cross before they took the eight-hundred-kilometre road north through the stony desert country to Agadez, the gate of the true desert, the Sahara.

The first village they came to was Yendi, where the head Chief of the Dagomba people lived with his twelve wives. His house was the largest in the village, with a tiger's head carved on the door to his compound. The only larger building in the village was the mosque.

Most of the houses were round mud structures with thatched pointed roofs. Poor families lived in a single hut. Richer families had several huts built around a covered courtyard. Along the road, hawkers sat beneath umbrellas with their goods set out on tables just as Kisa had seen in Tamale, Salaga, Kumasi and the coastal towns. Some things, it seemed, never changed. The women were dressed in flowing dresses with elaborate cloth headdresses. The men favoured loose pants and long-sleeved shirts to protect them from the sun and small skullcaps that indicated their Muslim faith.

'Perhaps we should try and meet with the chief,' Kojo suggested. 'We have been hunting in his territory. It would be interesting to know whether he supports us or whether he profits from the slave trade.'

Meeting with the chief turned out to be quite a task. His guards were not keen to admit the strangers and especially someone who was so obviously a sorceress. Messages sent to the chief were unanswered.

'I don't think he is interested,' Kisa sighed. 'He must know about our raiders from the Dagomba men who fight with us. I think if he wanted to end the slave trade, he would have sent troops to us before now. Probably half his wives are captives. I think we are wasting our time here.'

After Yendi, the first long haul began. It was fourteen hundred kilometres from Tamale to Kano. They passed several slave parties, but Kisa's disguises and hypnosis techniques made it possible to ride past them without being recognised for who they were.

It galled Kisa to let them go. She knew her warriors back at the crossroads would take care of them, but it was hard not to pull out her sword and strike down the slavers as they walked by. She sent strengthening prayers to the captives to assist them in surviving their terrible journey.

All along the way, Kojo added to his map, putting marks on his cowhide to represent the roads and villages that they passed through on their way. After weeks of travel, they saw earthen walls in the distance. Amina's Walls they were called after the queen who had them built a hundred years earlier. They were the first lines of defence in the cities of her kingdom and destined to outlive her for generations to come.

To get to Kano, they had to cross the Niger River that had flowed here all the way from the fabled city of Timbuktu. The slow brown waters of the river were teeming with fish and home to long canoes, called pirogues, that carried much of traffic of West Africa and the goods that came from the deserts and beyond. Inside the walls, Kano was a bustling town with many shops and huts plus the compounds and splendid buildings belonging to the rich and powerful of this nation-state.

The people were dark brown like Kisa and her band, so they blended in well. There were a few slaving parties present, but they were treated with fear and suspicion by many locals. Kisa suspected that many of the captives that were kept in the guarded compounds came from the forest villages south of Kano.

Kisa decided to send Kwame in grasshopper form to spy on the slavers in their compounds. 'Just be careful that no one steps on you!'

Kwame returned with valuable information. 'The slave masters are talking about a Bandit Queen, a sorceress who is attacking their comrades on the Salaga Road,' he reported. 'They are discussing how they can be prepared if attacked and are thinking about alternate routes. They said that they are petitioning the Dutch to put a price on her head.'

'Bandit Queen? The name has spread far!' Kojo laughed.

'Yes. They think they are just poor traders going about their business and we are the criminals.' Kisa did not find it so funny. 'And it means our hunting will be more difficult when we return, if they are looking for other routes to the sea.'

'The other routes are harder and longer,' Kwame said. 'I think most will want to use this route. But they will be better armed and more watchful, which will make our job harder.'

After a rest they, turned northwest to the road to Agadez, a journey of hundreds of weary kilometres. The country dried out, with only scattered trees to give respite from the heat of the sun. The people they met along the way were lighter in skin, more like the Arabs of the north. They practiced their religion too. Each village had a small mudbrick mosque as a signal to the raiders that they were followers of Mohamed and so not to be raided.

It was a tiresome journey with little change in the countryside for days at a time. There were fewer villages. The fertile red soil of the tropics turned to a fine grey sand. The few trees were nothing more than withered shrubs in the endless waste.

Kisa amused herself by looking for the animals that roamed here. She practiced soaring into the mind of Udele while on horseback. Always in the past, she had curled into the foetal position on a mat in a safe place with Kojo to guard her. But now there was no time to stop, so she tied herself on Amara, who paced quietly beside Kojo and his placid mount Ayo, where he could keep an eye on her body while she soared away into the sky. In this way, she spotted Agadez several days before they reached it. It was a dusty town made of mudbrick houses and enclosures, some with animals in them, others with slaves, much as she had seen it when she first explored the country through Udele.

Kisa returned to her body and informed her companions that the end of their journey was only over a few more low hills. They were relieved to hear it. The barren countryside was weighing on their spirits. They wanted to go home. They rode into the town early in the morning to see locals sweeping dust out of their homes, but the wind was picking it up and blowing it back in as fast as they swept. The men were dressed in flowing robes and their heads and faces were wrapped in long scarves called cheches. Many of the men sported bright blue cheches that stained their skin blue. Everyone wore sandals and the heat was intense even though it was winter. Few women were seen, and they wore flowing robes also, with their heads and faces covered in scarves.

Agadez was old, with ancient walls surrounding a maze of narrow lanes, buildings, enclosures, and pens, all made of mudbrick. Everything was for sale: salt, gold, ivory, hashish, and slaves. Even water had to be paid for. In the centre of Agadez was the great mosque, surrounded by a mudbrick wall. It was the largest mosque the travellers had seen, and they gawked at it, but Kisa was not interested in sightseeing.

'We should find a campsite and then we must learn all we can about this place. We must meet the merchants and the townspeople and find out who are slave masters and where they live. I will find Badru and more important, I will find his father!'

They found a secluded spot for a camp, in a dry gully a safe distance from the heavily guarded town. Then they returned to gather information. It was not an easy task. The people of the town were suspicious of strangers and not inclined to talk about where the real wealth of the town came from.

Kwame was called upon to enter locust form and listen in on conversations in houses and in the marketplace. He came back with useful information.

'I learned that Agadez is called the gate of the desert because the lands to the north, all the way to the northern sea, are a dry and barren desert. I think they have been sending slaves north for a very long time, but now they talk of the Europeans on the coast instead. I also learned that everyone of any importance goes to the mosque to pray. I will spend time there and learn more, I am sure.'

***

They returned to their camp, then waited for Kwame's return. While they waited, they discussed what they had seen.

'It is built to withstand attacks from inside or outside,' Amador began. The others nodded.

'It is too far to march an army. The land is too dry and barren to support them and we could not carry enough supplies,' Kakande continued.

'And no army could approach unnoticed across this barren land,' Mulondo interrupted.

'We cannot take this place.' Kojo finished and the other men nodded in agreement.

Niena didn't nod but looked at Kisa instead, who was sitting and listening, with head bowed and fists clenched. 'It is true what you say,' she finally admitted. 'But I will kill Badru and his father at least. Let the other slave masters sleep less secure because of their deaths. Let them dream of death in their midst. I can do that at least. Disturb their dreams.'

She went silent and her friends sighed a collective sigh of relief. They had been unsure if she could be convinced of the futility of trying to wipe this place out. At that moment, Kwame arrived back.

'I saw him! The one eared man!' Kwame was breathless with excitement. 'I saw him in the great mosque, where I was just one small fly among many.' He laughed at the thought and the others joined in.

Except Kisa. 'Tell us more!' she demanded.

'He was standing behind a man who I think is his father – a very important man, perhaps the most important man in this accursed place. He prays right up the front - in front of their chief mullah. He acts very holy, but all fear him. You can see it in their eyes and the way they bow to him and move aside for him. His name is Mbwana Abbas.'

'What does he look like?' Kisa interrupted her little brother in her excitement.

'He is very fat. He profits from the slave trade, but he leaves the dirty work to others.' Kwame spat to show his disgust.

'Are you sure that is his trade? And how can you be sure Badru is his son?' Kojo, ever cautious, wanted proof.

'The old man called him over on the way out of the mosque after prayers. He asked Badru why he was not out raiding. Badru looked worried and kept addressing the man as 'my beloved father' as he made excuses. I sensed that he was lying, that he was covering up the real reason he is skulking here.'

'The sorceress who haunts his dreams would be the real reason,' Kojo smiled as he said this and looked over at Kisa, whose face was a mask of hatred.

'I will kill them both. They will both pay. The fat man shall find that his wealth will not protect him!'

'Of course, you will,' Kojo spoke. 'I know you hate this place and want to do this as quickly as possible. This information is vital, but we must plan carefully. Your safety comes first. It will do us no good if they are dead, and you are too. Winning the battle is not the same as winning the war!'

Kisa knew this was true and she settled under his words. Breathing deeply, she turned back to Kwame. 'Follow them both. Find out where they live, especially the father. Find out how I can gain entry. I want this done soon. I hate this place. I will not leave till they are dead but that must be soon. My army needs me!'

It took Kwame several days to find out what Kisa needed to know. There was a walled compound near the mosque where Mbwana Abbas reigned supreme. He was the most important slave lord in a city of slave masters and his premises reflected that. Inside lived his extensive harem of wives, concubines, their guards, and servants and all their children plus quarters for grown sons when they returned from raids. Their raiders camped in the furthest compound belonging to Mbwana Abbas and strengthened both his power and prestige in the community.

Kwame told what he had discovered. 'Badru is in there but in one of the outer quarters. His father lives in the inner quarters of course. He seldom comes out except to go to the mosque. He has a large room with many servants. He takes his meals there and conducts his business, which is extensive. Visitors come and go all day, many of them bring gifts, all of them bowing. He obviously considers himself a great man.

'His wives and slave girls come and go at his pleasure, but he is a fat old man. I do not think they take up much of his time. Still, he seems to take other pleasures with his women. He surrounds himself with beautiful young female slaves who fan him when he is hot, massage his hands and feet and feed him when he is hungry.'

'Then that is how I shall reach him.' A plan was forming in Kisa's mind.

'You want me to sell you to him?' Kojo was thinking along the same lines.

Kisa nodded.

'But what about weapons?' Kwame asked.

'I need no weapons with a man like that. I will strangle him with a scarf.'

'You must plan carefully, my love. You must kill him when he is alone and leave before they find his body. You may not have time or the means to find Badru too.'

'That would be a shame, but the father is more important than the son.'

Kisa spent some time preparing her disguise with Niena's help and they all discussed how to get her inside.

'You have to be a gift from someone … special…'
Kwame finished lamely, not sure what kind of special
would work.

'Yes!' Kojo grabbed the idea. 'Someone of a high
rank who lives far away who wants to curry favour of this
rich slave master.'

'Someone who has come all the way from
Timbuktu,' Kisa added eagerly. The others looked at her.
Only she had glimpsed the fabled city and only from a
great height, through Udele's eyes.

'Yes, Timbuktu. They are very rich there it is said.
One of them could afford to send a son so far.' Kakande
was nodding as he said this. 'You could be that son, Kojo.'

'And I will be the gift your father has given you to
take to him,' Kisa said excitedly.

'I will say that my father has sent me with a pouch
of gold and a beautiful concubine for the chief slave master
of Agadez. That is how we will get in.' Kojo was getting
excited by the plan too.

'And I will go in with you as your guard,' Amador
said. 'You must have guards with you if you are carrying
gold.'

'Me too, me too' the others chimed in.

'Kakande can come too,' Kisa intervened. 'That is
enough. Anyway, it is not as if you can really guard us.
You will have to leave me there. Then I will do what I must
do. And use my magic to return to you.'

'We have to have an escape plan after that,' Kojo
continued. 'We must be seen to march in from the west,

from the road that goes to Timbuktu. They will expect us to flee back that way after they discover the murders. While you are in there, we will prepare our exit along the southern road. By the time they realise we are not on the western road, we can be a long way south and on our way home.'

They prepared their costumes. Kojo dressed to play the part of the first-born son of a great warlord who wanted to break into the slaving business. To further the deceit, Amador and Kakande were dressed to play his bodyguards.

Kisa dressed to play a concubine. She chose a costume of silk and dressed in the style of the concubines of the Muslim traders: pleated harem pants bound at the ankles, silk scarves covering head and face yet see-through; layered blouses with long sleeves bound at the wrists, all slightly transparent and showing off her figure.

After making their preparations, they gathered once more. Kojo spoke to the others. 'Kwame, Niena, Mulondo, I want you to stay here with the horses. Pack up our camp and be ready to fly when we return. Kisa, Amador, Kakande and I will go to the road from Timbuktu and find our way into the city.'

Kisa rose and threw the bones. The signs were auspicious. It was time to go. Niena hugged her and then they rode out. Kisa led her party around to the road from Timbuktu. They found a safe place to camp and surveyed the western gate into the city.

'That is where we will enter,' she said at last, and the others agreed.

At last, all was ready. They rode into the city and left their horses outside the entrance of the compound of the great slave master, Mbwana Abbas. Kojo marched up to the gate with Kisa by the arm and Amador and Kakande behind him, holding the pouch of gold and other small gifts.

Guards answered the knock on the gate and led the small party into the waiting room. Mbwana Abbas was informed of his unexpected visitors and had them ushered, under guard, into his presence. The fat old man sitting in front of them looked briefly at Kojo and then ate Kisa up with his eyes.

She sent him a mental message, 'I have never seen a woman as beautiful before.'

Kojo told his story and offered his gifts to the slave lord. Abbas listened impatiently and then made a hollow promise about letting Kojo's rich father take part in the slave trade. After accepting the gifts, he imperiously waved Kojo and his servants out the door and then turned his gaze back to Kisa.

She stared at him, willing him to look only at her and sent him hypnotic suggestions that he wanted to bed her immediately. When his guards took the gold pouch up to him, she made sure that he took only a cursory look inside, since only the top pieces were real. It was easy to do – she had his full attention now.

She sent Mbwana Abbas the suggestion to have her taken straight to his inner rooms and he did so. For the rest of the morning, he took care of business irritably, with images of Kisa dancing in his mind and a sense of arousal such as he hadn't felt for years.

As soon as he could get away, he went to her. The moment he laid a hand on her, she killed him. Her eyes stabbed him first and he was frozen in sudden fear. A silk scarf wound around his throat and strong arms choked him as a knee sunk into his groin with a pain greater than he had ever felt before.

He struggled wildly but uselessly as the air was choked from his body and there was none to replace it. His eyes bulged in his fat head as he sank to his knees before the black woman who was killing him. Then they rolled back in his head as consciousness left him. With the superhuman strength of rage, she lifted him by his throat onto the bed and with one sharp jerk, broke his neck.

She left his body in the bed, covered as if in sleep. She stripped off her outer costume to reveal the garment of a simple household slave and made her way to the gate. She sent a suggestion to the guard that this slave was on a mission of great importance for the slave lord, and he let her out. Soon she was running with light feet through the alleyways and out of the city forever.

***

She found her band south of the city, packed and waiting for her, ready to flee. Kojo and the others had left clues along the western road to indicate they had gone that way before returning to the southern camp. As soon as Kisa returned to them, they set off at once and travelled all night, to put as much distance between them and Agadez as possible.

No one disturbed the slave lord for hours, fearing his anger. But late in the evening, when he did not call for his dinner, they snuck in and found him dead. They ran out screaming and shortly the household was in a turmoil. The news spread quickly through the town. 'Mbwana Abbas is dead!'

Few grieved but all felt fear that something like this could happen in their well-guarded town. Who had committed this crime? Rumours swept round but blame was soon laid on the rich man's son from Timbuktu. A search was carried out, but he could not be found. The slave lord's oldest legitimate son, Abbad, immediately stepped into the power vacuum when his father's body was found. Amidst the wild lamentations of the wives and concubines of the old slave lord, the new slave lord vowed revenge. He called all the younger half-brothers, and their slave raiding parties together to tell them what had happened.

'Our father has been murdered! You will find these dogs and bring them back for punishment.' He described the young lord from Timbuktu and the woman he had given their lord as a present. 'She killed him! And then they escaped. But not for long. Search the western roads find them. I order it!' They raised a cheer to their new lord. No one challenged him. All around them were guards with weapons.

Badru was frightened by the news. He was sure who the woman was, and he did not want to meet her. Nowhere was safe if she could reach into Agadez itself. There was nowhere he could hide.

While they were out searching for the rich man's son and his band, his older brother consolidated his power at home. There was a new Mbwana Abbad and nothing else changed. Abbad found his half-brother skulking in a courtyard behind the main house.

'Why aren't you out hunting for our father's killer?' Badru made excuses but the new slave lord was not interested. 'Your brothers are hunting to the west. Go south in case they take that road. And go now!'

Badru went. He found his lieutenant, Kondro, and ordered him to gather the men together. 'Our new lord, Mbwana Abbas, has ordered us to take the southern road in case our father's killer went that way. Prepare yourselves. We will leave in the morning.'

Badru had never been a religious man, but he went to the mosque next and prayed hard to Allah to protect him. It brought him no comfort. When he left, he knew somehow that he was going to his death but that he could not cross his half-brother. Orders were orders and he had been obeying them all his life. After a sleepless night, he rode out the next day on the southern road, hoping vainly that the Sorceress had taken the western road or was so far ahead that he wouldn't catch her.

Mbwana Abbas had seen the fear in Badru's eyes and called Kondro to him that evening. 'If Badru fails this mission, I will give his troop to you. If you kill those hyenas who killed my father, I will make you a rich man. Make sure that Badru does not skulk off and hide in the rocks. Make sure the southern road is searched!'

Kondro had hated Badru since he ran away and left Sefu and the others to die in the ill-fated attack on the village in the maze. The man was a coward and Kondro had no time for cowards. On the other hand, he had to make sure that only Badru died if and when they found the

Sorceress. Kondro too, was sure who the killer was and although he was not a coward, he was a practical man and could see no reason to die, if there was no real hope of killing her. If anyone should have been able to kill her, it was Sefu, and he was dead. Kondro had no faith in Badru's ability to fight and he was sure that the Sorceress wanted Badru dead, after kidnapping of that woman from the village. Had she not stalked them and killed Zuberi?

They had thought themselves free of her after Badru and Kondro returned to Agadez and got a new gang but by the time they went west again, rumours were spreading about a Bandit Queen who was attacking slaving gangs and freeing the captives. Like Badru, Kondro quickly decided that the Bandit Queen was none other than the sorceress from the village. Now that he was being sent to find her, he had to find a way to get away from her again when they did.

'We need a lamb to sacrifice,' he muttered to himself as he left Mbwana Abbas's quarters.

While Badru was tossing and turning in his bed, Kondro spoke to the others in the gang. They had not been with Kondro and Badru when Sefu had led the ill-fated attack on the village in the maze – everyone else in that gang had been killed. But whispers had gone through this isolated and gossipy city about what had happened there, and the rumours of the Bandit Queen were everywhere as well. Tonight, Kondro confirmed their suspicions that the sorceress who killed Sefu, the Bandit Queen and the killer of Mbwana Abbas were all one and the same person. None of them wanted to meet her or die by her hands but what to do?

Kondro explained his plan. 'If they have gone this way, we must find them but let them kill Badru while the rest of us escape. Our new master has promised me the leadership of this group if we make it back alive, even if we fail to kill the witch.'

The rest of the gang preferred Kondro to Badru because Kondro was one of their own, not a member of the ruling elite. However lowly Badru was, he was still one of them. And they too could see that he was a coward. Hopefully the witch had gone the other way, but if they had the bad luck to find her, the idea of sacrificing Badru seemed a good one. That decided, they finished packing and then slept far more comfortably than Badru. The next morning Badru led his gang out the gates of the city. Kondro was right behind him. Overhead a vulture was circling.

***

Kisa and her band were far down the road by that time. Kisa decided to fly with Udele and see if anyone was following her. She saw that most of the slave gangs had gone west but that one was heading south. And Badru was leading it. She resisted the urge to cry out but flew higher instead and returned to her body.

'The gods have answered my prayers!' she said excitedly as she sat up on Amara, who had been carefully carrying her sleeping body while she flew. 'Badru leads the party which is coming south. We are going to ambush them, and I am going to kill him!'

The rest of the day was spent finding a suitable site for the ambush. 'It is a large party. It will be hard to kill all of them, but the gods will protect us.'

When all was ready, they waited. It took three days for Badru to reach the site. He tried to ride slowly but the others kept pushing ahead. He watched uneasily for the sight of the vulture, but she did not appear. This day, as they rode through a jumble of hills, Badru's unease grew and then suddenly there she was, standing in front of him with the eyes of the leopard. His men shouted and drew their swords as Kojo and Amador came from one side while Kakande and Mulondo rode towards them from the other.

Badru drew his sword as the sorceress approached him. Her hands were bare. *Why?* He thought, *where is her sword?*

He wanted to kick his horse and ride forward, holding his sword high. But he found himself yanking his horse around to flee back to his men. But they weren't there. As soon as Kojo and the rest leaped out to fight them, they turned and fled back towards Agadez. Kojo commanded the others to halt. No sense in tiring their horses to catch those cowards. They turned back towards Badru who was now between the horns of the bull.

He turned desperately and spurred his horse forward but Amara raced after him, her smooth Arab gallop bringing her up alongside Badru's foundering mount. Badru swung his sword wildly, but Kisa was on his off side. She leaned over as Amara passed his horse, reached out and grabbed the reins. Amara turned and Kisa yanked the reins, throwing Badru's horse off balance. She let go as the horse stumbled and Badru, no expert horseman, tumbled off.

Amara stopped and Kisa slid off. Badru struggled to his feet, raised his sword and with a wild cry, attacked her. Smoothly she stepped aside and let him strike and strike again until he was exhausted. Kojo and the others watched impassively as Kisa danced around Badru. Then she stepped within range and used a foot kick to Badru's sword arm. He screamed as his elbow snapped and his sword fell.

Badru fell to his knees, blubbering, 'Mercy! Mercy!'

'I will show you more mercy than you showed my people,' she said as she struck. A blow to the head knocked him unconscious. She picked up his sword and drove it through his heart. She stood watching his death throes as Kojo walked up.

'Are you satisfied?' he asked. She shook her head as she turned away, mounted Amara and rode south again.

***

Afterwards Kondro returned to Agadez to inform the new Mbwana Abbas that Badru had been killed, that the killer of his father was none other than the fabled Bandit Queen on the western roads and that after killing Badru, she had escaped to the South. The new Mbwana Abbas cared nothing for the death of Badru but was angry that the Bandit Queen had escaped. He forgot his promise to Kondro and appointed another half-brother, Jakali, to lead the raiders.

***

Kisa sighed. Kojo heard it. He reached across and took her hand as the horses walked slowly down the track.

Kano was near. Kojo was anxious to reach the town, have a wash and a rest.

'What is the problem, my Love.'

'Yasuki was right. It solved nothing,' Kisa sighed again.

'Did you really think killing the slave lord would do anything more than satisfy your blood lust?' Kojo squeezed her hand softly.

'I don't know what I thought. It didn't even feel that good when I strangled him. I thought of all those whose lives were shattered by his greed, but it could not help them. It could not bring my father back.'

'And as soon as he was dead, another took his place,' Kojo finished the thought for her.

'Yes,' Kisa replied with another sigh. 'We cannot stop this thing, can we?'

'I never thought we could, my love. All we can do is fight a great evil and hope that the gods will reward us.'

'As long as the white men remain in their castles, this will go on. Somehow, I must find a way to take them.'

'We tried that already. And that was a small fort. It would take a great army to seize Elmina. And there are more like it now, all along the coast.' Kojo did not like where Kisa's thoughts were going.

'Then I will build a great army.' Kisa pulled her hand away and clicked to Amara who trotted out in front.

It was Kojo's turn to sigh as he followed her.

***

Kano provided a brief respite for the weary travellers, but Kisa was restless and would not stay long. She pushed them hard as they journeyed west. Every morning she was up before the sun and she pushed on long into the evening, stopping only when the light failed. They arrived back in the Salaga Road camp without fanfare. Shani saw them first and called out. Everyone gathered around, relieved that the party had returned unharmed. After words of greeting, Kisa retreated to a hut to rest.

That night, around the campfire, Kojo and the others told of the journey, and how Kisa had killed the slave lord. 'But his son rose up and replaced him,' Kisa interjected bitterly, then added, 'I killed Badru. Afia, at least, is avenged.'

'But the war goes on,' Kisa finished and rose abruptly. All eyes watched her return to her hut.

'Perhaps it is time to go home.' Kojo said. 'I think we all need a rest.'

Chapter 26

A New Hunting Season

Kisa, Kojo and her lieutenants sat around the fire, eating porridge at the Warrior's Village. The hunting season from March to August, the rainy season, was about to start. The deathly dry winds that blew off the endless desert country to the north were being driven back to the deserts by the great rain clouds from the south.

The band had made a leisurely trip back north. It had grown and was a now formidable force. Kisa was planning to divide them into five groups this year, since so many young people were flocking to join up and help fight against the slavers. All had suffered losses from the slavers, whether they were Nzema or Ashanti, Ga or Fante, Dagomba or Gonja.

In each of these tribes, there were people who benefited from the evil trade, but not these people. These were men and women, most young but some old, who had lost family, friends, fathers or mothers, sisters and brothers, to feed the insatiable demand for slaves in the New World.

***

The first year brought only rumours of what was happening on the roads to Tamale and Salaga. By the second season, everyone knew. Slavers were putting a price on the heads of the bandits while villagers were feeling relief from attacks by slaving parties that had been erased on the northern roads. Rumours spread far and wide of a Bandit Queen and her army pillaging the slave masters on the roads to the coast. Even the white men, safe in their castles, took notice and put a price on her head.

So, in the second and third dry seasons after the war began, a steady trickle of people from tribes around the Nzema – Ashanti, Ga, Ewe, men and women both, who wanted to fight against the slave masters, found their way to Kisa's village. They stayed long enough to receive a warm welcome and a share of the villager's food. Then they were given some training in the ways of a mysterious fighter with the unusual name of Yasuki, the Black Samurai. They learned to fight with hands and feet, learned to defend themselves, and then were given weapons training though some of the young men were already skilled in the use of spear or knife. Then they were sent north to meet envoys from Kisa's army on the road north of Kintampo, the village where Kisa and Kojo kept a sizeable herd of riding and pack animals.

They were brought to the Warrior's Village, given huts and food and then trained some more. They met Kwame, who had also trained under the Black Samurai, and he drilled them mercilessly on their newly learned skills.

Then the newcomers met their own people who had come here earlier: Fela the Ashanti, Kwame and Shani the young Nzema fighters, people of the Ga and Ewe and tribes further south with strange names and stranger tales of being rescued by the sorceress from a slave ship far out to sea.

At last, they met the sorceress herself. First Kojo prepared them, telling them of her powers and her deeds in saving her village, penetrating the slave castle, leading a mutiny, taking a fort, and then marching north to fight this war.

When she finally emerged, carrying a great black staff, from a tree they were told that had been struck by lightning to create it. At her side they saw her strange slim sword in its stranger sheath, covered in foreign symbols but with a dragon clearly marked in gold. She was dressed for war, with a leopard-skin headdress from which her eyes glowed leopard-gold.

She strode forward and they fell back, often down to their knees, in worshipful fear. A great yellow dog paced beside her, with matching yellow eyes. Above her three ravens swooped and called out. She stopped before them and raised her right hand high. Fame shot up from her bare palm, a bright golden flame that hurt their eyes. Those still standing went to their knees.

'Behold the sorceress!' Kojo cried out and the army behind him echoed it.

'Behold the sorceress!'

The new recruits joined in until she raised her spear for silence and cried out:

'SOMUNYE!''

All echoed the word that meant we are one, over and over, men and women of a hundred tribes gathered together against the evil.

As abruptly as she came, she turned and disappeared. The new recruits were ready. They were part of the army. All that was left to do was find them places to fit in, other men to fight with, chores to help with until the bright day when they went into battle with their sorceress or her generals to kill the slave masters and free the slaves.

***

One night, Kisa lay in bed with Kojo, musing while lying in his arms. 'Have you noticed how they are all different colours?'

'What do you mean, my love?' Kojo said distractedly, being more interested in her breasts at that moment than her words.

'All the different people, from the south, from the north, from the far river to the east, the Nile they call it. Some are red like the Gonja, some are the colour of cocoa – rich brown. Others from the jungles of the south – why they are as black as coal – some of them are so black that they are blue!'

Kojo laughed but she pushed his hand back and sat up, 'Some are like the colour of sand and there is even an albino. His skin is like the white men, but his hair is white too and his eyes are pink. We have every colour here, Kojo, like the rainbow.'

Kojo laughed harder and wrapped his arms and legs around her, mock wrestling her down on their sleeping mats. She laughed back and mock attacked him with her leopard claws only half sheathed.

'We are all black to the white man, I know,' she purred as she burrowed her head into his neck. 'But to me we are a rainbow of colours, my army – different colours, different languages, but we share a common purpose and so we are one.'

***

By the end of that year, all roads were held by Kisa's army. The slave masters were denied their traditional routes and both Tamale and Salaga were suffering depressions in their economies as the slave trade dried up. Badru and his father were dead, and the coastal forts were being starved of slaves, but Kisa was not satisfied.

'We are already seeing fewer and fewer slave raiders coming this way, so I am sure they are finding other ways. They will just go around us, as long as the demand is there on the coast. We must find a way to attack the castles and the forts of the white men. We are protecting some of our people, but we have seen that they are taking people from everywhere. There will never be an end until the white devils are thrown into the sea!'

But no one had an answer to how that could be done.

Chapter 27

Journey of the Mossi Drummers

Far to the west of the Warriors Village on the Konkari escarpment, word was spreading among the Mossi people that the old chief of chiefs had died. After the mourning there was to be a great ceremony at the enthronement of the new head chief. Drummers from many villages gathered to be part of the celebrations.

Kouka, the master drummer of his village, got a special invitation. The Chief's own master drummer had passed away and there was no one to replace him. Kouka didn't like to travel but he would make an exception for such a special occasion. He packed up his favourite sangban and then approached some of his drumming team.

'I am going to the Chief's enthronement in Ouagadougou. They need drummers. Would you like to come?'

Two of his djembe players, Salam and Karim, said yes. Tiiga the djun djun player and Wendmi, who played the kidi drum, also wanted to go.

'You are not well, Wendmi. Perhaps you should stay here,' Kouka protested.

'No, I want to come. To play for the Chief of Chiefs! I cannot miss that.' Wendmi grinned but Kouka had a bad feeling about it. Nonetheless, Wendmi was there on the day they left.

The walk was slow due to the drums. They were heavy to carry and because of the strict hierarchy of the Mossi, only nobles and soldiers could ride. The heaviest drum, Kouka's sangban, was strapped to a donkey. Balanced on the other side was Salam's large djembe. All the other drums were carried by the men, along with their supplies for the journey. Their village was far to the east of Ouagadougou, on the edge of Mossi country, and it took several days of walking to reach the capital.

The trip was worth it. Kouka and his drummers were warmly welcomed, especially the master drummer. They were given a fine hut in which to stay, fed good meat and plied with palm wine. Kouka met the other drummers who had come from across the region and melded them into a tight drum core.

The feasting and celebrations went on for days and drumming was an essential part of the procedures. During the days, the drums accompanied the marches of the sub chiefs into the town and the enthronement of the new head chief at the grand durbar. At night the people danced to the beat of the drums. Everyone agreed that Kouka was an excellent master drummer who brought together all the different drummers and produced fine music.

The new head chief rewarded them with gifts and asked Kouka to stay, but Kouka begged forgiveness to return to his family. Family was of the highest importance to the Mossi, so the chief reluctantly let Kouka and his drummers go home when the celebrations finally ended. Several other drummers decided to make the return journey with Kouka, intending to turn off as they reached their own villages.

Jakali, new leader of Badru's gang, heard of the gathering too and decided it was worth riding further west for some raiding. The drummers had finished playing at the celebrations and were on their way home when Jakali saw them marching and was impressed by the strength and good health of the men.

He waited until they camped for the night and then attacked. The drummers were asleep when the raiders poured through their camp. They were musicians, not fighters and it was easy for the raiders to overpower them. Like the Dinka boys, they were chained together with collars around their necks. Then the raiders drank the palm wine in their jugs and in a drunken frenzy broke all the drums. Kouka felt his heart break as his precious sangban was smashed and trampled.

The march to Pikworo was heart breaking too. Wendmi, the Kidi player, was too sick for the journey and died one cold night along the way. Kouka watched with mixed feelings of sadness and anger as the slavers removed Wendmi's chains and tossed his body aside. Kouka and the others said prayers for their friend's soul as they were dragged away for another day's hopeless march.

At Pikworo, Jakali found that Samori and Babatu were willing to pay a good price for these men, saving him the dangerous march through the Bandit Queen's country. After what had happened in Agadez, Kondro and the others were relieved at this decision. The drummers were big strong men, the sort that would bring good money in the Salaga markets. Samori and Babatu Sato could sell them on to the southern slave masters and make an excellent profit on their investment.

The drummers were chained to the great granite boulders in the valley away from the slavers' huts. Their food was poured into shallow depressions in the rocks for them to eat. There was no protection from the relentless heat – no shade in the daytime, no blankets at night. Kouka did his best to keep his friends' spirits up. He insisted that they share the meagre food and water equally.

One hot day, to take their minds off their plight, he said, 'We should practice our drumming. It will give us something to do.'

His friends looked sceptical, but Kouka began to softly hit the rocks with his hands, setting up a simple rhythm. Salaam took it up immediately followed by Karim and Tiiga. Each man slapped the rocks as if it were his drum and soon the others joined in. The guards were bored and found the soft drumming pleasant, a reminder perhaps of their own village lives so long left behind. No one interrupted Kouka and his drummers.

After the daily meal, Kouka told his friends, 'We will do this every day. We will practice our routines. This is our trade. We must not forget our purpose in life even in this hell.' And so it was. It gave them comfort as they waited for the day when they would be chained together once more and marched south to an unknown fate.

Chapter 28

A Warrior Queen hears of the Bandit Queen

Far to the south of the Sahel, there lived a great queen, a warrior, who had fought the Portuguese for almost sixty years. Her name was Nzinga, and she was the queen of the Ndongo and Matamba peoples of Southwestern Africa. Her title was Ngola and from this, the Portuguese invented the name Angola for the country that she ruled.

One hot summer day, Ngola Nzinga was bored. The daily minutiae of running a country were annoying her. She was restless and longed for the battlefield and a good fight. Instead, she had to sign papers and listen to petitions all day. Now her ambassador to the Portuguese government in Luanda was reporting to her. Most of the news from the outside world came through this ambassador and there was a lot to tell, but it was hot, and the rhythmical swishing of the great feather fans was making her sleepy.

First, he explained what the Portuguese were doing and then the Dutch. As usual, they were busy attacking this village or that fort, or they were building new barricades or adding more cannons. It was all so drearily familiar.

They are like a plague, these white men, spreading their pestilence everywhere, she thought as she stifled a yawn.

'There is intriguing news from the north, Great Ngola.' The ambassador could see it was time for a change.

'There are reports of a 'Bandit Queen' who has a band of warriors and attacks the slavers on their way to the Castles. She seems to be having some success. Rumour has it that she is raising an army to drive out the White Devils.'

'A good name for them,' Nzinga said as she leaned forward, her interest piqued by this curious piece of information. 'I would like to meet this Bandit Queen. What else do you know of her?'

'They say she is a great sorceress and that she uses magic against the slave traders. They hate her and have put a price on her head, but it does them no good. She appears out of nowhere, like a whirlwind. She and her band are great swordsmen and they cut through the slavers like sheaves of grain. She frees all their captives and takes the bravest into her band, so now there are a great number of them. They kill all the slavers and take everything they own. They say she has gold bracelets on her arms and gold necklaces that shine so brightly that they blind her enemies.'

Nzinga came alive at that news. She clapped her hands. 'Fetch me my harem-master!' she ordered her attendants. 'And take the good ambassador to his quarters.'

She turned back to him. 'There is a state dinner tonight. Your presence is required, so go now and prepare yourself.' The ambassador bowed deeply and backed formally out of the room. He was pleased that his news had been received so well.

The harem-master arrived and went down on one knee before his Queen. 'How may I serve you, great Ngola?'

'I have the need of a strong resourceful man, someone with brains as well as muscles.'

The Queen seemed to be musing to herself as much as to the harem-master. 'It is a long journey he must take to find this Bandit Queen. I will send him as an envoy, one Queen to another. I will give him letters of introduction and safe passage for him to show the Europeans. They must not know who he is searching for if she has a price on her head. He can just say he is looking for some peaceful ruler who has goods I wish to buy.'

Nzinga raised her voice in command. 'Tell the men of my harem that they are to perform tonight at the state dinner. I want demonstrations of their fighting ability of course, but also mind games and oratory. Tell them I will choose the best for a great reward. A night with me and then an interesting journey. And on his successful return, he will have earned a house of his own and a commission in my army.'

Only the best and brightest were chosen for Nzinga's harem and it was considered an inevitable step if a man wanted to succeed in this woman's army. It was humiliating, having to wear women's clothes and live in a harem, but the rewards made it all worthwhile for the winners. They had to be skilled in many arts beyond just brute strength. She was choosing them for brains as much as anything. The first reward was a night with the Queen. She enjoyed her sexuality and the freedom that she had as the Queen to choose young and virile lovers whenever she felt the desire.

The harem-master went back to the men, who lived in special quarters within the palace grounds. They had

298

luxurious rooms with all manner of extras that normal soldiers never saw: good food served on fine plates, wine in silver-laced cups, cool sheets on comfortable beds, gardens in which to wander and a training ground on which to keep all their fighting skills sharp and muscles strong.

Since Nzinga clearly desired intelligence in her generals, there was schooling as well, and after dinner, there were nightly debates on all manner of topics. The harem master made it clear that these were the skills most to be looked for this night so some of the men gave up early.

'Only those with sharp wits need bother to come tonight. There will be wrestling matches for show of course, but it is how your words perform that will get you chosen tonight.' The harem-master finished and left them to their preparations.

Young Mbandi decided this was the mission for him. He was not that good with weapons and hopeless on the wrestling mats, but he could match minds with any other man in the harem. Mbandi had joined the army with the sole purpose of getting into the Queen's harem and so get the chance, as the son of a poor farmer, to prove his worth in her court. He learned to read from the local merchant in his village and had absorbed several different languages at an early age. He was bright, ambitious, and now his moment had come.

Mbandi's advantage in any debate was his sense of humour. He could turn even the most serious topic into a laughing matter, often at the most unexpected moment. He would use this skill tonight in a debate to make his verbal opponents look foolish and get the attention of the Queen.

All went as planned. The state dinner began with much eating, drinking, and gossiping among the court nobles and the few bureaucrats who were important enough to get an invitation. Then they demanded entertainment. There was drumming of course, and beautiful women danced. After that, the men of the harem came on stage. They started with a few exciting wrestling matches and then the harem-master informed the court that, with respect, his men wished to engage in debate to entertain them.

Mbandi had no trouble talking his opponents in circles no matter what the topic and before long he had his audience laughing at his verbal antics. They clapped, cheered, and declared him the winner for the evening. He approached his Queen and knelt before her.

Nzinga smiled at him. 'The nobles have chosen, and we agree with their choice. You will be given an important mission and a great reward if you are successful.' She turned to the Ambassador who was seated beside her. 'Tell the nobles and this soldier about the Bandit Queen.'

He willingly recounted his news and then the Queen stood up. 'I wish to meet this warrior. We have much in common because we are fighting the same war.'

She turned to Mbandi, who was still kneeling before her. 'You will be given the rank of Royal Envoy. You will have clothes to match that role, a ship to carry you north and gold to buy your way into the castles and cities you visit. You will find this Bandit Queen and convince her to accompany you on your return journey, in order that she may meet with me. Tell her I have the same goal as she: to rid our lands of the invaders!'

At this her nobles cheered. 'If you return successful, with the Bandit Queen at your side, you will receive all that you desire in life: a position in court, a fine house, and a noble wife. If you fail, do not return! Will you do the bidding of your Queen?'

Mbandi leaped to his feet and proclaimed: 'Great Ngola! I will serve you even if it leads to my death!' Then he fell at her feet and kissed them. The nobles responded with loud cheering and clapping.

'Await me in my chambers,' the Queen dismissed him into the care of her harem-master, who would see him bathed and then delivered to her bedroom after the feast.

Nzinga turned back to her guests, but she soon retired for the night. That night was the best of Mbandi's life. She was an experienced lover and knew what she wanted. His experience was limited but he gave her his all and she was satisfied.

A few days later he set sail for the North.

Chapter 29

Battle in the Hills of Fear

Another rainy season drew to a close. Kisa's foot soldiers patrolled all the roads to the Salaga slave markets, and the cavalry controlled the south-western road to Wa. Anyone bringing captives from any direction or returning from the south with their profits was attacked.

Kojo and Kisa met regularly to discuss strategies with the twins, Kwame and Shani, in their roles as group leaders, plus the others who had leadership roles in the army: Majeed came as the leader of the Dagomba; Bolley as the leader of the Gonja, and Nawi, the captain of the Fon women fighters. Other important warriors such as Fela the Ashanti, Okocha the Ibo fighter, Kakande the Buganda man who led the eastern warriors, and Amador, who commanded his Sao Tome fishermen joined them too.

They discussed all the factors that affected their various hunting grounds. The weather, the travel habits of the slave masters, the conditions of the people they were driving and the conditions of the roads on which they travelled were all topics to discuss. Fighting techniques and attack strategies were also discussed endlessly around the campfire, usually with cups of palm wine in hand, as the meetings went on long into the night.

This kind of communication between the groups was paramount so Kisa pulled them together as often as they needed and then sent them back to carry on their attacks.

'If we expand our reach to the eastern roads as well, beyond Yendi, we can strangle the snake,' Kwame said one night, while looking at Kojo's map.

The first objection came from the ever-cautious Kojo. 'How can we communicate over such long distances? Even with the vulture and the ravens. Kisa cannot fly all the time! We need a better system of communication first.'

Kwame was going to argue but Kisa shook her head to all of this. 'I think that first we must make the northern road ours. We harry the slavers there, but it is not ours yet.'

'How do we do that?' Kwame asked.

'We take Pikworo – the Hills of Fear.'

Everyone fell silent, thinking about the infamous slave camp. It was not an easy target.

'We can do it!' Kisa countered the silence. 'The gods are protecting us. Has anyone been hurt in any of our battles?'

No one answered because it was true – not one soldier had been so much as scratched in all the years of fighting. Superstitions featured in all their tribal pasts. They did not think that only their own prowess kept them safe. It had to be more than that. Her generals and her troops all believed that it was the power of the Sorceress that protected them.

'We would need everyone.' Kisa continued. 'I saw Pikworo from the air with Udele's eyes. It is well guarded. It looks like a fortress of rock and stone, but it has many holes in it. There are no walls around it. We could do it. We could come in from all sides and crush them.'

'We can use the cattle and the herd boys,' Bolley said. 'The boys are small but strong and they are good riders. They have trained their cattle to do their bidding and we have used them many times on the Wa Road. The boys are clever. They have even taught their cattle to trample the guards while leaving the captives unharmed.'

'They will be useful,' Kisa agreed. 'Let me tell you what I have seen,' she continued. 'There is a great rock that stands in the centre, with guard is always on it. But the country around is covered in trees, cut by gullies and rough with hills, so he cannot see everything. We must get as close as we can without being seen. Then we distract the guard while the cattle and horses come up from behind.'

The others nodded. Plans began forming in their minds.

'We will be the distraction,' Nawi announced. 'Let them see women coming. We hide our weapons. We weep and beg like mothers for our lost children. When they come forward to capture us, we will show them our teeth.' She grinned, showing a perfect set of white teeth in her beautiful but deadly face.

'Yes!' Kisa agreed. 'I will come in from the front with the women. Kojo and Kwame – you will divide our foot soldiers into two groups, one to come from the east and one from the west.'

'The horns of the bull,' Kojo said, and Kwame nodded in agreement.

'I will take our mounted soldiers around behind them, from the north,' Bolley continued as Kojo drew a battle plan on his map.

'We will take the dinka herd boys and the cattle too,' Shani added. By now all were nodding in agreement. This could work.

Hours were spent discussing all that was needed to make such an audacious move. The Hills of Fear were a long way up the road between Bolgatanga and Tamale. Half the soldiers were on foot, while the cavalry would be slowed to the pace of the cattle so time was needed to get everyone into place. First, each leader had to fetch his soldiers and bring them back from their camps on the various roads. Then here was the preparation for the march north, which would be made overland to maintain secrecy for as long as possible. All supplies had to be carried with them.

At last, when Kisa and Kojo were satisfied that everyone knew their respective tasks, they went to their sleeping mats. Sleep was hard to come by in heads filled with thoughts of the coming battle. The next day, the preparations began. Everyone in the Warrior's Village was informed about the coming battle. It would be the greatest blow they had yet dealt to the Slave Masters, and all of them were so convinced of the power of the Sorceress that there was no disagreement or fear, only excitement and anticipation.

Messages were sent out to the various camps and all the soldiers brought back to the Warrior's Village to be prepared for the battle to destroy Pikworo. Weapons were sharpened and the warriors practiced their hand-to-hand fighting skills each day, while their leaders planned each detail of the coming operation.

The army of foot soldiers was divided into large two groups: one under Kojo and the other under Kwame. They chose captains for each of the groups assigned to them and told them how they would participate, what their roles were and how to get to their allotted positions in the battle.

Supplies were gathered and packed for the journey. The cavalry men prepared their horses, and the herd boys honed their skills of sending the cattle where they wanted them to go and rounding them up afterwards. Even the pack of pariah dogs under the leadership of Chaga caught the excitement of the coming battle.

Kisa and Nawi planned their frontal attack. The women soldiers were given loose robes that made them look like simple peasants and allowed them to conceal their weapons beneath. Other women fighters joined Nawi's troops so that the frontal attack would be punishing and keep the slave masters occupied, while the foot troops moved in from the sides and the cavalry and cattle came in from behind.

At last, when all was ready, Kisa performed the rituals for the success of the battle. She lit a sacred fire and observed the patterns in the smoke. She said prayers to placate the gods and threw divination bones in the sacred circle at the center of the village to find the most auspicious day for the attack. She poured a special libation on the ground for the gods of war and then Kojo's drum called all to the last feast before they began the journey north.

The Gonja horsemen and Shani left first with the Dinka herd boys proudly mounted behind them and the cattle moving before them. They had the longest distance to cover since they were circling around to the north of Pikworo to surprise the slave masters from behind. Many of the horses were draped with cattle hides. Weapons were hidden beneath the hides so the soldiers looked like nothing more than simple cattle herders who would raise no suspicions if they were seen on the way.

After the cavalry left, the foot soldiers lined up behind their leaders: the Fon women behind their captain, Nawi, and the rest behind Kwame and Kojo. Kisa led the way on Amara. She was dressed as the sorceress, with her leopard headdress and prepared for battle with leather greaves on her legs and swords strapped to her waist.

Their sorceress raised her black spear above her head and cried out, 'Somunye!' to start the march.

Her soldiers echoed her, 'Somunye!'

The march took several long days across the open plains. Like the cavalry, they avoided the main roads so that word would not come to the slave masters of their peril. The troops started early and marched late into the evening, for all were fit and eager for this ultimate show of their power and determination.

Their camps at night were simple affairs. It was warm enough that no fires were needed, and they ate simple meals from their prepared supplies before wrapping themselves in blankets and sleeping on the bare ground. They made their final camp a half day's march from Pikworo. They hid in the trees and lit no fires. No one slept but all sat silent, waiting.

On the warm, rising air of dawn, Kisa rose on the wings of Udele to survey the slave camp. All was quiet with no sign of alarm or awareness of their impending danger. Slave masters slept in silk tents while the miserable captives huddled naked, chained to the bare rocks.

Udele moved north and circled above Bolley and Shani, to signal to them that the foot soldiers were in position. She found the horsemen hidden in the trees north of Pikworo, with their cattle and the ever-watchful Dinka boys.

Kisa cried out in Udele's voice and Shani looked up and waved. Satisfied that they were ready, Kisa flew back over Pikworo. She could see the guard sitting on the highest rock. On a slightly lower rock ledge, she could see traders gathering to inspect the captives. None of them looked concerned and there were no extra guards. They were sitting themselves comfortably under umbrellas held by slaves while other slaves fanned them to ease the oppressive heat. It seemed certain that they had no warning of what was to come.

The captives on the flat rock platform below the slave masters had no such protection or relief. The slaves had been chained to the rocks beneath the ragged Loa trees overnight. At dawn, the guards took them to the feeding areas where they were fed maize meal and given water. The food and water were not provided in cups or bowls. The miserable captives ate and drank out of depressions in the rocks. Then they were driven by guards to the rock platform where they were to be sold and left standing in the hot sun, bowed with grief while waiting for the auction to begin.

Kisa called out to them, but they heard only the dreaded cry of the vulture and did not understand so she wheeled Udele south. Quickly she flew back to the camp, returned to her own body. and reported to her commanders, who were ready to lead the attack.

'The gods are with us. There are many traders in the camp buying slaves. There is a guard keeping watch on the highest rock and there are guards herding the slaves around, but they have few weapons. They depend on their whips and chains to keep order and they are not expecting to be attacked.'

'Kojo and Kwame, take your troops around to the east and west of the main road out of Pikworo now. Station yourselves out of sight and wait till you hear us wailing and begging for the release of our children. That will draw their attention our way and allow your troops to draw near. I have signalled to Shani and Bolley to begin their approach from the rear.'

Everyone set out to follow her instructions and soon all were approaching their positions as Kisa and Nawi set out up the main road to the entrance of Pikworo.

The owners of the camp, the slave masters, Samori and his brother, Babatu, were following their normal routine. First. they prayed and then took a cup of tea before going to inspect the captives. Suddenly Samori heard a cry from the sentry on the high rock. He looked up to see the man laughing and pointing to the south road. Samori climbed up to the rock to get a better look. What he saw caused him to laugh too and call for his brother to come see the ridiculous sight. A band of women were walking up the road. He could just hear them crying and begging for the release of their children.

Fools, he thought and then he called out to his guards. 'There are women on the road. Go down there with whips and chains. We will have more slaves to sell to the traders before they leave!'

Babatu went down to lead the guards. All eyes were on the south road now. The traders stood up to watch. The captives too turned to watch the strange women coming up the road. Babatu approached the women with the guards close behind him. He saw nothing to alarm him. The women were of no tribe that he was familiar with and they had blankets wrapped around them, even in the heat of the early morning. One of the women walked forward to meet him. He waited with a sense of pleasure for her to beg him to release her children.

Instead, she threw her blanket off to reveal a great black spear. She held it high and shouted: 'Surrender or die!'

The other women didn't give their enemies the chance to surrender. They threw off their blankets, revealing their swords and spears, and leaped forward. They rushed around their leader and shouted 'Kill!'

The guards, suddenly facing shouting savages instead of helpless mothers, drew their knives and prepared to defend themselves. Behind them the slave traders began shouting at their own guards and soldiers to find their weapons and prepare to fight. Just as the women were nearing their targets, arrows flew out of the surrounding trees and guards began to fall.

Out of the trees, armed men came running towards a now frightened and confused Babatu. To add to his terror, they were shouting, 'Death!'

Kisa swung her spear and knocked the wind out of the slave master, who fell to his knees. She stepped over him and left him to Nawi, who quickly separated his head from his body. Other guards ran forward to assist Babatu and his men, but they stopped when they heard screaming behind them. They turned to see wild cattle running towards the camp. Their horns were painted red and gold and they were being chased by boys on foot. Behind them were men on horseback wielding wicked looking swords. They too were shouting 'Death' as they galloped forward.

Samori was the first to fall beneath the hooves of the cattle. He was a fat man and had been moving towards the back of the camp when he saw the weeping women turn into an army of warriors. As he waddled back to what he thought was safety, the cattle suddenly appeared before him and in a thunder of hooves, bowled him over and trampled him. The cattle veered between the captives who were scrambling up onto the relative safety of the rocks to which they were chained. Guards were running and screaming, trying to draw their weapons and avoid the stampeding cattle.

Just at that moment a strange thing happened. Some of the captives – the Mossi drummers - began to drum. They had nothing but the bare granite rocks to which they were chained and the small rocks on the ground. When Kouka saw Kisa and the women marching towards them, he felt the power of the Sorceress and for the first time in many days, hope rose in him. He could offer no other help to these strange women warriors but the power of drumming.

'Drum!' Kouka shouted to his fellow drummers as he picked up a stone and began beating out the rhythm on the rock. Soon all were drumming as loud as they could. The other prisoners began to chant with the drumming and the sound rose above the beating of the cattle's hooves.

To the sounds of the drumming, the warriors fell upon the guards and the slave masters. Swords flashed and bodies fell to the ground. The chained slaves climbed up on their rocks to escape the hooves of the cattle. When the guards and the traders tried to join them, they pushed them back. And all the while the drumming continued, louder and louder as the battle raged.

Behind the cattle, Shani came with her torch blazing. With her were Bolley and his men, slashing at the slavers with their swords. Shani's torch shone bright even in the morning sun, lit by magic, and blown by the speed of her horse. Beside her, Bolley's sword cut down all in her path.

Those slave masters still on their feet turned and ran down the hill to escape the cavalry but that led them into the swords and arrows of Kisa's foot soldiers. There was no safety no matter which way they turned.

The Dinka herd boys rounded the cattle and headed them back through the camp again. Shani and Bolley turned and charged towards the last of the slave masters huddled in the dubious shelter of their tents. Their guards surrounded them, driven now by the need to survive and determined to fight hard.

Bolley's men dismounted and fought hand to hand, determined to reach the slave masters behind them. Shani's mare reared behind them as she screamed her support. 'Kill them! Kill them all!' Kojo and Kwame ran up with their troops to help finish the job. The few remaining guards were no match for the enraged soldiers coming at them from all sides.

Below the slave camp, Kisa marched forward. She felt invincible. Behind her came her foot soldiers, who were still slaughtering the soldiers and guards who had come forward to capture helpless women. They fought hard because their lives were threatened but, unlike Kisa's soldiers, they had not dealt with an army before, only helpless villagers and chained captives. One by one they fell.

Untouched and untouchable, Kisa marched through the melee. One look at her was enough to stop any of the slavers from approaching her. She left them for her army to deal with. Instead, she marched to the highest rock and climbed up to where the sentinel was cowering, trying to hide. With a swipe of her sword, she took off his head. As he fell, she mounted the rock and stood, tall and proud.

As her soldiers finished off the last of the guards and slave masters, she raised her sword and cried out: 'Victory! Death to all slavers! Somunye! Somunye!'

Her army and the captives below picked up her cry and repeated it over and over to the sounds of the Mossi drummers, who, using only the granite rocks, were drumming out the victory chant. At last, they fell silent and looked about them. There was no one left to kill. Overhead Udele and her family circled, crying on the wind. They would be feasting tonight, but not on the flesh of the captives this time.

Kisa remained motionless on the rock while her army moved about the camp. They found the two owners of the camp among the dead. The dreaded names of the

Pikworo slave masters, Samori and Babatu Zato, would strike no more fear in their captives. Kisa's army found keys to the shackles and began freeing the captives. Others set fire to the slavers' huts and tents and began throwing the bodies on the flames. Kisa remained proud on her rock and Kojo joined her there.

'Others may try to rebuild it after we leave,' Kisa said to him as they watched the Dinka herd boys rounding up their cattle. 'But we will leave nothing behind that will help them.' The captives joined in as they were released, burning the tents, and stabbing the bodies. They looked up to the sorceress, standing on the highest rock above the camp.

'Kisa! Kisa! Kisa!' Her army shouted her name to the rhythm of the drums. The captives picked up the chant.

'Kisa! Kisa! Kisa!' Her name was carried on the wind. She raised her sword in salute.

'Let the slave masters beware!' she called out at last. 'For the sorceress will find them and they will die as they lived! By the sword!'

The cheering was louder for that and then the dancing began, in celebration and release. The slavers' bodies were piled high, and kindling stacked on them. Oil was poured on top so that they would burn, and more fires were lit. The freed captives danced around the burning bodies in wild abandon. Then they ransacked the slavers' possessions, drinking their wine and gobbling down their food.

All through the night, Kouka and his drummers continued drumming on the rocks, celebrating their

314

freedom. The captives and their liberators danced in the firelight till the sun rose. As the fires burned to ashes, they sat at last in silence and looked at what they had accomplished. Then, exhausted, they slept.

The Vulture Falls

Chapter 30
What Next?

In the days after the battle, when the thrill of victory eased and they were ready to think about the future, Kisa met with her generals and planned their next moves. The freed captives were the first concern. Most needed rest, food, clothing, and medicines to recover from their ordeals and this was provided. Others wanted to join the army.

Some of the women were so impressed by Nawi and her warriors that they asked to join her, and Kisa agreed to that. Several of the male captives wanted to join with the Gonja and those who knew how to ride were allowed to do so. The rest of the captives were given the choice to try and find their way home or go with the army to the Warrior's Village. Most chose to stay with the army that had saved them.

The best find for Kojo was Kouka and his Mossi drummers. Kouka approached him first, when he saw that Kojo had a talking drum slung over his shoulder.

'I am Kouka, master drummer, and these others with me are also drummers. We are Mossi men. We were returning from a celebration of our people when we were taken by these sons of whores.'

Kouka spat and then continued. 'We drummed on the rocks when we saw you coming to rescue us because our drums were destroyed. Now we want to join you. Perhaps we can be of use to you.'

Kojo suddenly saw the answer to the problems of long- distance communication, if they were to extend their range of operations. He held out his fist in greeting. Kouka's fist met his.

'I would be proud to have you join us,' Kojo answered. 'We use the talking drums to communicate while we are out hunting slavers. You could help us.'

Kouka pointed to Kisa. 'Who is she?' he asked in awe.

'That is our sorceress. She leads us in this war. She has been chosen by the gods to fight against the slave masters.'

Kouka shook his head in wonder. 'My people follow the desert prophet now, not the old gods. But we stand with you against the slavers. We will follow your sorceress too.'

Kojo grinned. 'That is good to hear. Come with us back to our village. Bring your drummers. They will be welcome. I look forward to playing with you.'

Kouka looked at Kojo's drum. 'I see you play the Kidi. My kidi drummer died on the road. I look forward to having you join us also. If only we had our drums. The slave masters broke our drums when they took us. It broke my heart.'

Kojo nodded and held his drum tighter. 'It would be the same for me. I have had my drum since I was a child. It is all I have left of my family. They too were destroyed by the slave masters.'

Kouka put his hand on Kojo's shoulder and looked in the younger man's eyes. They bonded in their shared sorrow.

'We will find you drums in Tamale,' Kojo promised. 'Join us for the evening meal. The sorceress is also my wife.'

Kouka, curious to know more about the mysterious woman, was quick to accept.

***

Over the next few days, the last of the bodies were burned and the camp was sacked. The freed captives were fed and rested and then prepared to leave this place of horror. They were to be formed into units to march with the army on the way south back to the warrior's village. It was just as it had been done after many smaller battles over the past three years but this time there were far more captives than before.

Before marching south, Kisa decided to take some of her troops north to Bolgatanga. At the evening meal she said to her generals. 'Pick some of your best men. I want to go to Bolgatanga and tell them what we have done. I want them to fear us as never before. We are an army now – we no longer hide!'

They rode to Bolgatanga in force and marched down the main street, to the surprise and dismay of the merchants and townspeople who were benefiting from the slave trade. All the town turned out to watch the strange sight. Rumours had been flying about the events at

Pikworo. Now the causes of the destruction were here, and the citizens feared for their own lives. The army ignored them as they marched behind Kisa to the central market, where Kisa stopped and drew her sword.

'We have destroyed Pikworo!' she shouted and the townspeople who were following them stopped in their tracks to listen to her.

'We have made it a place of fear for the slave masters, and we can do the same to you. Be warned! Give up this evil trade or I will return and wreak the vengeance of the gods upon you!'

Her horsemen and her foot soldiers shouted in agreement. Several of Nawi's women held up the bloodied severed heads of dead slavers, just in case the townspeople didn't get the message. Kisa rode up and down between her troops and the stunned locals, who were silently praying that she wasn't going to slaughter them on the spot.

She raised her war cry. 'Somunye!' Her soldiers echoed it and to show their new loyalty to her cause, the townspeople quickly took it up as well.

Then as suddenly as she had come, Kisa turned and led her army back out of the town towards Pikworo, leaving Bolgatanga to spread the word to the north all the way to Timbuktu that it was no longer safe to bring slaves down this road to Tamale.

By the time they got back to Pikworo, the freed captives were prepared to march with them. So, the next day, Kisa rode at the head of a greatly enlarged army. The smoke of the fires in the Hills of Fear burned behind them in farewell.

The army marched in triumph down the road to Tamale. They set up a camp outside the town. Kisa led her victorious troops to the centre, just as she had at Bolgatanga and proclaimed her victory. Then she was met by the chiefs who had supported her cause, while those who were making money from slavery hid in their huts.

Most of the common folk were fully in support of Kisa's raiders and had family members who were part of her army. Majeed, Fuseini, Mahamadu, Niena and many more of the Dagomba had come from this district over the past three years to fight with her. They and the rest of the army were ready for a proper celebration of the victory at Pikworo.

Kojo went to the market with the slavers' gold and bought Kouka and his drummers new drums. That night the drums carried everyone away. Fires were lit and Kisa's Warriors and the townsfolk danced and celebrated the destruction of Pikworo. Kisa wore her leopard skin headdress and carried her great black spear. On her belt the samurai sword in its dragon-sheath glowed in the firelight. She stood immobile for the entire night, while everyone else danced. They brought her a chief's stool and in the early hours of the dawn she sat on it, acknowledging her equality with the local chiefs.

The partying went on for a week as all the tensions of the battle flowed out. The streets were filled with dancers and the palm wine flowed freely. Everyone in the town contributed food and tables were set up in the streets so that no one would go hungry. The Mossi drummers were used to playing at celebrations that lasted for weeks. They joined forces with the local drummers and took turns so that the drumming continued almost nonstop. A rough camp was set up near the town for the army so that they could rest occasionally but there always more in the town. Life and freedom were too precious – no one wanted to waste time sleeping.

***

At last, the party ended, and it was time for the next part of their journey. They took the freed prisoners of Pikworo to the Warrior's Village. There, another celebration was held, if anything bigger and better than that at Tamale, was held.

And in the Warrior's Village, Kisa could let her guard down and take part in the celebrations. Here there were no hidden slave dealers hiding in the huts, and no antagonistic chiefs watching her every move. She had maintained the role of Sorceress for the entire time from the aftermath of the battle to Bolgatanga and Tamale until their final arrival in the Warriors Village.

That first night back, she came forth again as the sorceress. She stood, silent and powerful, and each member of the army came forward, bent their knees, and pledged their loyalty to her. Once again, they marvelled that such a great battle could be fought without harm to the least of them. Then their sorceress, in turn, led the worship of the gods, the Orishas, who had given her the power to fight this battle. Dressed still in her fighting garb, with leopard helmet firmly in place, she said the prayers, made the offerings, rolled the knucklebones of an ancestor in the sacred circle, and prophesied the future:

'We will not stop here! We will throw the white devils into the sea!'

After the necessary ceremonies, she ordered the celebrations to begin. She watched for a while then slipped away. When she came back, the leopard skin was gone and the warrior's garb and Kisa was back – still young and willowy, just twenty-one years old – a woman who had won an unlikely victory and who just wanted to celebrate with her friends.

They ate and drank palm wine, laughed and joked, told their individual tales of the battle; the drums played a thousand different rhythms over the night. Kouka and his drummers playing their hearts out on their beautiful new drums and interwoven in their playing was the voice of Kojo's Kidi drum, weaving in and out different rhythms that was with the others and yet separate- always going his own way.

There was much work to do to help them build huts and integrate them into the group. They had to train them for warfare or get them to do farming and other chores.

When he had a chance, Kojo spoke with Kisa about the usefulness of the drummers. 'They can talk on the wind,' Kojo began with excitement. 'They can be an important addition to our army. We need to get the men talking drums and work out signals. We can put drummers with each band. With you on the wings of Udele and the drummers to pass the messages on, we can find them all. It will seem like magic to the slave masters. No matter where they are, we will strike!'

Kisa caught Kojo's excitement. They called to Kouka to join them. Kojo explained the plan to him and how Kisa could use the vulture to see far. Kouka remembered the vulture screaming above the camp while he was chained there and shivered, looking at the Sorceress with new respect.

'I will help you,' he said. 'Find me the drums and I will work with the other drummers. We will be your voices. The slave masters will learn to fear the sound of drums!'

Kisa told Kojo her larger plan. 'I have been thinking about this for some time,' she began. 'We have secured the main roads and destroyed the slave camp in the Hills of Fear. We tried to take the war to the slave masters, but they are too far away and too well protected.'

Kojo was silent, wondering where this was leading.

'You saw it again at Pikworo,' Kisa continued. 'None of our fighters were hurt. The gods see the justness of our cause. They are protecting us. The men think it is me and I know that it is not. But still... the gods must be protecting us! How else can it be explained?'

'We can continue holding the roads but that will solve nothing if the white devils continue to hold the coast. We must take the castle, Kojo. That is the only way to end this.'

Kojo shook his head. 'It is well defended, Kisa,' he said.

'But the cannons face the sea.' Kisa interrupted.

'What about the gates? How will we get inside?' Kojo's natural caution would have to be overcome.

'I have an idea,' Kisa mused. 'We do not have a cannon, but we have gunpowder. Not enough but we could get more. If we had enough, we could use it, just as Yasuki taught us and make a hole in the gate. Once inside, we outnumber the Dutch soldiers. They have guns, but that is all.'

'I don't know,' Kojo was shaking his head again.

'We must do something decisive. We have the advantage. Our soldiers are strong, they fight well, and the gods are protecting them. If not now, when? I say we march on Elmina. We force the gates and take the castle. With such a victory, others will join us. It is the only way. What we are doing will never stop this!'

Kojo looked with pride at his wife. She would never be diverted from her goal. He sighed. 'Perhaps you are right. Perhaps it is the only way. I wish Yasuki and Grandmother were here. I would like to know what they think.'

'But they are not. They left the war to us. And we have had great success. We cannot stop now!'

Kisa called a meeting of her leaders. Kwame and Shani were there with Bolley and Amador, Fela and Mahamadu, Mulondo and Kakande, Okocha and Nawi. She explained her plan to them.

'We are strong now. We hold the roads, and we have defeated the slave masters at Pikworo. It is time to take this war to the white devils on the coast. They think they are safe in their castles and most people think they are too strong to attack. Let us show them they are wrong!'

Kisa explained her plan. 'We will march on the coast, attack from two sides, drive the cattle down through the middle and so reach the gates of the fort. ' will use fire and the magic of gunpowder to break down the gates. Once inside, we can overwhelm the defenders for they are few and we are many.'

'And we have the power of the sorceress!' Amador shouted. 'The gods are on our side. Your magic protects us!'

The others cheered. The matter was settled. The meeting ended and the leaders went back to their troops to begin their preparations.

Chapter 31
Storming the Stronghold

Because all the troops were gathered at the Warrior's Village, it did not take long to organise them for the journey south. Word spread quickly that they were going to attack the slave castle of the white devils on the coast. Excitement ran high among the troops, now totally convinced in their invincibility as long as they fought for their Sorceress.

Kojo was still cautious. 'Why don't you fly with Udele over the castle and see how it looks these days? See if there are any changes?'

'There is no time,' Kisa replied impatiently. 'After Pikworo, they know what we have done and that we are here. We cannot give them time to amass more troops. We must strike now!'

Kojo shrugged and didn't argue. It was a decision he would come to regret.

On the departure day, Kisa lined up her troops. She put on her battle gear and leopard headdress, mounted Amara and with her spear held firmly in her right hand, rode up and down inspecting everyone. On one side were the horsemen. The Dinka herd boys were mounted on their own horses and had their cattle ready. The cavalry troops were mounted behind Shani and Bolley.

On the other side was the bulk of the army – her foot soldiers. Nawi had her women warriors lined up. Next to them were Kwame's Nzema troops, then the Dagomba fighters with Majeed proudly in front of them. Amador was there with his southern fighters and Okocha and Fela with theirs. Kakande stood in front of the fighters from the far East. With them were the Mossi drummers, ready to lead them forward into battle to the rhythm of their drums. As their Sorceress rode past, they cheered and called out 'Somunye!'

After the victory at Pikworo, none doubted her decision to take the castle. It was inevitable that it too should fall.

'We will throw the white devils into the sea!' she cried out. 'We will win!'

***

They marched on Elmina - a week's journey for men on foot. Those on horseback kept their pace so they would arrive together. They made no secret of their passage because word was spreading through the beleaguered tribes of the region that they were coming and many flocked to her cause. The army swelled in numbers, and they chanted to the drums as they marched. By the time they came within sight of Elmina, there were over a thousand warriors ready to fight.

The army camped in the last forest before the coast and marched out one cool clear morning. They stopped at the sight of the solid castle walls, gleaming white in the sunlight. Amara reared as Kisa spoke to them,

'Have no fear! The gods protect us with fire and magic! My magic will bring down the gates and we will take the castle!'

'Somunye!' She cried out as she raised her spear and started forward.

'Somunye!' They echoed her and marched forward with her.

The foot soldiers approached from two sides: northeast and north west- around the left and right flanks. Those on the beach side had an easy run and reached the fortress just as the cavalry, driving the cattle before them, surged down the middle and into the town. Kisa raced with them on Amara. In her arms was the magical explosive ball she had made, wrapped and ready to set at the base of the gates and blow a hole in it. Her spear was set in its leather sheath upright next to her knee to show the way. Kojo rode beside her as they swept through the village and up to the gates of Elmina.

The cattle surged through the tents and swerved past the gates, as Kisa reached her target. She leaped down from Amara's back, leaving her great black spear in its sheath on her saddle. She strode forward with the ball of explosive powder in her hands. As she reached the gate, she threw the ball down and used fire to ignite it, as she backed away again. The result was perfect, a loud explosion, a gaping hole, and a broken bar. Behind it, the Dutch soldiers were waiting for the onslaught as Kisa's foot soldiers raced through the now empty streets to join her and enter the castle through the broken gates. Then three cannons of the newly built Fort Christiansburg changed everything.

The cannons roared and cannonballs flew into Kisa's army. In the first volley, three holes filled with bleeding bodies were created in the ranks of the troops who were rushing forward to take the gates and the castle.

Horses screamed and dropped or scattered as the first cannonballs ploughed through them. Many of Bolley's men as well as the Dinka herd boys were thrown and then trampled as the cattle, maddened with the fear of the cannons, turned and raced back into their own troops. Amara panicked, reared, and then ran with the cattle, away from the sounds of the booming cannons and the screams of the dying.

The foot troops were surging in from all sides when the cannons opened fire and the cattle turned. Many fell: Mahamadu and the Dagomba fighters; Mulondo with his eastern fighters were massacred in the second volley of the cannons and then trampled by the frightened cattle. The Mossi drummers who had travelled with the cavalry to help drive the cattle and been drumming as they marched, fell too, their beautiful new drums, crushed and broken by the hooves.

The men closest to Kisa had surged forward through the broken gates with their swords and spears. The Dutch were ready, in formation, guns loaded. One line fired, then knelt to reload while the second line fired over their heads. Amador with his fishermen were hit by the first round of bullets, then Fela and his Ashanti warriors, and finally Sule with his fellow sailors. Bullets ripped through their flesh, and they fell and died inside the gates and the rest of the army, torn now by the cannons, could not help them.

Kisa stood frozen in the midst of the chaos, stunned by the sudden onslaught of death. Then Kojo pulled his horse around, steady, dependable Ayo, who stood unflinchingly in the chaos. He called out: 'Kisa!' as he put out his hand. Instinctively she grabbed it, and he pulled her up behind him. She came awake as Ayo wheeled away from the gates and surged back through the cattle and the cannonballs.

'Go Back!' she cried and Kojo echoed her words.

The remaining horsemen, with Shani in their midst, tried to turn but another cannon shot landed in their midst. Shani and Bolley disappeared beneath the bodies of their horses - white mare and black stallion. Kwame had been racing in from the beach side and his troops, his brothers and sisters from childhood, the cream of the Nzema youth died when the third volley of the cannons ripped through them. Kwame was stunned and fell beneath his companions' bleeding bodies. He passed out and saw no more of the battle.

Kisa called to her troops to come to her. She and Kojo retreated through the streets and as many as could ran with them. The Dutch troops in the castle ran out screaming over the bodies of those they had shot. The cannons were being turned and raised, increasing their range, slashing into the furthest of Kisa's troops.

'Get back, get back! Beyond their range!' Kisa screamed at all who could hear. They fell back as fast as they could, and a remnant of the original army made it to a distance beyond the reach of the cannons.

Kisa leaped down from Ayo, unsheathed and raised her sword and turned to face the Dutch troops. Kojo and all who remained stopped with her and formed ragged defence lines on either side of her. There, in the yam fields beyond the village, they stopped, ready to engage the enemy once more.

The Dutch halted just within the range of their single shot muskets and fired into the remaining army before retreating back inside the area protected by the cannons. Kisa halted and the remnants of her army stopped too. Then she signalled them to retreat further, to the safety of the forest.

The Dutch soldiers watched as the wounded army of the Bandit Queen retreated with their sorceress. When the threat disappeared into the distant jungle, they retreated to the castle, where plans were already being made to repair the gates and request more troops from Holland. As the Dutch came back, the slave masters, who had been hiding behind the castle walls during the battle, sent out their minions to search through the fallen. They killed those who were badly hurt, but those who were only concussed or superficially wounded were taken captive.

Kwame and Shani were found alive. When they awoke, they found themselves in the dungeons of Elmina - Kwame in the bottomless pit, Shani in the women's barracoon. In chains, bewildered by the sudden betrayal of the gods against their sister, their magic left them and they sank into despair with the other captives.

***

The remnants of Kisa's army had been scattered by the cannons and it took them several days to make their ways back to the forest in which they had last camped. Kisa looked round to see who of her generals had survived. Her heart sank when she could find no sign of her younger brother and sister. A Gonja man told her that Bolley had been killed but he did not know the fate of Shani. None of the surviving Nzema warriors knew what had happened to Kwame in the confusion of fleeing from the cannon fire.

She found Okocha. Kakande and Majeed. They had been wounded but not badly. All three were mourning the deaths of their fighters. After helping the wounded, the remnants of the army retreated north. More fighters died on the way but at last the survivors found their way back to the Warrior's Village. The women and children who had remained behind watched stunned as the remaining fighters returned, defeated.

'We were not invincible,' they muttered as they returned to their huts. 'Many died...we are all that are left.'

There were a few joyful reunions. Ugochi fell crying into Okocha's arms when she found him. But Niena searched in vain for Amador and many others mourned the loss of their loved ones. Moaning began and wailing as the full extent of the loss was borne home to them. Their friends and mates, relatives and parents of the children were gone forever.

In their midst came their sorceress, covered in the blood of her friends and followers. Kojo was beside her, but her great black spear was gone. They saw that with all her power, she could not protect them. Magic was not enough against cannons. They saw that it was only their fighting prowess that had protected them, not magic. But it was too late.

They gathered around her in silence. They seemed more hurt than angry by all that had happened. They were numb with grief and still stunned at their sudden and unexpected defeat.

'I did not know about the cannons,' Kisa said wearily. 'I am sorry for that.'

Niena walked forward and took Ayo by the bridle. 'Come, rest, sorceress. The gods have turned against you with the coming of the cannons, but you were not to know... only the gods can know everything...'

'Go home,' she said to the exhausted fighters. And they went.

Niena took Kojo and Kisa back to their hut. Water was brought to them for washing but Kisa rejected the food that was offered. She went back out to look for Shani and Kwame once again, but they had not returned. She turned to Kojo with tears in her eyes. 'They are gone. My baby brother and sister. I failed to protect them. Do you think they are dead?'

'Do you?' Kojo replied quietly.

'No,' Kisa said hesitantly at first and then with more strength in her voice, 'No! I would know if they were dead. I would feel their spirits if they were with the ancestors. But that means they have been captured.'

'Perhaps, my love. Or perhaps they are still making their way home. We will have to wait and see.'

At last, exhausted, Kisa and Kojo retreated into their hut to sleep.

All convened the next night for a village conference. Kisa was their leader, their chief – even in the face of her defeat. They had followed her out of love, they still loved her and her cause - to drive the slavers from their homes and save their people. They did not know what to do next and still depended on her to make the decisions.

Kisa sat on the chief's stool, but her head was bowed and her symbols of power, the leopard-skin headdress, and the great black spear, were gone. She had taken off her sword. She sat with them now as she was, a young woman.

Kojo stood up first to speak. 'You fought valiantly,' he began and then stopped for a moment. Everyone could see the pain he felt.

'We have suffered great losses for the first time. I tried to tell you before that it was not magic that protected us. The fighters started that story - not Kisa. They wanted to believe that nothing could hurt us. But it was the training we had that protected us. And I believe that we would have won again, but for the cannons.

'Now we have all lost family and friends. The pain is great, and we must say many prayers and talk through what happened. We must make offerings to the gods and then when all is done properly, we can decide what we will do next.'

Heads nodded in agreement, and all waited for Kisa to speak but she remained silent. Kojo raised his speaking stick and said instead, 'who wishes to speak?'

One by one, the remaining soldiers came forward to tell of the battle, what had happened to them and their friends, to praise the fallen and to offer prayers for their journey back to the ancestors. At last, when all fell silent, Kisa rose.

'Do not think that the Gods and the Great Mother do not see what you have tried to do. You fought bravely. You suffered great losses. This way has not worked for us. The castle still stands, and the white devils remain. Our army has been destroyed. I cannot ask you to do more. You are tired and full of grief. It is time to sleep and then to go home to your families. I think you will be able to defend them now against the raiders. If you wish to remain here, do so. This is a good village and we have made it a home. But for me, I am going to go home. There I will pray and wait for the gods to tell me what I am to do next.'

Over the next few days, decisions were made as to who would stay and who would go. Goodbyes were said and tears fell. In the end, only Kojo and the remaining members of her original band stood beside her.

'It's time to go home,' he said.

Chapter 32
Hope Returns

Mbandi, the envoy of Queen Nzinga, found Kisa one day on the road south from the Warrior's Village. He had made his way to Tamale, where he heard of the great battle in the north when the slave masters were defeated and how the sorceress had marched south in triumph to throw the white men into the sea. There she had been defeated and was now thought to be hiding in her camp to the west of the mountains.

He journeyed to Daboya and got a guide across the Konkari Escarpment. The guard on the hill saw him first. He was unarmed and dressed in strange red and gold clothes. They were not like the robes of the Arabs nor the garments of the people of the moon, nor yet the clothes of the local tribes, but different from anything they had seen before.

Niena met him as he entered the village.

'What brings you here, stranger? We want no trouble.'

'I am looking for the Bandit Queen – a great sorceress I am told.'

'Why?' countered Niena, with suspicion.

'I represent a great Queen far to the south of this land. She has been fighting the white men in her land for sixty years. She has heard of this Bandit Queen and wishes to meet her.'

Niena looked him up and down in silence.

Mbandi pulled out his papers and showed them to her. 'I am an Envoy. I have travelled for almost a year to find her. I cannot return home unless I fulfil my duties to my Queen. Please help me!' he begged at last.

Niena could not read but she could tell an honest man when she saw one. Besides, she still believed in Kisa's magic and was sure she could handle such a small weedy man with little problem. He had no weapons, only papers and his strange clothing. Perhaps this was a message from the gods. She decided to tell him.

'She has gone south. Follow the road to Kintampo. If you travel quickly you should catch up with her. She only left recently.'

'Thank you! I will go immediately!' Mbandi could feel the trail getting warm and was eager to set off.

'First we will feed you and your horse.' Niena answered. 'We will pack food for you to eat on the journey. Start early in the morning when you and your mount are fresh. A good night's sleep will help you travel faster, and I am sure that the sorceress is not travelling at night.'

Mbandi reluctantly admitted how tired he was. His hosts provided warm water for washing, a good hot meal, and a comfortable sleeping mat in a clean hut. Before dawn, Niena woke him. His horse was saddled and the packs full of food to eat as he travelled. She pointed him on the right track, and he set off at a gallop.

***

Two days later he came up behind his quarry. They heard him coming and turned to meet him, weapons drawn. Seeing that only a single man was approaching, Kisa moved forward and hailed him.

'Stranger! Stop! Tell us your business!'

The man stared at her in joyful amazement, mouth wide open. And then to the astonishment of Kisa and her band, he jumped off his horse and fell to his knees, tears started streaming down his face.

'You are the sorceress! The Bandit Queen!'

Everyone in the band froze. Who was this man? Kojo raised his spear and rode forward.

'I am the Envoy of the great Queen Nzinga! I travel under the flag of diplomatic immunity. She sent me to find you. I bring you greetings from Ngola Nzinga, leader of the Matamba and Ndongo people and an enemy of the cursed white men that plague both our lands. She has heard of your fight in the north and extends her hand to you in peace and friendship.'

Kisa extended a hand to him. 'You are welcome here. Come with us now. I offer you my protection. This evening, when we camp, you can tell us your story. I wish to know more about your Ngola Nzinga.' Kojo looked doubtful but Kisa said to him, 'He is an envoy, a diplomat of a government. I believe he has been looking for me for a long time. I will trust him. What does it matter now anyway?' She turned and started south again. Mbandi and the others followed her in silence.

That night in camp, after dinner, Kisa invited the Envoy to speak at the fire and tell his story.

'My name is Mbandi, and my people are the Matamba. We live far to the south of this land ,and it has taken me the rising and falling of the moon nine times to find you. 'He pulled out a map from a scroll case and gently unfolded the thin leather document. 'This is a picture of our Mother Africa. Here is where you live,' he said pointing to one place. 'And here is where I come from,' pointing to a place far from the first.

'My Queen, the great Ngola Nzinga, heard the story of a sorceress to the north of our country, who was fighting a war against the slave masters and their evil trade. My Queen has fought the Portuguese for many years and her lands are known to take in those who escape from their captors.

'Most of the news from outside Matamba is bad. There are more and more forts built every year and more white men coming for slaves. At first it was just the Portuguese and then the Dutch. Now the English, the Danes, the Swedes, and the Germans come also. My Queen believes that we must band together to fight this war. She has sent me to find you and ask you to come to Matamba and meet with her to discuss how best to fight this menace.'

Kisa stared at the map. 'So far,' she muttered and shook her head. 'I must have had a big effect on the slave masters if news of me has spread all the way to your land.'

'It is so,' Mbandi answered her. 'And if it be your will, I will take you to her.'

Kojo shook his head. He was always the cautious one. 'Think on it first, my love.' But he could see that her mind was already made up. He sighed but thought, *perhaps it is meant to be. She has lost the battle here but somehow, she wants to keep fighting. Perhaps the gods have sent this man to her for that purpose. Maybe she is meant to go south and continue the fight.*

The journey south was slow after Kintampo, where they left their horses behind. Kisa held Amara's head as they parted. She paid the farmer in gold to put Amara out to pasture. 'You have earned a rest, great heart,' she whispered to Amara as she said goodbye.

They continued on foot and came at last to the forest that held the village deep within the maze. Mbandi was confused as the path twisted and turned and suddenly disappeared, only to reappear through the scrub as those who knew the way led them into the center where a village suddenly appeared before him. At the centre of the village was a great tree whose top was blackened by a long-ago lightning strike.

The villagers came out to greet their sorceress but there was no singing or dancing this time. All had heard of the defeat at Elmina Castle. For the first time ever, their sorceress was returning in defeat not victory. Kisa moved to the center of the village and found Chief Abrafo. She wasted no time telling him what had happened.

'It is true that I was defeated when I attacked the Dutch stronghold. My army is no more. But although I have sent them to their homes and brought our people back here, I intend to keep fighting somehow. Until a few days ago, I did not know how but the gods have sent me a messenger.

'A man from the south has come to me. He is being welcomed by the villagers now and I want you to meet him. He comes from a kingdom ruled by a great warrior queen far to the south. She heard of me and sent this man, her envoy, to find me and invite me to meet with her. He has been on the road for many months. He says that Queen Nzinga has been fighting a war against the Portuguese for sixty years. She wants me to fight with her.''

'And what about your village and your people?' Chief Abrafo asked. 'We are no longer protected by the maze. The slave masters know we are here. What will we do without your protection?'

'I have a plan. My magic has failed me. I grew too proud when I attacked the castle and the gods have punished me. Yet I think that they still have their plans for me, and I must serve them. But first I must protect my people.

'Gather the village together for a meeting. I want to take them home to the village by the sea. We left there long ago to come here but I want to take them back. I will set up magic protections there so that the slave masters will see only emptiness instead of a village. They will see that you are gone from here, but they will not find you.

'Put it to the people at the meeting. If they agree we will go back to our old home and the good life we had by the sea. You will be right under the noses of our enemies, but they will not see you. I promise it.'

***

That night Kisa and Kojo rested in each other's arms in Grandmother's old hut. It felt good to be back if only for a short time.

'Will you come with me to the land of the Ngola?' Kisa asked him.

Kojo laughed and held her tightly in his arms. 'You are my sun and my moon, you are my life, my beautiful wife. I would be nothing without you. Wherever you go, I will be there, as long as the gods allow it. Only death can separate us, Kisa.'

Kisa made the sign of the evil eye and blew at it to scare the spirits away. 'Do not say it, my love. I never want to be separated from you!'

Kojo silenced her with kisses, and they spent the night making love, all the more passionate for the great losses they had suffered.

The next night the village came together. Chief Abrafo took the chief's stool but Kisa and Kojo were also seated on stools of honor.

Chief Abrafo spoke first. 'All of you know how our sorceress saved us from the slave masters. Many of you have fought with her since then and defeated many more of the evil ones who would take our freedom and our lives from us. It is true that she suffered a defeat when she attacked the castle. I believe this means that the gods have decreed that we must continue to suffer their presence in our midst, but that does not mean that we will let them win.

343

'Kisa has presented a plan to me. The maze can no longer guarantee our safety and Kisa must take the war elsewhere for she is determined to carry on the fight for as long as it takes. She wants to take us back to our village by the sea. She says she has the magic to protect us, and I believe her. Discuss this plan among yourselves now. Come to a decision about the future of our children.'

The villagers talked for hours as villagers always do when a major decision must be made. All sides of the issues and situation were discussed until at last the Elders came forward to where Kisa, Kojo and Chief Abrafo were waiting patiently.

'We have decided,' the eldest said. 'We will trust our sorceress and our chief. We have longed for many years to return to the sea and the good life that we had there. Take us home, sorceress!'

Chapter 33
The Promise

She led her people to their old home country by the sea. She set up magic protections so the slavers could not find them. At last, she and Kojo packed their belongings. The people could see they meant to go.

'Come with me one last time' she said as she drew Yasuki's ceremonial sword from its sheath. 'Walk with me to the top of the hill where we can see the great Ocean. It is there that I will leave you and it is there that you can look for my return.'

Silently she led them up the hill. Silently she approached the great granite boulder that graced the top. With two hands she lifted the sword high into the air and then plunged it into the rock.

The sword, the old magical samurai sword from her teacher Yasuki, slipped into the great granite stone like it was made of cooked yam. It slid into the hilt and the watchers thought they could see the granite turn briefly to a thick grey liquid that welcomed the sword and then closed back around it into solid rock again. Kisa lifted her sword arm to the sky, first her fingers stretched up to the gods and then balled into a defiant fist.

Silence, breathless silence by all who watched: Kojo and Afia, Chief Abrafo and all that remained of the village and the army.

'I see the future! This terror will end! The white men will leave this land forever but you will remain.'

Her other hand pointed at the hilt of Yasuki's Sword, gleaming in the morning sunlight. 'As long as this sword remains, you will prosper. Your children's children will see freedom.' Slowly she lowered her sword arm and stretched out both hands to her People.

'I will always be with you in spirit, but now I must follow my heart. I will carry this war to the south. I will raise the captives and lead them to Freedom. When the war has been won, I will return to you. Look for me wherever the winds of freedom blow!'

Suddenly she drew her remaining sword, turned, and strode off into the forest, back straight, long legs taking great steps, sword swinging as if she was already cutting the heads off slavers and slave-masters. Her people watched her go in silence. Only Kojo and the envoy Mbandi ran after her.

End Book 2

Coming soon

African Sorceress

Volume 3

Fighting For the Ngola

AFTERWORDS

Disclaimer

Years of research has been invested in this story, but if I have made any sensitive cultural errors I apologise and ask readers to alert me to them

People can say that the story of Kisa is pure fiction, but I prefer to go with the 'what if' theory of reality. What if there were great sorceresses who tried to save their people from slavery? How would we know from conventional 'history', which teaches only a white, male-centred view of the past? What if women were not always suppressed? And what if their powers were of the earth, water, wind and fire and not just witch doctor hokum?

The history of the Atlantic Slave Trade is real. As for the great prophetess that I heard about from one man in Africa, who knows? For me the story has come to life in the person of Kisa.

2. The Other Sword in the Stone Legend: Komfye Onokwe

I visited Africa in 2014. I heard a legend about a great female sorceress who had lived centuries before and had fought against the slave traders… a freedom fighter.

This was the story of one small tribe in a nation with many tribes. I was in Ghana – a nation the size of my home state of Oregon - on a continent bigger than North

America and Australia combined. There are around 60 different language groups in Ghana alone. The dominant culture in the centre of Ghana has a story about a sorcerer - a man, whose statue you can see today in Kumasi, the capital of the Ashanti nation.

If you go to Kumasi you can see a native sword planted in a stone, protected by a museum in the gardens of the Komfye Onokwe Hospital. The hospital was named after the great sorcerer who put the sword in the stone and vowed that as long as it remained, the Ashanti Nation would endure. His proud statue stands in honour in the centre of the city, holding up the Golden Stool that he brought down from the heavens by magic It is the holy proof for the Ashanti people that their kings would endure. He was a great hero who fought the slavers and the colonialists. No matter that he did not entirely succeed. He was and is a great hero of his people.

My story is not about the Ashanti sorcerer. It is a work of fiction based on an oral tradition story told to me by a man of a different language group. In his story, the protagonist was a wise woman, a prophetess was his word for her, who fought for freedom against the European's Atlantic Slave Trade and set a sword of her own in stone to mark the survival of her people.

3. On Slavery

Because slavery is now illegal, we think it has disappeared and we forget the effect it had on millions of lives over thousands of years. It wasn't just in Africa, although Africans have arguably suffered more than most. It began about the time that we as a species turned from a nomadic, hunting and gathering lifestyle to growing crops and becoming settled farm and city dwellers.

Slavery and warfare probably go together. When we began fighting each other and seeing other tribes as different, it was a logical next step to take women from conquered tribes to be concubines, sexual slaves and house servants while their men could be used to do farming and laboring work.

By a thousand AD, the Arab Slave Trade was in full swing. Slaves were taken from Africa, Asia, India, Europe and China. It is estimated that from 1000 AD to the 1800s some 14 million people, were victims of the Arab Slave Trade.

The Europeans were late-comers to the trade but they made up for it between 1500 and 1850, when the Atlantic Slave Trade saw the forced migration of some 12 million Africans from their homeland to North America, the Caribbean and South America.

Slavery was always a nasty cruel business. It is something we as a species cannot be proud of. Yes, ants and termites do it too. Sure, it made a lot of economic sense at the time. The scary thing is that it still exists. It's now illegal in most countries but an estimated 45 million people are slaves in this modern world.

Kisa's fight must continue. We cannot call ourselves civilized until this scourge is eliminated from our world.

4. A View of Sorceresses

In the oldest societies there is evidence that religion began with the concept of fertility goddesses and the holiness of the mother earth.

Herbal knowledge was always first and foremost women's knowledge, even though they certainly passed it on to both male and female children. Primitive people are not stupid. They know the names and uses of every animal vegetable and mineral resources available in their territories. In Africa, South America, North America, many tribal systems were matrilineal and the more remote the community and the less it had to fight with other people in order to survive, the more matrilineal they were likely to be. It was the norm and that meant powerful older women, elders, who held the knowledge of the tribe, the vital knowledge about the world around them: what they could eat, how to catch, grow, prepare it. Which ones were poisons, which medicines? How to make those medicines, etc.

These old women were the doctors of their communities, now called 'witch doctors' in as derogatory tone as possible. They delivered the babies, nursed them in sickness, passed on the knowledge of previous generations, told the stories that were the basis of the tribe's identity, healed the sick or buried the dead. They walked in both the physical and spiritual world. Many people want to denigrate the spiritual side and say it is all hocus pocus. But they have no valid alternative to a higher plane in which miracles are possible. I could never come at atheism because, deep in my heart, I feel the spiritual. For me and for the sorceresses of the past, the spiritual realms are as real as the physical.

I believe all women are sorceresses at heart. They have the power to make magic if they want to. And I believe it is time we give them their due and their place in history instead of leaving them out.

5. A new understanding of African history.

When I was in high school, we learned about the history of Americans, Europeans and sometimes China, but never Africa. As late as the 1990's some white historians were still insisting that Africa did not have a true 'history' because of some racist prejudice they had that it was all darkness in Africa.

I knew something about the history of European colonization of Africa. In fact, when I was in high school, many African countries had yet to win their freedom and Nelson Mandela was still in a South African prison. When studying the American civil war, I learned about the Atlantic Slave trade but only from the New World side of things. About its effect on African societies, I learned nothing.

Visiting the Elmina slave castle in 2014 started me on the journey of learning African history. What I found when I went back before the Portuguese started building trading forts along the Atlantic coast of Africa in the late 1490s blew me away. Kingdoms, cultures, art, music and dance, a thousand different languages representing a thousand different cultural heritages and histories.

I also found matrilineal systems in many old cultures, some of which still exist. Men and women are roughly equal though with separate roles, which makes sense because both are necessary for the tribe to survive. These people, without exception, honour their elders and their ancestors. They are deeply spiritual, have rich oral histories and stories and live in societies that, far from being 'savage' are very civilized in their way of life. They live in houses, albeit made from mud and thatch, are often multilingual, and they live in what were the first democratic societies.

In scientific jargon, the term I found was Acephalous, meaning not having a head of state. Researching this, what I found was societies in which everybody had a say and at village meetings they discuss situations and the Elders, possibly through a chief, make a decision for the greater good of the tribe. This sounds pretty democratic to me - not perfect certainly, but a system where everyone had their say and the elders included both women and men. Not too surprisingly, they were relatively peaceful and are now endangered because of militaristic patriarchal systems around them.

But the old ways, the old beliefs persist in many parts of Africa. We denigrate their wise men and women by calling them witch doctors and treating their stories as mere primitive myths to be discounted and ignored. It is time to re-evaluate because African history is OUR history!

Out Now:

FIGHTING FOR THE NGOLA

Part 3 in the African Sorceress Series

by M.E. Skeel

(From L'Homme de la Terre,
Elysee Reclus 1896)

www.ingramcontent.com/pod-product-compliance
Lightning Source LLC
Chambersburg PA
CBHW070043120726
47909CB00002B/284